Terry Sue Harms

Pearls My Mother Wore

A Novel

TERRY SUE HARMS
PUBLISHING

FIRST EDITION

This is a work of fiction. Names, characters, places,
and incidents either are the product of the author's imagination
or are used fictitiously. Any resemblance to actual persons,
living or dead, is entirely coincidental.

Harms, Terry Sue,
Pearls My Mother Wore / Terry Sue Harms.

ISBN 978-0-9826070-0-8

Cover and book design by Norma Tennis

Printed in the United States of America

10 9 8 7 6 5 4 3 2 1

This book is dedicated to my husband — my prince
and to my mother, Dorothy Jean Schmidt
September 21, 1933 – February 13, 1977

Pearls
My
Mother
Wore

Chapter One

Landing on the solid floor did not stop the freefall I was in. I laid my cheek against the chilly tile and closed my eyes. Behind my eyelids was a head full of whirling thoughts, cruel incessant chatter: "Why did I say that about returning the favor? I'm so dumb. What was I talking about? Who else have I offended today? It's all my fault." It was Sunday late afternoon and had been almost seven days to the minute that I had found my husband, lifeless on our bedroom floor.

Grayson, my husband for twenty years, had been my dam. His love and our sweet life together held a world, the first third of my life, a world of unresolved and difficult memories, at bay. My defense against those old memories had always been to do that "stay in the moment" thing. If I stayed busy in my everyday life, then I could push away some of my bitter past. But those old memories were patient; they waited until staying in the moment was just as awful as looking back. I wanted nothing to do with the present moment that I found myself in, so terribly alone. And the future, it felt threatening, huge and vacant, something I wouldn't possibly survive into. I could neither stay in the moment, nor contemplate a future without my husband. What was left was the history that I had run from, a history that ended when my mother died thirty years earlier, and I was fifteen years old.

I squeezed my eyes shut against a throbbing ache in my head and turned my face to press the other cheek against a fresh, cool spot on the tile floor. Moments prior, I had given the last of our acquaintances, Grayson's employer and his wife, Mike and Lindy Skilken, a hearty reassuring wave goodbye. What the Skilkens wouldn't have imagined was me sliding my body down the solid oak door frame. I had pretended to be stronger than I was. I pressed myself into the doorway corner and almost instantly dropped into a sleep. When I woke, knees curled to my chest, the sun had set and the house was cold and dark. I didn't want to move. I didn't want to cooperate with life under those empty circumstances. My body, however, was not in agreement with my heart or mind; it insisted on my getting off the floor. My hand was numb from being lain on, my neck and back were stiff, and my feet were swollen and screaming from so many hours of being clamped into the unfamiliar, black-leather dress shoes.

With a groan I extricated my feet from the merciless high heels. With another groan, I got up and walked down the hall to the main bathroom. A floating zombie, I opened the medicine cabinet and dared to swallow three aspirin; two had stopped doing the job earlier in the week. I was afraid of using prescription drugs and alcohol to kill my pain. That combination had destroyed my mother. Progressing from two aspirin to three put me close to the slippery slope of escalating desire and need that I had feared my entire life. Surrounded by the loss of my husband, it was obvious to me that there would never be just one glass of wine or just one drug prescription. One would never be enough; I would want more, and I would take more once I started. Feeling better would not be a part of the equation; total annihilation would be.

In that hour I had little need for coping concoctions; Mother Nature had provided me with an altered state. I moved around the house as if I was having an out-of-body experience. I was drained, yet my body parts moved me with little conscious thought. My hands turned on the water and took off my clothes; my legs stepped into the shower. I didn't bother turning on the lights; my eyes had adjusted to the darkness. The hot spray of water dissolved whatever makeup was left on my face, whatever hairspray was left in my hair; perfume and deodorant ran down the drain. I stayed under the pelting showerhead until the water heater ran cold.

When I dressed again, it was in a forest-green sweat suit belonging to my husband. With scissors, I cut a raw edge into its fabric at the arm and leg lengths to fit my size. I crawled into his side of our bed, cradled in the remaining indentation of his larger body. Lying inches from my normal spot on the mattress rearranged my orientation to the room in a way that reflected my odd, new orientation to the world around me; everything was familiar but different. The bedroom curtains were open, and framed in the window I watched wisps of clouds slowly change shape and drift past a luminous crescent moon; the brightest of the stars shimmered far off in the distance. Catching sight of a shooting star was a sign of good luck, Grayson believed. I searched, but none appeared.

When my mother died, I didn't feel this way. Her death did nothing to prepare me for the iterating stings, jabs, and deep body blows of loss that were punctuating every minute of my recent days. When she died, I was relieved. Her nightmare was over. My nightmare was over. It didn't matter that I had lost my mother. Those first breaths of freedom were more exhilarating than any gloom I should have felt. I looked sad and held my head down, but in my heart I was saying, "Thank you, thank you, thank you." I entered my new life looking forward, pushing forward. She died; I lived. I was just as trapped by her drinking as she was. She wasn't living, she was surviving. Every day was Russian roulette; every drink, and every drunk put bullets in the chamber. It was simply a matter of time. As time went on, she got drunk more and more often. By the end she was drunk every hour of every day; nevertheless, I wasn't ready.

Losing her was just as sudden and unexpected as losing him. As my thoughts churned, I realized that in both cases, different as they were, there had been no goodbyes, and that fact broke yet another piece of my heart. I had to draw the curtains closed to give myself a chance to sleep. I got up and stood at the window. Outside, the street was bathed in moonlit shades of x-ray gray; instead of teeth, femurs, and rib cages, there were automobiles, front yards, and houses. I pulled the cord to draw the heavily lined drapes closed, then slipped back into the warm spot under the covers. I pressed my face into his pillow. A week earlier I could almost taste his smell, but that was already going away, and it smelled more of me than him. I had put his wedding band on a long, gold, necklace chain and wore it under my clothes, against my skin. I reached for the ring, held it to my lips, and within a minute was asleep. I slept as if I had been drugged—deeply, effortlessly; it was a gift.

Chapter Two

The next morning, restless and exhausted at the same time, I didn't want to be awake, and I didn't want to be asleep. Despite schizophrenic spurts of adrenaline that encouraged me to get out of bed, this tug-of-war battle had sleep winning. I had gotten in and out of bed a couple of times during the morning and it was in the middle of the afternoon that I was back lying down. I was drifting off, falling, falling, into deeper and deeper sleep when the doorbell rang. Was I dreaming it? The funeral was over; the people were all gone. I held my breath. Nothing. I had dreamt it. No, it rang a second time.

Being startled fully awake by the sudden noise after so many hours of penetrating quiet was disorienting. I held still, my heart thumped rapidly in my chest, my hearing tuned acutely to whatever noise would come from outside. I willed whomever it was to go away. There was literally no person on the planet that I wanted to see or talk to.

Again the doorbell rang, this time accompanied by a rather persistent knocking.

"How obnoxious," I thought. "Who in this odious world could that be." In the Rolodex of my mind I flashed on possibilities. Was it the police, fire department, or one of the paramedics checking up on me, the recent widow? Was it a delivery of some kind? Maybe it was a Jehovah's Witness pedaling those Awake magazines and whatever else it is they pedal.

The next thing I heard was rustling in the bushes right outside our bedroom, the one I was hiding in. My hammering heartbeat doubled its pace. Was somebody getting ready to jump over the fence? Had some crook studied Grayson's obituary in the newspaper to discover that a lone woman now occupied this house? Was I on the verge of experiencing a home-invasion robbery? I tried to think, was there a weapon nearby? Should I run to the kitchen and get a knife or a frying pan? Should I yell out in the huskiest voice I could project, "Who's there?" What if it was just some pesky do-good neighbor who wanted to give me a nut loaf or Tupperware of soup? Then I would be found out. They would know I was home, and I would have to open the door and show my cobbled and crumpled, slept-in sweat suit, my uncombed hair, and pillowcase-creased face. It was the middle of the afternoon.

"Uncle Gray! Yo, Uncle Gray, are you back there?" he called over the fence.

For God's sake, it was Mitchell, Grayson's nephew. Mitchell. Shit. Shit. Shit. I hadn't seen him in over four years, not nearly long enough. It was back then that I declared I would never speak to that kid again, as long as I lived, so help me God.

"Yo, Yo, Yo, G-Man, where are you?"

The rustling moved away from the bushes, away from the fence, and then again he was at it with the doorbell and the knocking. He was determined not to take no for an answer, but he was going to have to. I stayed put until all was quiet outside. Where had he come from? Obviously he had not seen Cheryl, his mother, my crack-cocaine addicted sister-in-law. She was checked out, but surely she would have remembered her brother had just died; surely she would have said something to her son about it. Why had he dropped by? What did he want? A handout no doubt. Did I care? No. He was trouble, and I didn't need any of that. He was on his own. I didn't care what he needed or what he wanted to say. I sat at the edge of the bed and wrapped a pillow around my head, rocking back and forth in an attempt to shut him out of my thoughts.

Down feathers were no match for guilt. I started thinking about what Grayson might have done if he were alive. Grayson wouldn't have let the young man walk away. Sure, he would have considered my position. He would have known that I didn't ever want to see that cowardly thief again. But he would have gone out there and, casual as ever, suggested they hop in the truck and go for a drive. Grayson wouldn't have harbored a grudge. He would have let the kid back into his life. Even if he knew another disappointment was bound to come, Mitchell was family, and that was that.

I waited probably thirty minutes from the last knock before I came out of hiding, confident that Mitchell would be long gone. I nearly fell on the floor when I peeked out the toile café-curtained window in the dining room and saw he was sitting quietly on the front step. The movement of the curtain caught his eye, and he saw me peering out at him. He had jumped up and was facing the door when I slowly opened it. I didn't open it all the way but stood wedged between the door and the jamb, filling the space through which he might spy a house filled with condolence bouquets. I didn't say a word and hoped my scalding look would drive him away. My thought was, "Bad timing, bad, bad timing." So intense were my feelings of I-hate-life-and-everybody-in-it that I could have spit bullets. So intense was my hate for Mitchell that I could have spit grenades. My eyes locked onto his and I stared, unblinking, daring that sticky-fingered punk to speak.

It had only been four years since we had last seen one another, but on a busy street I could have walked right past him unaware;

his appearance had so changed. The plump and shine of his early youth had long ago left him; so had the sass and spirit of adolescence, even the I-know-everything, you-know-nothing attitude from his late teens was different.

I figured he was in his twenty-third or -fourth year, but stood there looking much older. He was Holocaust-victim skinny, with a pasty, sick complexion. His face looked haggard, oily and pockmarked; it was pierced with three small, silver rods at his brow, two rings through one of his nostrils and another in his lower lip. A crowded, tarnished collection of small amulets, studs, bars, and hoops punctured pretty much every part of one ear and the other was less crowded but still looked like he had a miniature wind chime hanging from it. He had a side tooth missing and the others seemed to dangle from his emaciated gums. He wore a goatee, but several days of not shaving gave the appearance of a nearly full beard. A seaweed-colored tattoo crept up his neck from under the collar of a stained but once white, torn tee-shirt that hung over his protruding shoulder blades. He had a grimy black baseball cap on backwards; I could see his hair was long and slicked back into a braid. His pants, worn out black jeans, limp, baggy and also smeared and stained, barely held up over his hipbones. Mitchell fumed the malodorous stench of the street life he had no doubt been living.

Unwilling to say a word to him, I stared at his face. For a moment I think he optimistically expected a happy homecoming. He became nervous and looked down at the pavement; he bobbed and shifted his weight from side to side. An idea occurred to him; he looked up at me from the bottom step of the front porch and said, "Hey, Auntie Kell. It's me, Mitchell."

I looked at him as if to say, "So?" but still did not speak.

It always caught me off guard to hear him say Auntie or Uncle, especially when he had become such a toughie, but his grandmother Helen, Grayson's mother, had taught him to do it while he was still a child. He called her Gram and his aunts Auntie. Helen would say to him, "We only have a handful of relatives, honey; let's address them accordingly. There will be plenty of folks down the road who you can call by their first names."

There had been a hint of awkward embarrassment in his expression, like a smile he was trying to suppress, but he read my humorless demeanor and rearranged his own. He looked out to the street at Grayson's truck. I noticed it was already dusty from being parked for over a week.

"I saw Uncle Gray's truck. Where is he?" Mitchell asked with the arrogance and sense of entitlement I knew so well in him.

Unflinching, I continued to stare into his aged eyes. I had been overly accommodating to his wishes in the past; I was desperate to be loved by every member of Grayson's family, but that didn't matter anymore. Mitchell always seemed to get whatever he wanted in the end. Four years earlier, he lived with us for a brief period of time, but even before that, he never doubted that he should be provided for, and I played right into his assumption. Cheryl didn't give him that. Helen, his legal guardian, did. Helen couldn't stick to her no.

"No, I am not going to buy tennis shoes for 150 dollars. No."

"But I need these for gym. The coach said this was the kind I should get," he would persist.

"Oh, alright, what size?"

He had come wanting something, I was sure. Ever since Helen died, five years ago after a painful but quick invasion of pancreatic cancer, Grayson and I were who he turned to for bailouts. My guess was he wanted money.

"What is it you want, Mitchell?"

"Where is Uncle Gray?"

"He's not here."

"When is he coming back?"

To that I did not respond, but shifted my weight to the other foot. I looked past him to Mr. Finch and Mr. Ritell, the two old guys who live together in the house across from ours. They were at their daily post, two folding chairs in their open garage, ever surveying the limited action of our normally quiet street. I don't think they realized I was talking to "the nephew boy," which is how they referred to him. Mitchell had helped them do some heavy lifting while he was living here for that unforgettable period of time, and the old guys thought he was a fine young man. They would inquire, "How's the nephew boy?" I never revealed to them the circumstances under which he had left. The old guys weren't gossips; I wasn't worried about that. They were two distinguished gentlemen; it was just that the theft seemed too tawdry to retell. Normally I would have given a wave to them, but under the circumstances, I didn't bother. I did wonder, however, what the two sentries thought of all this.

Mitchell either didn't notice or didn't care that he was being observed. He became more animated and agitated that I was not answering him. He paced a couple of steps out and back on the walkway. I was not going to be the one to break it to him that Grayson wasn't coming back.

"Aw, man. Why are you being so cold? What did I ever do to you?"

There was a hook, but I refused to bite. I continue to look at him but shifted into a blasé gaze.

"Shit, forget you then," he said and threw his hand in my direction as if to be done with me. He walked out to the sidewalk and just past the yard. His lumbering swagger almost made me laugh. I felt completely disengaged from his agitation. I was just beginning to feel relief that he was leaving when he stopped and turned back to me. He slowly approached the front porch, his eyes cast down and with a seeming humility I couldn't have imagined, he said, "I'm sorry."

I had to think about that for a minute. I was never going to forgive him.

"You're sorry. I don't believe it. What do you want, Mitchell?"

"I need a place to stay. I know you don't believe me, but I'm done running. I haven't picked up in eight days; I'm clean and I am going to stay that way. I mean it; I want to get my life back. So do you think uncle Gray would let me hang here for a while?"

"He might, but I'm not. Once a user, always a user. Mitchell, I'm not going let you rip us off again. I'm not going to finance your next little drug spree with my belongings."

"Aw man, that's messed up. Listen, I promise, I'll get a job. I can work around here. I'll pay my own way. I'll pay you back. I really don't want to go to my mom's. Can't we try this just for a day? Can we see how it goes? Can't I come in?"

"Goddamn you Mitchell, no. I won't let you in."

I struggled to keep Grayson from my thoughts. He never would have turned his nephew out. Mitchell was my nephew too, but by marriage, not by blood. We had never bonded. He was four years old when Grayson and I started dating, and he resented Grayson's diversion and showed it in the tactless ways only a child can. If I wore perfume he would wait until plenty of people were around and then tell me I smelled funny. If I had my hair styled in a new fashion he would ask with a pinched expression on his face, again while all eyes were on him, "Why do you look like that?" I had robbed him of his number-one-buddy status and he didn't like it; he didn't like me.

But Grayson wouldn't let me do it. He wouldn't let me turn my back on family, blood or otherwise, but he also wasn't there to protect me from this derelict either. I had to decide, and with Grayson weighing on my conscience, I told Mitchell he could go around and let himself into the backyard by the side gate. That was as far as I was willing to go.

"I'll let you stay outside in the backyard if you want. I'm sure it's much nicer than the places you've been sleeping. I want you to get the lawn mower out of the cottage shed and start working, though. Oh, and if you think you are going to smoke any cigarettes around here, think again. Take 'em around the block."

"Ooh, that's so harsh. But it's cool. Thank you. I promise, I'm not going to do anything to screw this up. I promise." And he skipped around the garage corner to the gate and flagstone path that led into the backyard.

Mitchell made his way around to the back of the house in about the same amount of time as it took me to walk through to the living room and draw closed the sheer curtain that hung across the sliding glass door. Certain I was making a mistake, I jerked on the drawstring cord. I watched through the swaying, diaphanous fabric as he bounded into view. The first thing he did was to help himself to gulps of water from the hose. He moved into the cottage shed with a high degree of confidence, extracting the lawn mower, checking it for fuel and starting it up.

I figured his enthusiasm would probably last about a day, if that. It was possible that as soon as he broke sweat he would give me the finger and hit the road. Undetected from my side of the curtain shade, I scrutinized his every move, waiting for him to make a mistake: mow over a bed of zinnias, step backwards into some plant and crush it, topple over one of the birdbaths.

Disconcerting was the fact that, despite being emaciated, he resembled his uncle as well as grandfather. The Tremblake men are tall and they carry themselves as if ducking through a doorway that isn't quite high enough. The family genes were also apparent in the hook of Mitchell's nose and the angular ridge of his cheekbones. Richard Tremblake, my father-in-law, has old, straight-faced daguerreotype images of his father and grandfather, and the same nose and cheekbones can be seen down the line.

I watched the clock as Mitchell muscled through his chore, counting the minutes until he had a tantrum, but he didn't. It was the later part of the afternoon, but the heat of the day was still high. He managed to keep Grayson's meticulously maintained, vintage John Deere lawn mower running and got the yards done, and, to my surprise, under his own initiative, he edged and swept as well. He emptied the clippings into the garbage can on the side of the house, returned the mower to where he found it in the shed and seemed well content to settle onto one of the lounge chairs shaded by a tall birch. His whiskered face was beet-red from the heat and effort. He fell asleep instantly. It occurred to me that if he truly had eight days off drugs then his sobriety date and Gray's death date were the same.

It wasn't a good match, Mitchell in my garden. It was like watching someone read a newspaper from a church pew, play canasta wearing boxing gloves, or smoke a cigar next to a baby's crib.

Grayson and I bought this house over twenty years ago, right before we were married. We were so excited. It was a run-down mess, but we loved it back to life, toiling day and night, proud of our progress. We were just a little older than Mitchell is now, by probably two or three years. The large yards and the two-hundred-square-foot bonus cottage with electricity, a wood-burning stove and a small bathroom sold us on the property. Our home-improvement efforts included several dump runs to dispose of the rusty junk that had accumulated around the exterior: tires, bicycle parts, a clothes rack, a collapsed swing set; it was all hiding in unchecked waist-high grass and ivy. Over weeks and months we filled a box with lost toys found in the dense weeds. Long forgotten by the children in the former owner's life were tiny green plastic soldiers; rusty, miniature fire trucks, tractors, and cars; and dozens of balls: dirty, deflated rubber balls, tennis balls, Super Balls, baseballs. There were five-cent bubble gum rings and trinkets, dismembered dolls, a head here, a leg there.

Mitchell, in his threadbare clothes, tangle of tattoos, scraggly hair and beard, suited the old backyard better, with all its trash and disorder. He rested on a vibrant, fern-patterned lounge cushion, his form dull in contrast to the lush colors and textures surrounding him. In the flower beds, in-between the perennials and ground covers were mix-and-match annuals. Cardinal-red cyclamen that had bloomed all winter were still showing strong. The spring bulbs were in their glory: golden daffodils, blue hyacinth, red narcissus, purple bearded iris, and multicolored tulips. Marigolds, zinnias, dahlias, petunias and portulacas were beginning to sprout and bud.

As he slept, his relaxed expression appeared smug and entirely too comfortable for the imposition he was causing me. I didn't know what my future plans were, but I was sure they didn't include him. I could see he was in pretty bad shape and needed some rescuing, but I didn't want to be the rescuer; I had done my stint. He had earned a night's stay, but that was going to be it.

Grumbling as I went along, I gathered into a bucket a bar of soap, a disposable shaver, shampoo, a towel, a pair of Grayson's jeans and belt, a tee shirt, socks, underwear, a stick of deodorant, toothpaste, an unused toothbrush, and a comb. I also put in the bucket a large garbage bag for Mitchell to put his soiled clothes. When I opened the sliding glass door, he jumped at the sound. I wondered for a split second if he had been crying but decided the shimmering droplets on his lashes and cheeks were sweat. He pulled up his tee shirt to wipe off his face, exposing his caved-in stomach and rib cage. I set the bucket on the patio table.

"You need to clean up. You smell bad. You'll have to clear away the spiders from the shower in the cottage shed, but it should still work. Turn up the water heater if you want it hot. I'll feed you when you're done." All of this he took in without looking at me, his face unreadable as stone.

I returned to the house suspecting that he might gather steam and yell at me to go to hell, the hairs on the back of my neck raised like hyper-alert insect antennae.

It was over an hour before Mitchell reappeared on the lounge chair, washed, shaved, and in baggy but clean clothes. He looked better, but he still looked like a hollow-eyed runaway, a street punk.

Left over in the refrigerator was an absurd amount of food. The kindness of Grayson's friends and family, the people I work with, and complete strangers was carried into the house via finger foods, casseroles, homemade tamales, pizzas, salads, loaves of fresh-baked bread, chips and dips. From a cold-cut platter I put together two sandwiches, absentmindedly picking at the cheese and salami as I put together a tray of food for Mitchell. Along with his sandwiches, I added a pile of potato chips, an apple, and a slice of homemade cherry pie that had come from I don't know who or where. The housewife in me was glad to see some of the food be eaten, even if it was by my archenemy.

Balancing the tray in one hand, an act familiar from my old waitressing days, I walked from the kitchen through the dining and living rooms without spilling. I drew the curtain a few inches, unlatched the door lock and slid it open. I set the food on the patio table and pointed to a large cooler that had been used for all the people who came by during the previous week. I told Mitchell that he could help himself to the drinks inside. I raised its lid and saw there were still plenty of cans and bottles floating in icy water.

He raised his brows and widened his eyes at the bounty.

"Damn! Looks like you had one hell of a par-tay! Whaz up?"

The shower had lifted his spirits. He was bopping around trying to catch my eye. I got the sense that he felt he had discovered the reason for my foul mood: it had nothing to do with him; I must have just been hung over from some wild party the night before. That would be the lens he would see the world through — parties and hangovers.

He had placed the garbage bag of his dirty clothes on the table in the same spot where I had set the bucket. He expected me to take the clothes in and no doubt clean them. I snatched the bag and went inside without responding to his party query. After locking the door I drew the curtain shut again and watched through it to see what he chose to drink. Inside the cooler were bottles of uncorked wine, beer, a variety of sodas, and bottled water. He chose soda. I walked the bag of vile-smelling clothes straight through the house and out to the garbage can, then wheeled it to the curb for Tuesday's pickup, something Grayson had always done.

As the sun was setting, Mitchell moved around the backyard,

from the patio table to the chaise lounge. He went in and out of the cottage shed, eventually dragging out an assortment of outdated magazines I had at one time intended for collage projects. A couple of times he belched loudly. One time I caught him hawking up a wad of spit that he let fly into the blue hydrangeas. Reluctant to reveal the surveillance that I had been doing, I turned away from the phlegmatic glop with one thought: "Twenty-four hours, that's all you get."

As the sun was setting, I had to deal with the fact that the visibility advantage through the sheer curtains would shift when I turned on any lights. Mitchell would then be able to see in my direction, and I wasn't going to have that. I decided to nail some blankets up to completely and opaquely cover the sliding glass door and its sheer curtain. Mitchell was asleep on the lounge again. The tray of food had been devoured. I quietly slid open the door so as not to wake him and took the meal tray; in its place, I left a couple of the blankets.

Through the kitchen I entered the garage to collect a hammer, nails, and a tall stepladder. It was Grayson's domain. The concrete floor, racks of metal tubing, bins of miscellaneous supplies, and smells from machine oil and cleaning solvents all seemed ready to be enlivened by his touch. Under its car cover was Grayson's "baby," a cranberry red, 1960 Aston Martin DB4. It's an adorable vintage sports car with the original old-fashioned dial radio, switches and gauges, cracked black leather upholstery, and a real wood steering wheel and gearshift knob. We would take it out for long Sunday drives. It's a conversation starter, that's for sure.

In Grayson's garage, everything has a specific place. It's a mini metal shop. Much of the same equipment that I had seen at Skilken Metal and Machine, where he had worked his entire adult life, is out there, but smaller in scale: lathe, welder, mill, belt sander, etc. Everything was there but he. Stricken by yet another aspect of longing, I sniffled back new sorrow. Saddened by the full yet vacant shop, I gathered what I had gone in for. From a drawer labeled Screws Hooks Nails, I found a box of heavy-gauge, two-inch common house nails, the hammer hung from its place on a pegboard, and the stepladder which was mounted on the wall next to the water heater. Forcing myself not to linger, I turned out the light and returned to the living room.

I used two heavy, navy-blue wool blankets, slightly overlapping to block all of the glass doorway. Wobbling on the stepladder, I licked back warm, salty tears that dripped over my lips. As I tapped with the hammer, the defenseless bed covers sagged under their own weight at each nail piercing. I didn't look out to see what Mitchell did when my hammering began. If he realized what I was up to, and if he thought it was extreme and a little nuts, I didn't care. Grayson, I was sure, would turn ill with disbelief at what I was doing.

I was unskillfully working the last couple of nails into the wall plaster when the phone started ringing. I intended to let the answering machine get it. Grayson's voice delivered the recorded greeting; I couldn't bring myself to change it although I supposed I would have to one day. After the electronic beep Grayson's eldest sister, Margaret, was there. Margaret and Grayson's other sister, Clair, live together in Ashland, Oregon. They both do theater work: acting mostly, when they can get it.

"Kell. Kell. Pick up. Where are you? Are you there?"

At fifty-two years of age, Margaret is seven years older then I am, and she sometimes makes me feel immature. I didn't want her to know I had been crying. I got myself under control and picked up the phone with a not-a-care-in-the-world, "Hello."

With the cordless phone to my ear, I returned to the living room and turned on a light to inspect my handiwork.

"Hey kiddo, how you doing?"

"Oh, I just walked in. I was at the grocery store."

She'd know that was preposterous, given all of the food she had helped put in the refrigerator the day before.

"Oh?"

"Ah, I wanted to get some more laundry soap. I decided to spend the day washing and ironing all of the window coverings, you know, to keep busy," I lied as I smoothed the hanging wool.

She responded with a skeptical, "Hum."

To change the subject I asked her how the long drive home had been. It takes about seven hours to get from here in Sonoma, California, to Ashland, Oregon. The sisters had departed early in the afternoon during the memorial gathering because of "professional commitments," whatever that meant. My father-in-law, Richard, also left early. He had to catch a flight back to Florida where he lives with his latest wife, Shirley.

"Oh please, don't get me started," Margaret began. "Clair nearly killed us just outside of Shasta City. Didn't you?" she directed at her sister who was obviously nearby and listening.

I could hear Clair say to Margaret, "Shut up."

"Shut up? You shut up," the three-way conversation continued. "If I hadn't screamed my head off, we would have driven right off the edge of the road. Like an insane fool she tried to reach into the backseat to get that stupid enormous purse of hers."

Again I could hear Clair, "Oh, stop it."

At that moment a loud clang came from Mitchell in the back yard. My eyes widened and I jerked aside the blanket coverings.

He had managed to knock over a wrought-iron patio chair and was scrambling to upright it, calling out, "Sorry," when he saw me glaring at him. I released the curtains and tried to muffle the receiver so that Margaret wouldn't hear him. I didn't want to tell them about Mitchell; I didn't want to get into it. He would be gone soon anyway. Mitchell and his mother were forever topics of long discussions and psychological analysis between the two sisters, and I was loath to get a dissertation started.

"Is someone there?" Margaret asked.

"Ah, no. That was me. I bumped into the dinner table and the napkin holder fell over."

She made another skeptical sound but didn't pursue it.

"Well, we just wanted to call and say hello and to check up on you. How is it going?"

"I think I should get a gold star for answering the phone if that tells you anything."

"What?"

"Nothing."

"What did you say about a gold star?"

"Forget it. I was trying to be light."

"When do you go back to work?" Margaret wanted to know.

I'm a hairdresser, and the thought of standing in front of a mirror, feigning concern over the length of someone's bangs made me want to leap off the nearest bridge. The sisters have a strong work ethic, as did Gray, and I feared a lecture about idle hands. The truth was that I had already been thinking about quitting my job at Beau Tique, but rather than tell her that, I told the other truth, which was that I had requested a month off. I had already mentioned the bereavement leave to Margaret at least twice during the previous week while she and Clair were staying here at the house with me, but for some reason she either didn't believe me or she was testing to see if her incredulous memory was accurate.

"A month? Are you sure? What are you going to do for a whole month?"

A shuddering sigh came with my next breath and tears began to flow silently. I asked Margaret if we could change the subject, and to her credit, she apologized and backpedaled as much as she could.

"Hey kiddo, you do whatever's right. What do I know? I'm sure you know what you are doing."

No, I didn't, but I wasn't going to admit it in that moment. I regretted having answered the call, and simply wanted to hang up.

"Hey, we were wondering something and wanted to ask you about it," Margaret fished casually. "Daddy's silver. We were just wondering what your plans for it are."

"Daddy's silver?" I repeated with stunned brevity.

"Kell, that silver has been in the Tremblake family for four generations."

"You mean the Tiffany silver flatware that Richard gave to both Grayson and me as a wedding gift?" I said with an audible strain.

"Kelly, don't take this the wrong way. We understand that it belongs to you now, but Clair and I both feel it should be bequeathed back to us in the event that something should ever happen to you. Since you don't have children, is what I mean. We'd like to know if it has been accounted for in your will, that's all we're asking."

She was talking so fast. I couldn't keep up. My words formed and were spoken slowly. "Are you saying that the two of you think something is going to happen to me?"

"No, no, no. But realistically, something is going to happen to each of us one day, you know that. It would be a shame if our great grandmother's china and crystal stemware was never reunited with her silver."

There must have been oxygen in the room, but I was struggling to find it. "Reunited?" I managed to get out, as the word ricocheted around in my head several times.

"We're talking about final wishes, setting things right."

"Right," I repeated. "Did Richard ask you to call? Does he think something is going to happen to me?"

"Kelly, you're missing the point. This isn't about Daddy. Clair and I aren't asking you to do anything tomorrow. We just thought now would be a good time to bring it up. To let you know what our wishes are with regards to our family heirloom. If you haven't thought about it, we'd like you to, before it is too late. If the state gets ahold of it in some probate court, it could be lost forever. We can't leave it to an estate auction or, heaven forbid, some garage sale or flea market."

"But I'm not dead."

"You're not listening. Kelly, this isn't about you. Are you alright? I didn't mean to upset you. We had no idea that old silver even meant anything to you. Don't get yourself all worked up over it. We can talk about this another time, O.K.?"

"O.K."

"Kiddo, I hate to hang up on such an uncomfortable note, but we're not really getting anything accomplished here, so how about we just stop for the night, O.K.?"

"O.K."

"Hugs."

"Hugs back. Bye"

In the silence of my kitchen, I couldn't believe the conversation that had just taken place. We had buried Grayson's ashes only the day before. She was there. She and Clair were both there. Had she really said her request had nothing to do with me, that the time was right to bring this up? When I thought about all of the family treasures the Tremblakes possess, not just crystal, china, and silver, but paintings, photographs, books, framed military citations and medals, antique furniture, fur coats, and jewelry, I had to think about the sole treasure I had once owned belonging to my mother, her pearl necklace and earring set. As I rattled off each category of riches amassed by my husband's family, the searing resentment I held over Mitchell's theft roared to life. He, their blood relative, had robbed me of my mother's finest belonging, and Margaret and Clair knew it. How could she suppose I wouldn't care?

My stomach fluttered with anxious energy as I turned out the kitchen and living room lights. I wanted a brick of food to weigh down my angry jitters. I opened the refrigerator door and a wedge of light beamed across the floor. With trembling hands, I stood at the fridge and stuffed myself with the smorgasbord that had been brought in. I picked from under sheets of aluminum foil, from disposable plastic containers, from cellophane bags. I didn't use a plate. I didn't sit at the table. I barely tasted what I put in my mouth. I grabbed several shortbread cookies and took them to bed. Crumbs and teardrops rolled off my cheeks and landed on my husband's pillow. One after another I crammed the sweet, buttery shortbread into my mouth, expecting its mellow flavor to comfort me. With each mouthful I tried to swallow my anger and shame. I was ashamed of not sticking up for myself with my sister-in-law. I was ashamed of allowing Mitchell a single toe onto my property after what he had done. I was ashamed of the lies that were building up around me, and I was ashamed of the secrets I had carried for decades.

Chapter Three

A t 5:00 A.M. I bolted out of bed after hearing Mitchell whooping and hollering in the backyard. It hadn't occurred to me to turn off the automatic sprinkler system until it was too late. I dashed outside to trip the timer, but by then, Mitchell and the chaise lounge were fairly well soaked. I wasn't going to start the day with apologies, not to him. He shouldn't have been there anyway. "Oh brother," was all I could say at first as he cursed and hopped around in the cold, shivering underneath a soggy blanket. The second blanket, bright pink and thoroughly saturated, was sprawled across the lawn like a deflated hot-air balloon.

"What the fuck was that? Shit."

"Mitchell, lower your voice. It's automatic."

"You did that on purpose," he accused with both ferocity and hurt.

"No, I did not do that on purpose. It's set to come on by itself."

"You're pissed that I'm here, so you forgot on purpose to turn that shit off. Fuck."

"Think what you want, but I'm telling you it was an accident. It's off now. It won't happen again. Flip over the chaise pad to the dry side. It's only water. You'll be fine. Quit swearing, and I'll find another blanket."

When I returned with a fresh blanket, my nephew jerked it away from my hands with some kind of self-righteous indignation. By then I was wide-awake and neither humored nor sympathetic to what was going on. I hadn't asked him to show up. What little hospitality he received from me was far more than he deserved.

"Hey, hey, hey grabby-hands. I'm not your mother. You don't get to snatch anything from me, do you understand? Change your attitude or go find somewhere else to crash."

"But I'm soaking wet."

"That's not my fault," I said, emphasizing the word "not."

Mitchell tossed the damp blanket across the top of the fence before wrapping himself in the new one. Again, for a flash, I could see his skeletal figure as he stood un-self-consciously in his uncle's boxers. For a few seconds he agonized over what to do next. He squirmed and twisted as if his fingernails were being removed one by one, but then got to a point in his internal conflict where he was able to say, "I'll chill out." He tiptoed into the wet lawn and adjusted the dripping chaise, then sat on the solid green, dry side of the fern-patterned cushion and hung his head dejectedly.

This acquiescence wasn't like him. Something had broken him, at least for the time being. I wasn't willing to feel sorry for him, however. I was sure that whatever he had gotten, he had deserved. I released a heavy sigh, then turned on my heels. Inside the house, mimicking his indignant grabbing gesture, I flicked off the patio light and returned to bed.

In my dark room, behind closed eyes, complete and incomplete thoughts swirled together, preventing me from falling back to sleep. Thoughts about my husband, thoughts about the silver my sisters-in-law wanted, thoughts about my hairdressing career and going back into the beauty business, and memories of my mother all collided into one another.

The day Mitchell made off with my mother's jewelry echoed over and over. Four years earlier, I had gone along with the plan of letting him move in because I wanted Grayson to be happy and I wanted to come across as a cool aunt. Immediately upon his arrival, I was sorry. He would do stupid and infuriating things such as walking away from a wide-open refrigerator door, or urinating on the floor around the toilet then leaving the seat up, or biting his fingernails and spitting the bits in the air. Conversations with him consisted primarily of yes and no grunts. The day came when I arrived home from work expecting to find him doing some screwball thing but instead was stopped in my tracks by what I dared not think him capable of. In the hallway, on the carpet was a fine gold necklace that he had no doubt dropped in haste. Instantly I knew where it had come from, a jewelry box that I rarely used. He had been scouting through my drawers. I'm not sure what all was in that jewelry box except for sure my mother's pearl earrings and their matching necklace. They were gone. I looked in the guest bedroom where he had been sleeping and saw the bed was unmade. I saw the closet door at some point had come off its track and was leaning against the hanging clothes. I saw scraps and trash from fast-food joints and a crusty bowl of sour milk and cereal, but what I didn't see was the army camouflage duffle bag Mitchell had with him the day he moved in.

When Gray got home he found me sitting at the kitchen table, the empty jewelry box in my lap. His Hi-Honey-I'm-home face quickly turned to a look of guarded restraint and he wanted to know what was going on. I had been rehearsing to myself what I was going to say when he came through the door. I was going to calmly state that Mitchell's things were gone and so were some of mine. If I could stay as matter-of-fact as a judge about the material theft then I thought I would be able to cope with the sentimental loss. I didn't want to think about how little I had of my mother's. I didn't want to think about having one less item, one less thing to touch that she too had touched. But as soon as my husband was next to me I burst into tears. I didn't have to say anything. He brought me to my feet and hugged me tight as I sobbed into his chest. It wasn't until later that evening that we discovered he too had taken a loss. Several of his metal-working tools were missing: dial calipers, digital micrometers, drill bit sets, and metric tap and die sets, all kept neatly in their original cases.

I could not forgive Mitchell. Time was no palliative; in fact, the opposite was true. He was wise to stay away; reappearing only showed his absolute stupidity. Did he think I would have forgotten what he did? Did he think like his Aunt Margaret when she suggested I might not care about such old things? I wanted to get even with him but could not think of how to exact my retribution. In a lifetime he could not replace what he had taken from me; he could never repair the damage. The best I could come up with was that if he stuck around, I would make him work. I wanted him to suffer. If he left, it would be good riddance even if he hadn't paid his debt. Either way, stay or leave, he was never going to make right the wrong he had done.

As the morning hours progressed into day, I eventually heard Mitchell rattling around out back again. The birds, squirrels, neighboring dogs and chickens had no doubt given him his second wake-up call. Reluctantly, I got out from under my down comforter and headed for the coffee pot, scrupulously avoiding the area in the room where Grayson's life had ended. The sight of cold coffee from the day before was exceedingly disappointing. My usual routine belonged to another lifetime. Neglecting to prepare the maker the night before was upsetting beyond reason. I tossed the day-old brew into the sink with such force that much of it splashed back up at me, staining the front of my hastily-tailored sweat shirt, further exacerbating my foul mood.

I ate a slice of cold quiche as I heated some for my ward in the backyard. On a disposable paper plate, I included a slice of ham. I considered adding a donut but changed my mind and kept them all for myself. I poured coffee into a thermos and carried it all to the patio.

Maneuvering out the sliding glass door was slightly more challenging then it had been before I nailed up the thick wool blankets. I pulled a round end table closer to the door where I could set my tray. Using my body to hold open the window coverings, I kept my hands free to open the door and retrieve the breakfast tray. Mitchell had showered and shaved again. His hair was wet and pulled back into a loose braid. The sopping-wet pink blanket joined its mate draped over the fence to dry. His dry blanket was folded into an approximate square on the lounge. Mitchell was sitting at the patio table. He had been flipping through a magazine but stopped and was watching me as I squeezed the tray and myself through the narrowest fissure. The fragrance of shampoo, soap, and deodorant lingered around him. I set the tray down without bothering to say a word. He stopped me from going back into the house by gently taking ahold of my arm.

"Aunt Kelly, where is my uncle?"

I still wasn't ready to have that conversation, so I struck back with an offensive attack. I jerked my wrist from under his hand, "Where is he? Where is he? You tell me where you've been. Where have you been for the last four years? Where did you go after you stole my mother's jewelry? Where did you go after Grayson bailed you out of jail in the middle of the night? Do you think he came home and just fell back to sleep? No! He cried for you that night, and he cried for you after that. I know Gray gave you money. Where's the payback you promised? You are never going to pay that money back. Who do you think you're fooling? You're the fool. You're always asking, can we do you a favor, this or that. Where were you when I needed a favor? Where were you when Uncle Gray could have used a hand? He loved you! He wanted to share his life with you. Goddamn you! Why weren't you here? Why? I didn't ask you to come back. I don't owe you any answers."

The young man sat stunned and possibly frightened by my shrill assault.

He was looking at the ground, and for the second time in less then 24 hours he said to me, "I'm sorry."

"That's not good enough," I snapped as I stomped back into the house. I locked the door with a shaking hand, fumbling to get untangled from between the glass door, the sheer curtain, and the dark-blue wool blanket that had been hastily nailed into place.

I ran a bath for myself, convinced Mitchell would drink the coffee, eat the food, take what he wanted from the cooler, and leave. I slipped into the steaming water and tried to settle down. I lay back and let my head, pounding from that relentless headache, float while I waited for the latest round of aspirin to slacken the pressure behind my eye sockets. My nose and mouth were just at the surface of the water. My immersed ears heard strange and amplified sounds, drips dripping, air bubbles rising, and pipes creaking, each sound aquatic and mysterious; normal sounds disappeared. I crossed my hands over my chest and tried to control the flutter in my eyelids. Until that moment I had never considered the similarity between a coffin and the bathtub. I tried to imagine what it would be like to rest eternally in a box. My thoughts were, "Take me, God. Let me fall asleep and drown. If it's possible to drown in a few tablespoons of water, then it can't be that difficult in all the water I have right here. Spare me. This is agony. Take me right now."

After about an hour of soaking, the tub water had cooled, my skin had shriveled and my death wish had not been granted. I lifted myself from the lukewarm bath disappointed, disappointed that I was still among the living, and disappointed that Mitchell was still in the backyard. I could hear him in the cottage shed. He had turned on a radio I keep out there and took the liberty of changing the station from light jazz to the drilling litany of rap. That music sounded like I was being yelled at, berated, and lectured. If it had been any louder I would have gone out there and smashed the radio to pieces.

I re-dressed in Grayson's clothes, the ones I had cut to fit. Nothing of my own would have been as comfortable. If I couldn't have his arms wrapped around me, then I was willing to settle for his warm sweat suit. To that layer I added his Pendleton shirt. The added weight suggested a desperately longed-for caress. The sleeves were long, and the scissors were still nearby, so again I trimmed off their excess. There was something of reckless abandon in what I was doing, and to that end, ironically, it gave me a sense of control.

From the guest bedroom window I shifted the window curtain a half an inch to look out and saw Mitchell was cleaning the cottage shed. The front of the cottage is essentially a wall of paned windows. Through them I could see the gardening tools were all hanging from their hooks, the potting table was wiped down, the aluminum garbage can that holds fertilized soil had its lid on, and terra cotta pots were stacked in their different sizes in descending order. The broom was leaning against one of the outside flower boxes, and he was currently working on cleaning all of the glass windows. One windowpane at a time he was polishing to a streak-less shine. He was trying.

I didn't think he would stick around after all of the verbal artillery I had thrown at him. I had to remind myself that he deserved every word of what I had said. I had nothing to feel guilty about. He was the guilty one, the liar, the thief. Nevertheless, there was a nagging part of my conscience that wanted to beg forgiveness for myself. I couldn't stand confrontation. Grayson and I were not fighters. Far away in my past was the little girl voice that said, "I'm sorry. I didn't mean it. Please tell me you're not mad." It was my mother who I had to beg forgiveness from. "Please don't be mad at me, it was an accident..." breaking the water glass, losing my sweater, burning the toast. Her fury could erupt with the slightest provocation. When it did, all I could do was cower and plead for forgiveness. Angry confrontation put me back there.

I was beginning to wonder if I could trust any word that came out of my mouth. I felt so out of control and exposed. Giving Mitchell a piece of my mind, I ended up feeling like I had filleted myself. I had laid into him; he needed to hear what I had to say, but not like that, not with a barrage of accusations and insults. I worried that he could see inside me and would know I was unraveling. "What must he be thinking of me? He thinks I'm a hysterical b-i-t-c-h. He thinks Grayson was a fool to marry me." I didn't know what he thought, but it couldn't be nice. He had no idea where his uncle was, but surely he wouldn't have left without connecting. He'd want to tell on me and recount my rudeness. If he could have reunited with Grayson, he'd have wiggled his way back in the house, gloating with spite.

Beyond feeling invaded, self-conscious, defensive, and resentful there had always been a layer of fact that got to me and prevented me from hating him to the core. It repeatedly gave me a reason to take a higher road.

Comparing childhoods, it was difficult to say which one I would have preferred, his or my own. Mitchell was born in prison. Not exactly in prison: Cheryl was moved to a community hospital for the delivery. She had prior convictions for petty crimes on her record, but what got her incarcerated was possession of stolen checks, possession of drug paraphernalia and, the most serious, armed robbery of a liquor store. Her parents couldn't get her out of that one. Cheryl is the perennial child. She has never matured past the development of a five-year-old, the I-want-it, and the you-can't-make-me stage. Consequently, Mitchell remained in his grandmother's custody even after Cheryl had been released from prison. Richard and Helen had long since been divorced, and my father-in-law wanted nothing to do with the new baby, his grandson. And Mitchell's father, he continues to get arrested, and continues to live in prisons all across the country. My father, I never knew him. I was told that he was married to another woman.

In my case, my mother was all I knew. In Mitchell's case, he was tugged on by two vastly different women. Growing up, I didn't know that my home life could be anything but what it was. Mitchell, on the other hand, was routinely Ping-Ponged between the crazy world of his biological mother and the relatively stable and affluent world of his grandmother. For me, I think ignorance saved me. I didn't have to routinely choose between my mother and safety; he did.

Pearls my Mother Wore

On some level the nature of his birth and the circumstances of his parents entitled Mitchell to a free pass, not only with me, but with a lot of people, family mostly. We felt sorry for him, and never expected much. It was as though he was handicapped. His life had started off on the wrong foot and we all tried to make up for it by not pushing him. Nobody openly admitted this of course, but it seemed to always be there. He had a king-sized excuse for being a screw-up, and we all let him use it.

So that kid, whose world had been turned upside-down before he took his first breath, was in my backyard. He needed to know about his uncle. Furthermore, it wasn't for me to deny my husband Mitchell's respects. Mitchell was deeply bonded to Grayson, even though he did a crappy job of showing it. I didn't know exactly when Mitchell was going to leave, and I had no idea where he would go. I couldn't be certain he would go to his mother's, but if he did, I didn't want him to learn about Grayson's dying from her. And if he turned to his other aunts for refuge and they found out he had been here and I hadn't told him, then I would have even more explaining to do. I sure didn't want them nosing around and wondering why I had denied him the facts.

It became clear that I should tell him. I didn't want to think about what I would say, how I would say it. I didn't want those words to appear scripted or contrived. I didn't have the energy to imagine the dialog anyway. I tried to ignore the whole thing and take a nap, but I couldn't fall asleep. I got up and found a copy of the newspaper with Grayson's obituary in it. I took it outside and sat on the lounge chair. Mitchell looked up from his window washing and came over to where I was sitting. I lifted the paper, folded open to the part he should read. "You missed it," I said unsympathetically.

He took the paper from my hand, unsure but curious. Following the first sentence, he sat himself next to me on the chaise. He read without making a sound. His Adam's apple raised and lowered as he read on, swallowing his emotions. He finished the obit and set the paper at his feet, then buried his face in his hands. A few seconds later, he was crying. I went to get up and give him some privacy, but he reached for me to stay. A pang of maternal instinct passed through me. Despite all of his bad behavior, Mitchell did love his uncle; he idolized him, and I couldn't ignore the shock and pain he was feeling. I remained seated.

I don't know what I expected Mitchell's response to be to the news that Grayson had died, but I didn't expect the crying. Nobody was watching. He didn't have to put on a show for me. From experience, I didn't trust him. I couldn't trust that his response was genuine, that he was actually distraught. But he was crying. Tears dripped through his fingers and ran down his wrists. He couldn't speak. He made very little sound, but his upper body convulsed in spasms of anguish. Even when Helen died he didn't cry, not that I saw. I remember he asked his Aunt Margaret, "Did Gram leave me any money?"

I thought to myself, "Don't feel sorry for him. Once a user always a user, if you give him an inch, he will take a mile. I will not let him take over this house again just because he has been dealt yet another blow." Mitchell didn't ask to be born in prison any more than I asked to be born a bastard. Mitchell didn't have a dad or family from his father's side. None of his father's relatives had ever come forward. He appeared to be broke. There was no telling if he was a fugitive from the law. His doting grandmother was dead, and now so was his Uncle Gray. But, "Do not let him in. Do not," I continued to affirm in my mind.

I attempted to leave his side again, but he wiped his face with the collar of his (Grayson's) tee shirt and turned his head towards me. He was looking over my shoulder, not in my eyes, as he asked if he could still stay. He realized that we were relatives by marriage only, not blood, and in his tears he was considering his next move. He didn't ask me how I was doing. He didn't ask me what I was going to do. He didn't ask me to assure him that I was going to be all right. He asked about covering his own butt, which was normal; that was what I would have expected.

"Yes, I guess so, if you're comfortable enough outside. I'll let you stay a little while longer. I think you're still my nephew after all."

He had plenty to think about, and I didn't care to sit in his silence. I returned to the house feeling like I had been punched in the stomach, not from anything he had just done or said, but because of a deep constricting ache in my gut. I sat in my chair with my arms wrapped around my middle, bent over, holding myself, trying to catch my breath, holding on.

Chapter Four

My days with Mitchell in the backyard quickly fell into a dull routine, and the week passed with only a vague awareness of each specific day. We didn't have much to say to one another. Early on, I warned him that if he wanted any more food delivered he would need to remember how to say thank you. I thought perhaps that demand would send him packing and then I would be free again, but he obeyed. The strain between us was dulled by our mutual grief.

Every day I swapped out clean clothes for Mitchell to wear. Every day I was surprised to find him still hanging around. It was a relief to me that he was finding ways to occupy himself — I suspect more out of boredom than any interest in pleasing me or atoning for his theft. I could remember my intention to punish him, but my stamina was waning. It was easier to tolerate him than it would have been to ask him to leave. He'd putter with projects around the exterior of the house, and that pacified me superficially. He finished nailing up the last segment of fencing Grayson had been working on. He pulled weeds and scrubbed out the birdbaths. He watered with the hoses and washed the two cars, my Volvo and Grayson's Ford truck. He also killed time with all of the back issues of Vogue, Harper's Bazaar, Condé Nast Traveler, Architectural Digest, People, and Sunset that I saved in the cottage for crafty projects. He would roll the chaise around the yard to get the best sun or shade and read from magazines that were two and three years old — putter, read, doze — putter, read, doze.

Inside the house, I slept large chunks of the day away. My bed had a pull twice the force of gravity, such that lifting myself out of it required great strength and concentration. Once up, I found myself accomplishing very little. I was battling a headache that refused to go completely away despite the fact that I was taking several aspirin morning, noon, and night. I sat at the kitchen table and tried to deal with the mail that was accumulating at the base of the front door where the mailman passed it through a slot. I wanted to sort out the nonessential junk mail from the essential, but halfway through I could see I was mixing up the piles and had the gas and electric bill in the discard pile. I started over, and again I checked the stack of junk mail only to discover a letter from our attorney was in it. I became so irritated by the whole mess that, childishly, I scattered all the mail across the table, some of it spilling onto the floor, and I gave up.

Handling the accumulation of mail was similar to handling money; en masse, it struck me as filthy. I wondered how many people had put their hands on it and what else had they touched. For the first time, it made my skin crawl. The poor-quality inks had rubbed off onto my fingertips, adding to my sense that it was dirty. I couldn't wait to wash my hands and watch all the sudsy gray gunk swirl down the drain.

I came to waste huge amounts of time daydreaming at the kitchen sink. I'd stand there with the warm water running and wash my hands for ten to twenty minutes at a time regardless of whether I had a reason to or not. Over and over I would pump the detergent dispenser into my palm and work up lather after lather. The suds and water slipping down the drain would carry away all the nasty microbes that were only too eager to get under my skin. Pure, white, soapy bubbles would sometimes float up and then pop mid-flight. I did think at times, "I should stop this," but then I would give myself permission to continue for just another minute.

In a burst of stability or madness, I'm not sure which, I attempted to address something that had been gnawing at me all week. Clair and Margaret had taken it upon themselves to assembled a photomontage for Grayson's memorial; dozens of Kodak moments from throughout his life were mounted to six 32" x 40" poster boards. They had promised to return the pictures to their proper frames, albums, shoeboxes, and files, but with them, often, little promises were dispensed like Pez candies, sweet but quick to dissolve. The tribute had not been re-addressed following the service and the boards ended up partially hidden, sleeved behind the living room couch and against the wall. They were somewhat out of sight, but never out of mind. How long was I going to have to pretend that it didn't bother me that the vapors from so many unforgettable experiences hovered collectively around the room?

I was the only one who really knew where those pictures belonged anyway. What did I have to be afraid of? The tribute to Gray's life was appropriate. The poster boards were only part of what the sisters had pulled together to honor their baby brother in remembrance. Also on display were his baseball trophies, his downhill skis, his collection of model racecars and airplanes he had built, high school yearbooks, his guitar (not that he played it much anymore), his welding helmet and gloves. All of that stuff had been put back; it was only the pictures that needed to be returned to their proper places.

Pearls my Mother Wore

I washed down a couple of aspirin. Putting those pictures away would be my big task for the day. Before tackling the job, I finished off the last bits of taco casserole from a disposable, aluminum party pan. With my fingers, I picked at the wilted but once crispy cheese that had spilled over the rim when it was first baked. Not wanting to get filmy cheddar cheese oil on the pictures, I washed my hands.

I stood at the kitchen sink and washed my hands for several minutes. I squeezed and slowly rubbed my hands in the slippery soap. As my skin softened, I pushed my cuticles back, and chipped away at the stubborn remnants of fingernail polish that had been hastily applied over existing polish on the day of Grayson's funeral. The first coat was due to be taken off but I hadn't cared until it came time to dress for the service. Grayson liked how feminine my hands were. He would press his palm to mine and marvel at the difference in size and softness, giving my fingertips admiring kisses. For the funeral, it was quicker to put another coat of pink over what was still there rather than to remove it all and start over. My nails looked about as good as I did, presentable if you didn't look too closely. The sounds of warm running water pouring into the sink and down the drain and the foaming up of the soap were mesmerizing. I closed my eyes and continued the wringing massage. My mind emptied for a brief period of time. The reprieve ended when I noticed my finger pads shriveling into sensitive, fleshy, pink prunes.

I dried my hands and waited at the sink, looking out the window until my normal touch returned. I looked beyond the neighbor's tall fence out to Sonoma Mountain in the distance. The midday sky was yellow-blue, hazy, and pollen-filled.

I thought about all of the activity going on between myself and the mountain peak, people busy with their daily activities. Workers were working, drivers were rushing here and there, phones were ringing and children were playing. People everywhere around me were filled with their own concerns and events. It was musical chairs; the music had stopped and I had not caught a seat. I was out of the game. There was a swirling world out there. But so what? I told myself to turn away and go deal with the poster boards.

I pulled the photo essay of Grayson's life from behind the couch and laid each board across the living room floor. The full impact of those memories was immediately overwhelming. There he was as a little boy, face caked with mud on the bank of a river, then buttoned-up in a collared shirt on the first day of kindergarten, in his Little League uniform, prom night with full, bushy brown curls and a pale blue polyester suit. Birthdays, Christmas, Halloween — one year we were Rambo and Rambimbo. They were all there looking out at me, Grayson's eyes beseeching the onlooker to smile. There were pictures from our wedding day.

I shuffled and restacked the boards one on top of the other to reduce the surface area I had to face. I worked my way from the top board down to the last, resolving to pick each photograph from its holding tabs. Quickly, and in fact with my eyes averted and sometimes closed, I plucked every picture from the temporary display.

When I was done I had a pile of differently sized photographs and a pile of white poster boards. The holding tabs, black triangles, remained affixed to the white surfaces in stark contrast. The tabs hinted at the photos they had held. I remained on the floor next to the vacant poster boards. Now you see him, now you don't. My eyes blurred with more tears and the black tabs seemed to levitate and shift against the intense white. I wanted to let go, to drift into the undulating field of watery white. I rolled over onto my back and let tears stream off my face. I tried to focus on a cobweb wafting ever so slightly in a corner of the ceiling. I spoke to myself, "This isn't true. This isn't happening. This isn't real."

Eventually, I resurfaced from that spasm of grief and pulled one photo in particular from the stack of images, one I adore. It's a picture of Grayson, around ten years old, pulling his mom, who is sitting in his little red wagon. She is off-balance from his tug. One of her hands is holding her large, floppy hat from flying off; the other is clutching the side of the wagon. Her head is tossed back and she's laughing. He's checking over his shoulder; his sweet, innocent face is to the camera. His cheeks are pink, and his large, brown eyes sparkle from the joy of playing with his mother. He is wearing blue denim cut-offs, a red-and-blue, horizontal-striped tee shirt, and sneakers with no socks. The sinews of his skinny arms and legs are straining against her weight, petite as she was in the picture. She is wearing a denim halter-top and red hot pants. Her floppy hat also has red flowers painted on it. The reds and blues in the photograph are just as vibrant as the tall green privet hedge behind them.

The picture is so full of life; it's ironic that no one in it is alive anymore. I know that the person standing in the street taking this snapshot is Harry, Helen's boyfriend. Harry's life ended in a car accident a couple of years before Helen died. Helen and Harry never lived together, but they were devoted companions for over thirty years. Harry was a professional photographer who sold his images to corporations to use in their brochures and publications. He took many of the pictures that ended up on the memorial poster boards I had just dismantled.

Harry was the quintessential beatnik. He wore a dark-blue beret tilted towards the back of his bald head. He was a good fifteen years older then Helen, but such a hip cat that the age difference didn't matter. Harry was cool, never tried too hard. He was laid back and easy to talk to. Often, he would have a collection of budding photographers hanging around him. He was the nickname man, always giving people nicknames, and he had plenty of them applied to himself. Helen sometimes called him Handy or Handyman, but usually it was Bluey for his pale blue eyes. Sometimes she would also call him Thread because of his lithe, lean body and how he moved. Grayson would call him H-man. Harry called Helen Goggie, Goggie Girl, Goog, Sweets, Sweetsville, and Doll. He called me Kelly Bell and Jazzy, which I miss. He had endless names for Grayson: Champ, Sport, Scout, Boss Man, Daddy-o, Iron Man, Arrow, Gravy, Gray squirrel, Buster, Stretch. He'd call strangers Cats, as in, "I was talking to this Cat the other day…" Mitchell was Hops when he was little, then it was Foxy for awhile until Mitchell told him to stop calling him names. Harry had a very poetic and amusing way with words. I think he enjoyed words almost as much as he enjoyed photography.

The day before Grayson's memorial I noticed Richard, my father-in-law, looking at the photographs of his son that Harry had taken over the years. Whatever Richard's thoughts were, they didn't register on his face. His chiseled features remained true to form, handsome and unmoving. It was, however, on that day that he surprised me with a tender hug. That time I was the one to stand impassive while being embraced, not him.

My favorite picture of Grayson, Helen and the red wagon is kept in a frame on the nightstand on my side of the bed. Even after Helen died the old picture still filled my heart with joy because it was such a happy scene. Their guileless loving expressions had been captured on film; that look can't be faked. Holding the picture in my hand, I suddenly had a different response to it. Instead of joy,

I was angry, mad that they had all left and didn't take me with them. I returned the image to its frame and the nightstand, then lay down on the bed where I continued to look across at it. I pulled the covers up to my chin and imagined his high-pitched, little-boy voice saying something like, "Mommy, should I go faster?"

"Sure Honey, go faster. Go faster! Don't fall," Helen would encourage.

Mitchell hadn't asked how I was doing because it had been my endless goal to look like I had it together. He believed I was born on easy street; indeed, I had spent almost two-thirds of my life trying to convince people of just that. I shouldn't have faulted him just because he happened to believe me, but I did. I resented the fact that he couldn't read my mind as well as I could read his. The anger Mitchell displayed outwardly was equal in proportion to the fear that kept me in check. I didn't challenge; I withdrew. I didn't make scenes; I cleaned them up. I didn't scowl; I smiled. What made me that way was hammered out on the same hot anvil that made him — drama, deception, and disappointment. Good girl is the flip side of bad boy, but he couldn't see it.

His circling around the exterior of my home interfered with the total numbness I was seeking. Everything hurt. Without my husband and my routine I was like a tree with no bark, a planet with no sun, a lily without a pond. Like Cinderella's wicked stepsisters, I tried to cram the ugly parts of my life into a pretty glass slipper. Without Grayson, the glass slipper had shattered, and all the ugly parts sprang to life.

Chapter Five

"You're yelling at the wrong guy. I'm not that bastard's daddy," he had said to my mother. I heard that the night before I was to start kindergarten. My mother was arguing with a boyfriend, I can't remember his name. The problem that time was my clothes had suddenly become a crisis. Until that day, I had no consciousness about what my clothes looked like; they were there to put on in the morning and exchange for pj's in the evening.

Earlier in the day, my mother and I had been in a grocery store. She was going up and down the aisles picking out what she needed, and I was free to roam the toy aisle. The toy aisle was a fantastic place where I could get lost in my imagination. The items were too expensive to buy, but I could imagine owning the bubble-bath kit, complete with a tiny pot of powder, a tiny bottle of perfume, and a tiny bottle of little-girl nail polish. I could imagine owning the gold-glitter plastic high heels. There were pink necklaces, bracelets, and brilliant cut ring sets, jacks and jump-ropes, crayons and watercolors; there were so many beautiful things to touch, if I could get away with it. "Look, but don't touch!" she had warned.

I got caught fondling a pretend, lime-green feather boa. It came with child-sized, elbow-high, white gloves. I was daydreaming and twisting the soft feathers around my arm when my mother snatched it away, took ahold of my upper arm and marched me out of the store. She was walking so fast and pulling up on my arm so much that many of my steps barely touched the ground. I thought my offense had been touching something I shouldn't have. It turned out that what I had done was to bend over. I had bent over to pick up the luscious feathers from the bottom shelf they were on, revealing my underpanties, my underpanties that had more holes than fabric.

"I'm so ashamed of you! How many times do I have to tell you that a proper lady never bends over at the waist. You bend your knees! Now everybody in that store has seen your dirty fanny sticking up in the air. You wait in this car until I come back. I want you to think about what you've done. Now I have to go back in there and the whole world is going to know what a nasty little girl my daughter is. What am I going to do with you?"

Before we drove home, Mom stopped at the St. Vincent de Paul thrift store and quickly sized up and purchased the clothes and underclothes I would wear to school the next day.

That night Mom was seething. By dinnertime, her invidious wrath was directed at the boyfriend. "Rags, damn you. I had to buy rags for baby girl." Waves of amber liquid sloshed out of the tumbler she was clutching as she gestured toward the bag that still contained my new-used clothes.

"You bring your lard ass here every night and eat my food, but you won't give me a God damned dime to pay for it," she slurred.

"I gave you ten dollars last week," he slurred back.

"You never gave me shit! You're a penny-pincher and you're a liar!"

"What are you talking about? If you need money so bad, why don't you get it from her father? Where is he? You're yelling at the wrong guy. I'm not that bastard's daddy."

My mother called her boyfriends beaus. "I have a new beau," she would announce coquettishly. That was confusing at first because I thought she was referring to hair bows. I was just as tickled when I got a new hair bow as she seemed to be when she got a new man beau.

One evening, a new beau took us to the drive-in to see the Elvis Presley movie, Double Trouble. It was the summer between first and second grade, and it was my first experience watching a movie on a big screen. I was told to put on my pajamas and given a blanket to fall asleep with in the backseat of his car. At the drive-in we pulled between the parking lines next to the magical sound box. I was standing on the hump in the backseat looking out the front windshield at all of the other cars parked and parking around us. The beau looked back at me and asked what kind of soda pop did I like. I didn't know; at home Mom made Kool-Aid. Mommy told him I would like 7-Up. Before getting out of the car, he flashed open his wallet and made a joke about not being sure he could afford it. His wallet was thick with dollar bills.

Mommy pointed to the giant white wall and told me that was where the movie would appear. She flipped down the visor and checked her makeup and hair in the mirror before he returned. The mirror light illuminated her movie-star face. She pressed a wand of orange lipstick to her lips, then seductively blotted the excess on a tissue she had hidden in her cleavage. Her pearl earrings and necklace matched her bouffant pearl-white hair.

He approached the car gripping three icy cups and straws with his massive hands, and slightly crushing two red-and-white striped boxes of buttered popcorn between his ribs and biceps. The straw was the best part of the 7-Up. I found it captivating. What control I could exert over the drink, stopping the flow mid-stream! I was blowing bubbles in the cup when Mommy turned around and told me to "knock it off."

The crank to roll down his driver's side window was missing; it was in the passenger side glove compartment. He reached across Mommy to get it and brushed his hairy arm across her breast while doing so. She sucked in a little air at the thrill. I wasn't supposed to know what that was. He fidgeted with the window crank until he finally got it to work. A speaker box hung over the glass opening.

The lights in the parking lot went out, and the car filled with music. The big white wall exploded in color. An animated chorus line of happy candy bars danced across the screen, encouraging everybody to visit the concession stand. Mom looked back at me and ruffled up my hair; she was amused by my wide-eyed amazement. Elvis sang songs and grown-up girls and boys danced on the screen. Sometimes, Mom and I would dance in our living room; she showed me how to do the jerk, the pony, and the mashed potato. Mom and her beau bobbed their heads and torsos to the music, and I wiggled around in the commodious backseat area. As the singing lessened and the plot grew, I reclined into the worn leather seat, legs jutting forward, feet just clearing the seat. I used the blanket to protect my skin against the scratchy, peeled up upholstery. It was difficult to see the big movie with the front seats blocking most of my view. About the time Elvis was singing a snappy rendition of "Old MacDonald," I was falling asleep.

Several beaus later, I found myself again in pajamas with a blanket in the backseat of another car. I wasn't told where we were going, but I was hopeful that it was to the drive-in. I had crayons and a coloring book full of Walt Disney Jungle Book characters—Mowgli the jungle boy, Bagheera the panther, Baloo the bear. I didn't care where we were going. All I knew was that I was excited to be going out with my Mom and not left at home with a baby sitter.

The beau parked his car at a corner where two streets in an industrial area met. Straight ahead was the massive backside of some kind of factory; steam escaped from various places in the gigantic Erector Set structure; tiny yellow-and-red lights dotted along metal catwalks and around large holding tanks and towers. Down the street to the right was the only indication of life, a blinking neon sign that pulsed three red arrows in the direction of a door. Mom and her beau were going to go in for "a drink." I was to wait in the car until they came back. Mom, standing on the sidewalk, indicated with her frosty orange fingernail that I should push down the four door locks while saying to me, "We'll be right back. Be a good girl." I pushed the locks and watched them disappear through the black vinyl-padded door that swung in both directions.

A few minutes after they had gone in, the door flew open, cracking against its hinges and somebody stumbled out into the street. Fortunately, his car was parked in the opposite direction from where I was. If he had come in my direction, I would have scrunched down in the foot-well and covered myself with my blanket. Every time the door swung open I hoped it would be Mom and her beau coming to take me home. Mom stuck her head out the door and looked down the street at me. She smiled and waved with her fingers. I waved back. I didn't color; I watched that door for any and all movement.

A car pulled directly in front of the bar and a black man and lady got out. She was wearing a full length rabbit-fur coat and he was wearing black leather pants. They both styled their hair in full round Afros. From the factory, men in white hard hats appeared through a gate that rolled open. They trotted across the avenue and ducked into the bar only to reappear a few minutes later and jaywalk back to work. The street was not a busy one, and long stretches of time passed in between the appearances of one vehicle and the next.

My mother's beau came out carrying a small cardboard to-go box. I unlocked the door and he handed me a sausage sandwich and a ruby-red 7-Up drink, a "Shirley Temple," he called it, before leaving me. It had a sweet maraschino cherry in it, and a slim red straw. The sausage was spicy and the roll was dry, but I ate every bite. I drank the entire Shirley Temple in just a couple of long draws on the cocktail straw. As the ice in the glass melted, I blew bubbles in it to my heart's content. Once the ice had melted and I had slurped and swished the liquid until it was all gone, I then chewed on the straw and tied it into various shapes — a circle, a figure eight, a square.

Later Mom came out to retrieve the glass and check on me. She tipped off her high heels slightly as she walked towards the car.

"Can we go home now?"

"We're going to go home in a few minutes, Rudy is just finishing up a game of pool. We'll leave when he's done. Give Mommy a kiss."

We kissed on the lips and again she pointed to the door lock before swerving back to the bar.

After the few minutes went by and my mother and her date had not come out, my heart began to sink. A half hour went by and then an hour, and then another hour. The thought of running down the street and going inside the bar to get them crossed my mind — in fact it persisted in my thoughts, but I rejected it over and over again. Rudy's car was parked on the far side of the corner; I would have had to cross the street by myself. The factory, with its hissing vapors, was menacing; Cyclone fencing topped with razor wire surrounded it, and warned me that it was a dangerous place. At one point, I accidentally tooted his horn. There was no response, and I couldn't summon the nerve to try it a second time.

Hours passed. They must have thought surely I would be asleep. I wasn't asleep. I saw a man come out and urinate in the doorway next to the bar and then go back inside. The pulsating neon sign turned off, but an additional collection of neon lights poured color onto the sidewalk. Mom and her beau appeared through the door together. They slowly made their way to the car, bumping into each other. Mom stopped and fumbled in her purse for a cigarette. She dropped the purse and its contents lay scattered around their feet. She stood for a moment looking at what had happened and then bent over slowly to gather her things as he looked on. The two of them stood at the spot swaying from side to side. His lighter flared up and an effort was made to connect flame to cigarette. She reached up to steady his hand and together they succeeded in igniting the Pall Mall. In the flame I could see her face was lax, like a wilted flower.

I could tell they were arguing, but I couldn't make out what they were saying; they were both talking and mumbling at the same time. As they got closer to the car, I could hear Mom's voice go up and down from barely audible to shrill and then back again. I had been afraid all night, but the sight of them, her so intoxicated, made me shake with fear. I knew I was supposed to be asleep, so I lay down and covered myself with the blanket. He opened her door and she plopped inside. She was slurring and puffing out each word individually for emphasis.

As he got into the car she was saying, "You...God damn... no good...son of a bitch. Go back to your whore wife then. That's where you belong. You...rotten...slime. You make me sick! You know what you are? You're filth! You're shithole scum."

From a rip in the blanket, I watched her head move around like it was too heavy to hold steady. Her body heaved forward when she said "scum" so as to deliver the word with even greater gusto.

From the side, he looked like a pink balloon about to pop. Tiny red veins in his face glistened under his perspiration. As she was spewing her hateful words, he was trying to drown her out with his own. "You're drunk. You don't know what the hell you're talking about! Look at you! You're pathetic! Why don't you shut up so you don't scare your God damned kid? Yah, your God damned kid. Who in hell's kid is that anyway? I bet you don't have a clue who's the father of that bastard. You don't know shit from Shinola."

As the car lunged down the avenue, I squeezed my eyes shut and rubbed my hands against my ears so that I wouldn't have to listen to their fighting. Around corners he squealed the tires; I had to let go of my ears so that I could hang on and not roll onto the floor.

By the time he got us to the carport of our apartment building, their fighting had escalated to uncontrolled screaming. He grabbed her jaw and twisted her face to look in the backseat at her bastard. She began to flail about, swatting at him, she scratched three bloody welts into his face.

"Son of a bitch!" he bellowed.

I started screaming, "Stop! Stop! Mommy, stop it!"

He made an attempt to swat at me, but my mother blocked him. She gripped his arm with strength I hadn't known she possessed and said, "You'll have to get through me before you ever, ever touch that child."

"Get out of my God damned car! Now! Both of you!" he wailed.

The parade of recollections continued. I was in the fourth grade when my mother married Jack Perkins and we moved from the urban industrial sprawl of San Leandro to the rural hinterland of Napa, from a you-can-be-invisible city to an everybody-is-staring-at-you small town. Before we moved, one of the neighbor ladies watched me while JP and Mom went to Reno to "tie the noose," she said.

"Can I go?"

"No, of course you can't go. Reno's no place for children, silly."

"Where is Reno?

"What do you care where it is? You're not going."

"Is it far?"

"No, it's not far. Now quit bothering me. Go outside and play. It's a beautiful day."

"When will you be back?"

"Listen young lady, if you don't quit bothering me, I am going to send you to your room until it is time to go to Mrs. Furtado's. Have you packed your things?"

A paper bag held my wad of nightgown and a change of clothes. I didn't want to go outside. I didn't want to be that far away from my mother, knowing that she was going away. I lay on my bed and listened to her as she was getting ready. She sang and whistled parts of that song from My Fair Lady about getting married in the morning—ding dong, I'm gonna get really drunk, but don't let me be late to the church, that song. I could hear her curlers land one by one in the plastic case she kept them in; her silver clippies clinked and shifted in the pink glass dish she had for those. I could hear the snap of her stockings as she wrestled them on. The sweet, powdery scent of cosmetics and perfume floated from the bathroom into my bedroom.

There was a knock on the front door. JP had arrived.

"Baby, get that for Mommy, will you?"

She liked to keep her beaus waiting. She would wave frantically at me to go open the door while she herself ducked into another room. Not until he had been in the house for a few minutes did she make a staged entrance.

"Mommy's just about ready," I informed JP sheepishly.

"Yes, that will be fine," was his response.

JP was a man who didn't have much to say to people in general, and even less to say to nine-year-old girls. He had a gravely voice. "That will be fine" was one of his few phrases. "I told you no," was another. He also said, "Get out of the way of the TV," and "Go outside." Deep, curved folds of rugged skin flanked his thin lips. The fold lines gave his mouth the appearance of being enclosed in parenthesis, as if his mouth was an interesting but not entirely necessary addition to his face.

He was a Korean War veteran. Before we met for the first time Mom showed me a wallet-sized photo of him. It was his military service portrait from years earlier; he looked strong, proud, and determined in his uniform. "This one's a catch, baby girl," she had said to me.

JP was a stocky handsome-ish man; he looked like the older Frank Sinatra, not the young angular one. He wore his dark hair slicked back with Vitalis hair tonic; a flat-top with wings they called his hairstyle, flat on top with longer sides swept up and folded into a ducktail roll in the back. He had a scar that cut vertically across his forehead and gave one of his eyebrows a permanent high arch that made him look angry all the time. His jaw was square, and the muscles of it frequently twitched as if he were clinching his teeth. He wore perma-press polyester slacks, polished wingtip shoes, short sleeved-shirts ironed crisp, and he smelled of Aqua-Velva aftershave. He drove a chocolate brown, brand new Cadillac.

"Mommy, JP is here," I called out as if she didn't already know.

She entered the living room from the opposite side of where JP and I were waiting and paused long enough for him to let out a slow "um, um, um," like he was looking at a table set with a Thanksgiving feast. Her platinum hair was lacquered with hairspray, sculpted into overlapping petals. Her hair glistened like butter-cream frosting spread on a birthday cake. She looked like Marilyn Monroe with her ruby red lips and pale white skin. She was wearing a cream-colored sheath dress with a short matching jacket; chocolate brown piping ran down the sides of the petite dress and jacket sleeves. She had on her pearls. She stepped forward to give him a peck on the cheek, but he had bigger ideas. He grabbed her around the waist with one arm and pulled her tight up against himself. She made a slight whoop and giggle, but then swatted at him. "You're gonna wrinkle my dress. Now, let go so I can take Kelly to the sitter next door."

JP was a heating-and-cooling specialist. He installed and repaired heating-and-cooling units used in the food-and-beverage industries. Many of his customers were from dairy farms and wineries in the rural counties north of San Francisco. Often he would bring home fruit juice, cheese and butter or wine and brandy from the places he serviced. Sometimes a job would take him farther away and he would be gone for a couple of days, but there were also times when he wouldn't have any work and stayed home watching TV and drinking beer.

He met Mom at her work; she was a front-office clerk at the big tomato-processing plant not far from where we lived. In my neighborhood, the tangy smell of ketchup and tomato sauce hung in the air day and night. He was doing some work at the plant when one day he brought a box of chocolates to Mom's desk and asked her for a date. He was her beau for only a couple of weeks before he was her husband and we moved into his house.

They got back from Reno, and the three of us drove to Napa to live together. I had grown up in various apartment buildings, so the prospect of living in a house that had both a front and back yard, that I was free to play in, was exciting. From the backseat of his perfectly polished Cadillac, I strained to look up and out at the changing scenery. In almost imperceptible increments the congested homes and businesses that had been the only landscape I knew fell away. As we got closer to the place called Napa, all I could tell was that there was a lot more land, and a lot less life. Country music played at a low volume on the car radio but the signal was weak and much of the time there was static. Mom was full of ideas about how to decorate JP's house; she chatted at him almost the whole way about dishes, furniture, closets, and cupboards, what she needed and what wouldn't do. "That'll be fine," he said several times.

I was relieved when we actually pulled into a neighborhood. The more grassy the view had gotten the more I wondered what kind of Hooterville I was headed for. But in JP's neighborhood, the houses were on city blocks with sidewalks, intersections, and lampposts. I remember walking up to the new house. Mom put her arm around my shoulder as we went up the wide, wooden steps to the covered front porch; leaves and faded newspapers had collected in its dusty corners. The house was dark. Even once the curtains were drawn it was still dark with wood paneling and mix-and-match furniture that looked like it belonged in a hunting lodge.

"Christ-almighty JP. It's like a damn cave in here," Mom said, and I was glad because it was.

The moving van with our things wasn't going to arrive until the next day. That night I slept, or tried to sleep, on the floor of what was to become my room. It was musty at first when we entered it, basically an empty unused room except to store JP's hunting gear. The room was up four stairs off the kitchen; its windows looked out into the surrounding trees. I imagined it as my own private tree fort. Mom pushed open the windows, and helped me unroll JP's sleeping bag. With one hand on her hip and the other pointing around the room, she explained how my furniture would be arranged. "Baby girl, we'll put your bed here so you can look out at night. Wait 'til it gets dark, girlie, the stars are gonna knock your socks off."

That night the sky was blacker and the stars were brighter and more plentiful than the ones back home had ever been. Once Mom and JP turned out the lights and went into their bedroom at the other side of the house, everything became so quiet that I couldn't fall asleep. I missed the city drone, cars whizzing past, neighbors moving around in adjacent units, voices and footsteps from people coming and going. With my tree fort window ajar, I could hear crunching in the dry leaves below. I got out of the sleeping bag to look. From the light of the moon I watched a fat black cat slowly prowl around. A second cat appeared and they yowled and hissed at each other; then, after a quick tussle, they ran off.

Mom got me into school right away. It wasn't the first time I had started with a new class in the middle of the year, so I knew what to expect, and I dreaded it. The principal ushered me into the classroom, everybody became silent; I was introduced and given a desk, books, paper and a sharpened pencil. The students stared at me for several minutes and then stole glances again and again throughout the morning. At recess, the other children had already established their preferred playmates, and so I talked with the yard monitor, a small gray-haired woman, who was curious to know everything about me. I pretended JP was my real father. She wanted to know my name and where had I moved to Napa from, what my mother and father's names were, did I have any brothers or sisters, what kind of work did my father do, what was our address, did we own our home or rent, what kind of car did my daddy drive, did I have any pets. I answered all of her questions and was proud to be of so much interest.

JP strung a rope-swing for me from one of the two big magnolia trees in the backyard, the back half acre. The rope was thick and he put a knot on the end to provide a lump for me to sit or stand on. Mom watched him work and even took a spin on it herself before turning it over to me. We both tried to get JP to get on it, but he refused. Mom called the backyard "the south forty." I spent hours and hours back there. Against the back fence was a thicket of blackberries. I picked large bowls of them, getting lacerated in the process, but the pain was worth it. My stained and bleeding fingertips were a small price to pay for those plump, succulent berries that I would coat with sugar and milk.

We had only been living at JP's for a couple of months; I was still the strange new kid in my classroom, but I knew everybody's names and they knew mine. I ran home at lunchtime and after school because I knew Mom would be waiting for me. At that time, she seemed to like not working and being a housewife in the suburbs. She prepared nice dinners; instead of Spam, hot dogs, and Kraft macaroni and cheese, we were eating steak with baked potatoes, roasts with Yorkshire pudding, fried chicken with corn on the cob. We had salads and fresh vegetables, not canned. On Sunday mornings she fixed scrambled eggs with Portuguese linguiça sausage, or fried ham and eggs, with biscuits and gravy, or pancakes and bacon. JP had a washing machine and dryer in his garage and an ironing board that folded out of a cupboard in the wall. She would press his shirts and slacks.

Then she had a miscarriage.

That day, as usual, I eagerly blasted through the door after school but then stopped dead in my tracks. My mother was on the kitchen floor crying into the avocado-green telephone mounted on the wall, its spiral phone cord stretched almost straight to reach her ear. "There's too much blood," she was saying, and indeed there were drips of blood leading to where she was. Her housedress was hiked up and a bath towel was between her legs; streaks and smears of blood were crusting on her legs, fingers and on her face where she held the phone. I stood mute, staring at her. "My baby," she kept saying over and over. I didn't have any idea what this had to do with me; I was her baby, her baby girl.

Ambulance sirens were getting louder and closer. With a hand over the receiver, she finally acknowledged that I was standing there. In a no-nonsense whisper she gave me directions. "Kelly, I want you to hide in the closet. Mommy has to go to the hospital. I don't want them to take you. Be Mommy's good girl and don't make a sound."

"No, I want to go with you," I pleaded in a similar whisper.

"JP will be here soon. Now, do what I say."

A commotion was approaching the front door. She hissed at me and snapped her fingers at the coat closet. I darted into it and pressed myself behind the wooly, tobacco and Estée Lauder-saturated full-length coats as the doorbell rang simultaneously with the front door opening. I could hear Mom inform the person on the telephone, "No, doctor, I am not alone, they're here now." And then her groans were horrible. I wanted to do the right thing. I wanted to comfort her, but I was afraid. I knew better than to assert myself in her affairs. She wanted me out of sight. She said they would take me away; I was too afraid to move.

"Mrs. Perkins?" I heard a husky woman's voice say. From my hiding place I could hear several adults all talking at the same time. Loud, staticky, walkie-talkie radios were conveying coded messages; I caught our address among the jumble of letters, numbers and words. A fine edge of light outlining the closet door penetrated into my hiding place, but I could not see out. I stayed pressed against the back of the closet, still and silent.

"Everything is going to be O.K. Mrs. Perkins," I could hear the woman's voice assure my mother as she continued crying out, "My baby, my baby."

It sounded like a huge party was going on, but then the front door closed, the siren noise receded, and the house was empty. I stayed in the closet for what felt like hours before JP arrived home and called out my name. I was afraid of the blood on the floor. I didn't want to come out of the closet and be alone with it. When JP got home I leapt up and flew out of the closet straight into his arms. He held me for the first, and only, time.

It would be fair to say that my mother's marriage to JP, the industrial heating and refrigeration specialist, ran hot and cold. Their first fight came shortly after we moved into his house, a few weeks before the miscarriage. Mom had almost all of JP's furniture moved out to the front porch and later hauled away. Our furniture wasn't fancy, but it was better than the ratty Naugahyde and plaid stuff he had. She was going to J.C. Penney's almost every day to buy things for the house—curtains, rugs, kitchen, and bathroom items. Initially, JP liked what she was doing; he complimented her decorating skill and suggested she start a little business. But after a while, he didn't find it so great. She'd bring in bag after bag of stuff, but then leave it unattended to in a small office next to their bedroom. The first fight I heard them have was because she was spending too much money. He made the mistake of inquiring about something she was showing us. "How much did that cost?" he asked.

I knew better than to hang around after that crack. A couple of Mom's beaus had made similar remarks, and the sparks always flew once they had. I exited the back door as she was launching into him: "Oh, don't you start with that 'How much?' crap." I stayed in the backyard until it got dark. When I went back in, I entered the house gingerly. She was cooking dinner. At the sight of her, I could tell the fight wasn't over. She was holding a frosty cocktail glass in one hand and tongs in the other, standing at the stove, turning grease-spattering pork chops in a big, cast-iron skillet. "Go wash your hands," she commanded, and I was more than happy to get out of her way.

JP sat stone-faced in front of the blaring television; a brandy was on the coffee table in front him. That night, the three of us didn't sit at the dinner table together. She practically threw his plate at him; I heard it land on the coffee table. "Do you want to know how much your stinking dinner cost? Well, do you?" and she started rattling off prices.

I don't know how much he had said to her up to that point, but suddenly I heard the coins in his pockets jangle with more velocity than the usual noise they made whenever he stood up. His dinner plate and silverware clattered on the table, and there was a definite rustling of motion. I don't know if he took a hold of her or if he just got up quickly, but he hollered, "Enough!" with the booming authority of a military general. I think he grabbed her because she made a noise that sounded like more than just a startle, it sounded like it was being shaken out of her. There was a pause and then, quite calmly, she said to him, "You son of a bitch. Is this how it's going to be? Do you feel like a man now?" They must have been glaring at each other, but he didn't answer her. She walked into their bedroom and slammed the door, and he sat back down. I could hear the silverware tap on his plate as he ate his supper.

My opinion of JP shifted in that moment. I had thought he was somebody my mother had wrapped around her little finger. I had taken some kind of comfort in the new surroundings because I felt she was in charge. She was running the show, and she would protect us. But his yell was like an explosion in a gold mine, and I couldn't trust that it would never happen again. That night I choked my meal down. My fork shook while I tried to stab at the food. I did the normal dinner-hour thing, I ate my supper and then cleaned the kitchen. I didn't bother my mother for a good-night kiss.

The next day things were chilly between JP and Mom, but they were civil to one another. After a couple of more days, Mom's banter returned, and all seemed well again. She could tease JP and he would play along with mild humor. He might say something like, "Here we go again," or "Mother of God," but I could tell he wasn't angry because he'd give her fanny a little swat when he passed by, and she would jump in mock surprise. She gave him big lipstick kisses on his cheeks and forehead, or she would read something aloud to him from the newspaper that she found interesting to show her restored good nature. She absentmindedly sang her Peggy Lee and Connie Francis favorites as she got dressed in the morning, while folding laundry, or while stirring pots on the stove. He came home with flowers a couple of times, went back to calling her Doll, and regularly lit her cigarettes.

The temperature plunged dramatically just after she returned home from the hospital without a baby. JP was sleeping on the couch while she was supposed to be recuperating, except she wasn't recuperating. She would be in bed when I left for school in the morning and still buried under the scrambled sheet and covers when I returned home in the afternoon. I would knock ever so softly on her bedroom door and hope that she would say, "Come in." I didn't want to wake her if she was sleeping. I was her good little helper. When she asked me to get her a glass of ice water, I gladly obliged. I liked it when she'd pat my hand and tell me I was too good to her. Sitting on the edge of the bed, I'd check her forehead for fever, the way she had done to me when I was sick.

"Kelly, don't bounce on the bed like that. You know it hurts when I move." She grimaced as she washed down a couple of prescription pills.

"Kelly, get my wallet."

She gave me a couple of dollars to go to the corner market and buy three TV dinners for our evening meal and a little something for dessert, ice cream bars, cookies, donuts, whatever I wanted.

When JP arrived home at the end of the day, he brought cigarettes and vodka with him. He didn't knock to enter her room; but just opened the door and looked in. He might say hello to me or he might not. In the kitchen he mixed her an icy vodka and tonic, and in the living room he poured himself a brandy from the liquor hutch. By the time the TV dinners were done cooking they'd have had two or three drinks. I ate at the kitchen table, Mom ate from a TV tray at the side of her bed, and JP ate in the living room. JP and I could both view the television from our separate locations. Tommy and Dick Smothers, Dean Martin, Carol Burnett and Ed Sullivan filled the house with talk and laughter. Behind the closed bedroom door, Mom listened to a talk-radio station, or she read and re-read her romance novels.

Late, on many nights, I was awakened to the sound of the national anthem being played before the TV station signed off for the night. I'd hop out of bed before the blaring static noise could indicate the empty channel and possibly rouse one or both of them. I'd slip through the house quickly, turning out the lights. JP snored from the couch. His scar-arched eyebrow continued to hold his hostile expression as he slept. She, too, could be heard breathing heavily in the closed-off room. There were nights when I would wake up to the sounds of her making her way to the bathroom. She'd bump between the hallway walls. I could hear her slurring defiantly, "Don't touch me, God damn it," even though nobody was there. I never wanted her to catch me being out of bed when she made those staggering treks.

Eventually, Mom was getting dressed in the morning and JP was back sleeping in the same bed with her. Much of the time there was nothing but silent tension in the house and the television blasting. But periodically, some combination of resentment, innuendo, fabrication, perhaps a telephone call, the local or national news, the weather, the bills, something would set them off and the fight would be on. JP's payday seemed to precipitate many of their bigger fights. All the different ways money can be spent number all the different ways they fought on the subject. Her ranting seemed to fall on deaf ears. It was like she was a freak wind-up doll, yelling to nobody and everybody at the same time.

I always dreaded news flashes about Yoko Ono and John Lennon. For some reason, Mom hated Yoko Ono, and once she was drunk, the news flash would remind her to heave loads of anti-Asian vitriol at her Korean War veteran husband. That was her kerosene to his fire. He would ignore her up to a point, but inevitably the moment would come when he would blow. After he had heard "gook," "chink," "flat face," or "slant eyed slut" enough times, after he had endured her umpteenth lame impersonation of an Asian, "You like-ee yellow whore?" he would come alive with volcanic fury. I vividly recall her efforts to provoke him: "Is that the kind you want? You can't touch me because you want some yellow whore? You limp bastard."

His gruff voice, much louder than hers, would very nearly rattle the dolls off my shelf: "If you know what's good for you, you better zip up."

She wouldn't.

"I'm telling you, Wife, enough. If you want to talk about whore, let's talk about who's the stinking whore around here. I should have walked away and let you raise two God damned bastards. Now I'm stuck with you."

"Stuck with me! Ha!" she countered. "You're lucky I'm still here, you good-for-nothing worm. One of these days I'm gonna use that door right there and that will be the last you're going to see of Mrs. Jack Perkins. If you think I won't hire a lawyer to destroy you, you've got another thought coming my friend."

"I'm not afraid of no gold-digging, two-bit tramp. If that's your plan then leave now. Go on, get out of my house. I'll see you in court and we'll see who destroys who." The front door was swung open and crashed against the wall. A pane of decorative leaded glass busted out of the door and smashed to pieces against the hardwood floor. He was yelling something to the effect of, "There's the door, use it!" At the same time she was hollering about the glass, "Now look what you've done, you moronic horse's ass."

His participation took their fights from verbal to physical. He'd get right in her face and bellow threats at her. If she was sitting and tried to stand, he'd push her back in the seat. Many times he fumbled with drunken attempts to push her out the front door. It didn't take long before the physical exertion would exhaust them both and it would soon be over. She'd attempt to slap him or throw a drink at him. There were times when he slapped her right back, or he shook her, or smothered her mouth with his hand. He'd twist her arm behind her back and slam her against the wall. Unsteady on their feet, it wouldn't take much for them both to go tumbling against the walls and onto the floor. She would get in screams of "You bastard!" and "You son of a bitch!" and he would holler back, "Shut up. I'm warning you. Enough."

The neighbors did not live close enough to be woken from sound sleeps by the late-night fracases that were going on at the house I lived in. Eventually, Mom and JP would pass out and the next morning act as if nothing had happened. By the time they got out of bed, I typically had righted the toppled furniture, emptied and washed the ashtrays, swept whatever had been broken the night before, and cleaned whatever had been splashed on the walls. I thought if I could erase the evidence then I could erase the experience. Time and time again, I believed that the last fight would be their last, and time and time again, another vicious row sent me running for cover.

I hated myself for being such a chicken. As they fought I would stand in the dark at my bedroom door compelled to listen. Sometimes I'd dare myself to open the door a tiny bit and spy what I could of them. Or, just as often as anything else, I scrunched down under my covers and scrubbed my ears to drown out as much of what they were saying and doing as I could. I hated hearing him call me "bastard." Something about me being a bastard always entered into and escalated their fights. I wanted to march out there and stand up for myself, but I was too afraid.

They didn't fight every night by any stretch, but it is those insane nights that I remember most about growing up. Just about the time I would think I had seen the last late-nighter, and that they had figured out how to get along, a whopper would show up and blow my circuits all over again. The thing is, I was supposed to be sleeping in my room. I wasn't supposed to be hearing everything they were yelling at each other. I never wanted to get involved, but I was involved; I was there.

I knew I couldn't read, but my mother didn't, and if my teachers knew, they didn't say much about it. I was a polite and quiet student in the classroom. I did everything I could to blend out of sight. My fifth-grade teacher was especially impatient and cruel. Reluctantly, she would call on me to read out loud, but then she'd call on somebody else when my struggling with the words had brought me to tears. I can still hear her exasperated tone as she spoke the word I was hopelessly trying to sound out. The humiliation I felt in front of my classmates was crushing. The only thing that gave me comfort during those times was the fact that I wasn't the only one to have my head on my desk, hiding shame in the crook of my arm. Nelson Rialey also couldn't read. He was the first boy I ever kissed on the lips, a quickie in the coatroom on the last day of class before summer break.

School year after school year, I'd try to read, but I just couldn't remember the words or where I was on the page. The letters and words were like synchronized swimmers, pulling apart, coming together, and crossing over one another. I'd use a bookmark to anchor the sentences, but still the words would swap places. I couldn't keep track of all of the different phonetic rules—that ph's sounded like f's, g's could be silent, and cion, tion, sion were all pronounced the same. If I got through one word then I'd forget what the previous one had been. Because I struggled with the letters, I struggled with the words. Because I couldn't get the words, I couldn't get the sentences. I guessed at subjects and verbs. My chances of diagramming a sentence were about as fat as my chances of diagramming Apollo 11. Book reports and essays I plagiarized verbatim from a tattered incomplete assortment of old encyclopedias in JP's office.

Parent/teacher conferences, back-to-school nights, and report cards were irritating nuisances to my mother. She had very low regard for teachers or anything they had to say. "That woman is an imbecile," she often said about the different teachers I had. After one extra- long parent/teacher conference my mother said nothing to me about my grades, but cleared her throat as if to dislodge an unpleasant taste, "Ak! My life would be so much easier if I could only have her flea brain. Ak! officious nit-wit." Because there is a difference between poor grades and outright failing, and because I never actually flunked a grade, my low marks were not a source of concern for my mother or me. I wasn't complaining. Neither was anyone else. I was passed from one grade level to the next with the rest of the students.

As I got older and the dreaded reading aloud was less called for, school became a place where I could go and hide. I made a few friends, but nobody I would ever bring home. I played hopscotch and tetherball after school with a girl who once showed me scabbing blisters on her back. Her father had beaten her with his belt because she hadn't made her bed when she was supposed to. I felt sorry for her. Her mother hadn't protected her. My mother would never do that.

The last fight JP and my mother had was the worst one ever. I was a freshman in high school. I dialed zero for the operator that night and asked the lady to send police to our address (911 hadn't been invented yet). I thought they were going to kill each other. At one point, Mom reached for the phone and JP wrestled it from her and cracked her across the face with it. They were both very drunk. It was about three o'clock in the morning. She kept pulling open the silverware drawer threatening to get a butcher knife and he kept slamming it shut, crushing her fingers one of the times. I listened to her screams of agony the way one listens to a child crying after a fall; it's when they don't make a sound that you really become alarmed. As long as she was wailing, I had confidence that help would arrive in time. It was one of my greatest acts of courage to skirt past the battlefield into their bedroom where there was a spare phone and make that call for help.

I didn't say goodbye before she was taken away in an ambulance. I was afraid to see what he had done to her. JP was put in one squad car, and I was put in another. I was taken by the police to a juvenile protection facility in Martinez. I stayed in the girls' unit for two nights, not speaking except when absolutely necessary. Many of the girls were older than me. The showerheads lined an open tiled wall and the girls had full breasts and pubic hair, something I had yet to develop. I wasn't asked and I didn't argue when I was released into JP's custody late that Sunday afternoon. It was 1976; domestic abuse was considered a family problem, to be solved by the family. JP and I said nothing to one another during the long drive home.

Mom was sitting in her usual chair when I came into the house. JP kissed the top of her head and took the unread newspaper into his office outside their bedroom. She allowed the kiss but didn't say anything to her husband; instead she was focusing on me. She was happy and relieved that I was back home. She didn't stand up, but lifted her arms and bandaged hands for me to bend down and hug her. I was cautious in touching her; if the rest of her body looked anything like her face, I doubted she would be able to accept much of a hug. She had a couple of stitches on the side of her eyebrow and in her lower lip. Every part of her face was swollen and bruised—pink, purple, green, and yellow. Obviously, she wasn't alright, but I asked the stupid question anyway, "Mom, are you alright?"

"Certainly, baby girl," she said with a pasty mouth. She hadn't called me "baby girl" in years. I consciously tried not to look horrified, but my expression must have conveyed the dismay with which I was examining her. I was trying to look past the puffy mask of colored flesh and ointment to find my mother's true face. "Kelly, I'm fine. It's alright. I'm fine."

She was wearing a pale yellow flannel nightgown and matching chenille robe. With her legs curled up underneath her tiny frame she resembled a nesting bird in the middle of her wing-backed chair. I sat on its arm and leaned in towards her, supporting myself against the ample back, careful not to press against her. I stayed perched on the arm of the chair for several minutes. We didn't say anything to one another; nothing was said about the fight or my stay in the Martinez facility, but instead we watched Edith Bunker flutter around Archie in the TV show "All in the family." Mom and I laughed together at the funny parts. She gingerly rested her palm on my leg. I moved my eyes off the television screen and looked down at her battered hand; two fingers were bound together with white medical tape.

At the commercial break, Mom spoke to me in a low, calm voice. "Baby girl, I'm sorry you have to look at me like this. I know I look like I've been hit by a truck. But Kelly, will you do Mommy a favor? Will you get some tacks and towels and cover my dresser mirror (she pronounced it, mirrah) and the bathroom mirrah? Baby, will you do that for me?" I felt so sad and bad for her that I could have denied her nothing, but she knew that. My legs were pins and needles from sitting on the edge of the chair, so I welcomed an excuse to get up.

After draping the mirrors with long bath towels, I tried to act like it was a normal Sunday evening by explaining that I had homework to do for class the next day. I asked about dinner and she told me to call in pizza delivery. I answered the door with money from her wallet when the order arrived. JP came out of his office to eat at his usual place on the couch, Mom remained in her chair, a plate balanced in her lap, and I took my usual place at the dinner table where I too could view the television.

I think they crossed their own line with that fight. Something changed. Mom became just as taciturn as JP. They almost never spoke to one another after that weekend, and they never had another argument or fight. It was like a deep freeze descended on the house and we each went into verbal hibernation. After years of being on the alert for the next explosive drama, I almost welcomed the mute truce, except Mom's drinking took off; I didn't welcome that.

She started pouring brandy into her morning cup of coffee. I worried about her all day while I was in my classes. I would hurry home never knowing what condition I might find her in, sometimes naked, sometimes clothes inside out and backwards. Sometimes I'd pick her up off the floor where she had passed out and put her in bed. There were times when I cleaned urine and vomit around her. I assumed the household responsibilities, washing clothes, buying groceries and cooking meals. I even wrote out checks to pay bills; all my mother had to do was sign them. A part of me knew this wasn't right, but I didn't allow myself to dwell on it. I didn't want to upset her, never once having the courage to consider that she was upsetting me. I didn't dare confront my mother.

JP was taking jobs farther away from home, in other states, and he would be gone for weeks at a time.

It was Wednesday, February 9, 1977. I was in my sophomore year at high school. I was fifteen, eight months before my sixteenth birthday. I had come straight home after class. JP was sitting at his couch; a tall glass of Alka-Seltzer was fizzing in front of him. He had been in Ohio for three weeks doing some kind of training. I'm not sure if he was giving the training or receiving it. I wasn't surprised to see him. He called every few days and with as few words as possible let me know what his schedule was and what hotel he was at. He would talk to Mom for a few minutes when she was awake.

As soon as I came through the door, I intuitively understood something was gravely wrong.

"Hey JP," I said with hopeful lightness. "Where's Mom?"

"Your mother is dead," he stated. That was exactly how he put it.

"What?" I responded, not because I hadn't heard or understood what he had said, but because I didn't want him to cease speaking.

"I got home late. I missed the connection in Dallas. She was on the bed with two empty pill bottles next to her. An empty vodka bottle and glass were on the floor. They just took her away about twenty minutes ago. Now, go to your room. I want to be alone."

He wanted to be left alone, and I wanted to leave him alone. I had nothing to say to Jack Perkins. I had very few conscious thoughts to say to myself. In my small room with windows that looked into the trees, I didn't burst into tears. I didn't know what to think or what to say, but it was there immediately, a sense of relief. Maybe that sounds like I didn't love my mother; I did love her; I didn't love the life she was living. I was relieved that part was over.

JP had wanted to be left alone. I tried to put my adult self in his shoes. I now could completely understand wanting to be left alone. I wanted nothing else, myself. The tidal pull of grief was drawing me away from the worldly shores of family, friends, home and business. Cut adrift, I floated through the boundless universe of my own imagination, a universe studded with memories, painful and painfully sweet. Alone in my dark living room I wondered if he loved her the way I loved my Grayson. A loss that can't bear to be witnessed, pacified, or explained. What my mother and JP had seemed so different from what I had with my husband. The love I feel for my mother is so different from the love I feel for my husband, but I know they are both love. JP burrowed deeper into a place of isolation, a place so confining that his words could barely escape into the light of day without the aid of alcohol. I don't know what he thought; he couldn't tell me; I didn't ask.

The question I asked, and have asked again and again is, "Why?" What exactly had it been that put her over the edge? She was an alcoholic, at times angry, demanding, physically ill, irrational, unpredictable, jealous, maudlin. She was self-centered. I was of peripheral concern. That's not self-pity, it's fact. She thought of me when it served her need to feel like a mother. She was never discouraging, but neither was she encouraging, not to me or to herself. But that was what was normal. Were there signs? Should I have known this was coming? No matter how many times I try, I can't make sense of what she did. I cling to the unhappy echoes in her life as a way of justifying her actions. If I think about the happier times, her wedding day, decorating JP's house, lighting thirteen candles on my birthday cake, then I get further from understanding what she did.

In the space travel of my internal universe, I visited the place I have been many times; had her suicide been a sudden decision, an insane impulsive act, or had she been planning it, imagining what JP would do, how sorry he would be. Did she remember me in her planning? I couldn't remember her ever dropping a clue, not about suicide. I don't want to think that she had planned out the whole thing and disregarded what would happen to me. I want to believe she was staging a drama, but then JP arrived home too late.

Part of me becomes that fifteen-year-old all over again when I lock onto those distant memories. It is where there is a scratch in the record and I get stuck. If she had not died, I judge with my adolescent mind and feel absolutely certain I would have continued living with her or very close by. I would have had to choose between her survival and mine. And I would have chosen hers. How to account for this loyalty, I don't know. It was what I knew. I wasn't a rebellious child; I was compliant; I was "a good girl." I never brought girl playmates home, so it is hard to imagine that I would have ever matured to boys. I most likely would have found refuge in liquor just like she had. I could imagine working in some dead-end job, the nice minimum-wage-earning cashier that knows the customers' names by heart. I never would have found the courage to tell my mother that I wanted out of her insanity.

It is because of the forced separation, her death, that I was given a fork in the road. I judge what my mother would have done in my adult life, based on what she did in my youth. She would have fiercely resented any loss of control over me. She could be jealous of good things coming my way. Anything that would have taken the spotlight off of her, would have been twisted into something rotten during her drunken tirades. I understood this so acutely that I would try not to attract attention to myself when I was young. I preferred to fade out of sight, and for the most part I was successful.

I felt like I was stepping out of line when I would do things out of the ordinary, things like participating in the school spring musical, being invited to a birthday party or sleep-over, submitting a project in the science fair. Whenever I garnered a little attention, something would happen; Mom would back the car into a tree, her purse would get lost, she would find a stray animal and insist on finding its owner, or she would become injured in some way, nothing serious, just something that would require a makeshift sling or Ace bandage. By the time her crisis was dealt with, my event would have ended. Justified by the fiasco, she'd drink. Sometimes, in her cups, she would cry apologies over and over again. No matter how many times I would say it was O.K., she would keep crying about it. At other times, she could work herself into such a pitch of anger, the details of the day would contort and amplify until all I wanted to do was get away from her. This was why I said "Thank you" to myself when she was gone forever.

I never would have gone to a trade school or to community college. I never would have met a man as perfect as Grayson. I went to trade school and created a career for myself after she was gone. I can't imagine her supporting such a choice. She would have denigrated hairdressers mercilessly while she was drunk until I would have found it an impossible profession to pursue.

I went back to school, community college, to prove to myself that I could. I didn't want to be a dumb hairdresser. I took the classes because they were interesting, not because they would help me get a job; I had a job; I was a licensed cosmetologist. Without some crazy drama unfolding around me, I could actually concentrate on what I was reading. I took remedial classes, and I progressed. I could study and pass tests. I learned how to write papers without plagiarizing; I found I had opinions and was able to participate in classroom discussions. I read classic literature and found it fascinating. Those old guys, Shakespeare, Milton, Dante, with astonishing beauty and wisdom, portrayed a world of complexity that I understood.

The more I attempted to find my bearings, the further lost I became. I had the untold story of my past, but I also had years of successful living. Where had my ability to deny gone? I had stayed ahead of the wave for thirty years, only to discover that it was building in size and strength at my heels.

Chapter Six

Shortly after breakfast one day during that first week with Mitchell, I wandered out the front door in pursuit of something familiar. I was reluctant to go, and it wouldn't have taken much for me to ditch the idea entirely. There is a four-mile walk I'd typically do at the end of the day, after work. It might seem like a gentle enough proposition, but it wasn't. It wouldn't be the same; how could it? Yes, it was a different hour, but more to the point, I was different. I felt as though I was whistling in the dark, going about a normal daily routine when in truth I was scared out of my wits. I was terrified that this pleasant evening ritual of mine would ring false. I would no longer find the exercise and scenery rewarding. Besides, my head ached and my body felt like lead. It would be another aspect of my former life that didn't make sense anymore. I couldn't have said what exactly I was afraid of, but fear is what I felt. I couldn't imagine anything good coming of the walk, but I left anyway, not saying goodbye — Mitch didn't need to know that the house would be empty for a couple of hours.

The loop begins a half-mile up the road where I cut through a Presbyterian Church parking lot to access an infrequently traveled road that heads up Sonoma Mountain. As I approached the parking lot, a car pulled in the driveway and its driver waved casually. I scurried along with a preoccupied look on my face, not wanting to be addressed for any reason. Beyond the church, I resumed a slower speed. A couple of women were power-walking towards me on the opposite side of the road. They were in shorts and sleeveless shirts and engaged in a lively conversation. A brief pause was made in their discussion, just enough to bid me "Good morning" and give me a quick up-and-down glance. I was overdressed in Grayson's clothes and my shearling boots. I removed the Pendleton shirt and tied it around my waist.

Further up the way I came upon Riddles, a one-eared donkey corralled next to the road. I waited against the fence and watched as he nibbled at the ground. Slowly, he lifted his head and sauntered towards me. "Sorry Riddles, I don't have any baby carrots for you today." His black, doleful eyes expressed his usual bored disposition. He stood patiently, allowing me to scratch his nose and pet his neck. "Sorry old guy. I've got nothin' for ya," I said and held my palm out to prove it. His lips searched my outstretched hand just to make sure. When I began to walk on, he turned and meandered back to the shady corner he had been in, disappointed perhaps by so little reward for his effort.

Bits of gravel and asphalt crunched under my feet. I didn't look up at the sky, I wasn't listening for the convivial bird chatter, wasn't watching for squirrels that raced from tree to tree or lizards that dashed from rock to rock. Pine, eucalyptus and bay laurel scents went unnoticed, as did the trickling creek, landscaped yards, and small family vineyard patches. My eyes were cast down; I was somewhat mesmerized by my steps over the passing black roadway. Every few steps I swiped at perspiration inching down my hairline and neck, drying my wet hand on the aptly named sweat suit.

About twenty minutes into the hike I was uncomfortably hot and thirsty, and the mid-morning sun was almost directly overhead. A wild thought found its way into my head. "Go into the church where it will be cool and there will be a drinking fountain," the thought went. I had never been inside the church, not because of any extreme aversion, just indifference. Normally, at the end of the day when I would walk past, it would be abandoned for the night, no people in sight, no cars in the lot. That morning it was opened for business, so to speak, and so appealing was the thought of water and air conditioning that I turned right around and headed back down the hill.

As I got closer, I wondered if it was O.K. to go inside, it not being Sunday and all. My sense was that churches are semi-public places, not as public as a gas station or restaurant say, but also not as private as a home or office. Approaching it, all I could think about was how parched my mouth had become. When I saw a dozen or so cars parked in the lot, I panicked. I couldn't possibly go inside if a service was being held. A non-member, I would have been as conspicuous as a clown.

Surveying the grounds for an outside drinking fountain or hose spigot, I was feeling desperate and thought I could collapse without some water very soon. With astonishing relief, I spied a door to what appeared to be an events hall; it was propped wide-open with a chair; a round cardboard sign was hanging from its doorknob, and "AA" was emblazoned on it in red letters. That was where all the people were, and fortunately they were all facing the front of the room and away from me.

Quietly, I skirted past the hall and slipped through one of two tall, glass doors that entered the church lobby. Coolness immediately seeped through my sweat-dampened clothes and pricked at my skin. Two unisex bathrooms were to my left with a drinking fountain between them. The fountain might as well have been Niagara Falls for how marvelous it appeared. I sucked at the cold water for several swallows. Nobody was around, so I soaked my sleeve and whipped at my flushed face with the ice-cold water.

Four massive, I'd guess they were perhaps twelve feet high by four feet wide, clear-glass doors to the sanctuary were framed in lightly stained wood. Through them were rows of inviting pews. Shaken by my brush with dehydration, something possessed me to try a door handle. When it gave way, I pushed slightly and entered the sanctuary. A hydraulic assist mechanism hissed gently as the door return closed behind me. The simultaneous chorus of voices, "Hi Bob," and random applause from the AA meeting were completely extinguished by the door seals. My heart was jumping around in my chest because I was pretty sure, at that point, I was trespassing.

I walked up the center aisle and sat at the end of the first pew, where I could look out at a splendid view. In even taller and wider scale to the entry doors were soaring windows at right angles in the front corners of this great hall. Through the windows I could see a grassy knoll; beyond that was a horse paddock, and then even further stood Sonoma Mountain.

Once I felt somewhat revived, I took a minute to look around. What struck me about the sanctuary was how modern, spare, and well lit it was. Other than cushioned pews and the pulpit that was as basic as a college lectern, there was nothing ornate to be seen — no stained glass, no statuary, no tasseled, velvet runners, no candles or candlesticks, no Jesus on the cross. It wasn't musty; it didn't smell of old or new leather-bound Bibles and hymnals. The pews were not outfitted with oiled, fold-down kneeling benches. The ceiling soared at a 45-degree angle easily 40 feet above me, providing stellar acoustics, I imagined, when the room was full of people. But empty, the room enveloped me in silence. If I hadn't known better, I almost would have thought I was in an empty museum instead of a place of worship.

Closing my eyes, I drank it in. I felt oddly planted in the seat, nearly unable to move. A peacefulness tried to wash over me, but I resisted it. A should-I-stay or should-I-go debate was brewing in my head. A lifetime of spiritual indifference bordering on cynicism caused me to feel guilty. I had no right to take pleasure in the tranquility surrounding me, yet I wasn't ready to walk out. Conflicted over whether I could simply sit and rest for a minute, or should I get out before somebody caught me, I felt tears come up. My sniffles were amplified without any competing sounds. Empty of people, the sanctuary was so expansive that I felt myself shrinking; I was little more than a speck in the room.

Despite feeling intrigued, I reminded myself that I didn't belong there. Church was for other people, religion was a trap, and I couldn't let myself get sucked in. Holding back, I had the presence of mind to question whether I was making a lonely mistake, but the argument persisted. "I am alone. I am completely alone," I was thinking when the hydraulic hiss alerted me to the back of the sanctuary. "Oh, shit," I thought. I quickly looked back and saw a grey-haired man with rimless spectacles coming through the door. He wasn't in any clerical robes, in fact, I think he was wearing a Tommy Bahama shirt and belted shorts. He was slight in his build and tanner that I would have expected for an older gentleman. I faced forward and wiped my eyes and nose with my sleeve, and then I prayed he wouldn't say anything to me. I couldn't jump up and run out the door like some feral cat, I just couldn't.

His steps grew nearer, and I was indeed the reason he had come in. He sat a few inches away, half his body off the pew so that he could face me. Extending his hand with a benevolent smile, he said, "Hi, I'm James, pastor of this church."

I can only guess at what shade of tomato red my face was when I took his hand. I tried to arrange my expression to copy his but it didn't feel very natural. I fumbled grossly in my greeting, "Hi. I'm sorry. I know I'm not supposed to be in here. I, I haven't touched anything. I'll leave. I just needed to sit down for a minute, but I know I should have asked first."

He interrupted my string of apologies by saying, "No, no, no. It's quite alright. People come in here all the time. You're welcome to stay as long as you like. It has that effect on folks, this space, once you're here, you don't want to leave."

He seemed disarmingly amused by my graceless fumbling and genuinely sincere in his invitation to remain. I had done nothing wrong by entering the sanctuary after all. It was a relief that he wasn't upset with me for sneaking in without permission, but in the absence of penalty my gratitude quickly shifted to suspicion. His invitation to stay caused me to wonder if he came pre-wired with recruitment ideas. I wasn't staying, no way. I couldn't abide the notion of being wooed into becoming a church member, one of a flock. "I, um, I. You're right. It's very nice in here, but I better get going. I've got stuff to do." I was blushing more because I knew I had absolutely nothing compelling me to leave, and I wondered if he noticed the heightened flush.

"I don't mean to chase you off. Tell me, what were you thinking about before I disturbed you?" he asked with engaging interest. Had he been observing my actions before coming in?

"Oh, it's not like that. You didn't disturb me. This is your church. You're the one who belongs here, not me."

Scrunching his face in a mock frown, he dismissed my statements straight away. Smiling caused his rosy cheeks to lift and his bespectacled eyes to squint nearly closed. A roadmap of wrinkles on his face conveyed so much been-there-done-that that I was put to ease, and when he said, "There's room for both of us, I'm sure," I was glad he had been un-swayed by my oafish resistance.

I tried to meet his smile, but something about his warmth and there being room for both of us choked me up — it was in such collision with my knee-jerk cynicism. His statement more than choked me up; I had to look away because my eyes brimmed with fresh tears. I couldn't compose myself, but he didn't seem to mind. He sat back in the pew with his hands relaxed and resting in his lap. While gazing out the window he filled his chest with several deep meditative breaths. Meanwhile, the more I tried to control myself the harder it was. Pride in front of this complete stranger prevented me from totally breaking down, but I came close. My own breathing was strange; I inhaled with a shuddering flow of air, and my exhales came out as spastic huffs. Swallowing, my larynx felt like it was coated with rocks. My nose ran, beads of perspiration had formed over my lip, and I was crying — my face betraying a veritable flood of emotion.

After a long couple of minutes, once I had gained some control over myself, he asked, "Is there anything we can do to help?"

I barely could shake my head from side to side to indicate no. It was humiliating to be in such a ridiculous state. I squirmed under his caring gaze. I was afraid of my exposed, raw weakness. We were not on equal footing and I didn't know what to do about it. It is so much easier to give than receive. Clearly, he was well-intentioned, but I felt awkward and foolish. Unfamiliar with proper protocol or church etiquette, I tried to think up some way to re-dignify myself.

I didn't mean to be rude, but he winced slightly when I implied that his kindness was motivated by money. "I'm sorry I don't have my wallet. I know I'm supposed to give a donation." That was the wrong thing to say, and I wanted to take it back immediately. "I have no business being here," I declared again, and when he didn't respond, I reinforced it with, "I don't even know why I am here." The man still didn't reply, but nodded as if to himself. He leaned back again and continued considering the view beyond the windows. I followed his line of sight and saw two horses in the nearby paddock trotting around in circles, kicking up a cloud of dust. I couldn't find a graceful excuse to extricate myself from the pastor. I had the sense that he was trying to come up with a move of his own. His head continued to nod and he made a subtle "humph" sound, as though he were being given instruction and wanted the instructor to know he was listening.

"What's your name, dear?"

"Oh. I'm Kelly. Kelly Tremblake," I said, offering my clammy hand.

"Kelly, I want you to know you're not alone."

An involuntary snort of incredulity came out of me, and I was immediately ashamed of myself. I looked apologetically to him and saw that he did not take my gaff personally. I covered my face with my hands and begged his pardon.

"Kelly, wouldn't you like to tell me what you were thinking about when I came in? It looked like you were thinking about something important."

I couldn't answer him easily, but then mustered up the courage to say, "I, I guess I was wondering if I believe in God or not."

He fixed his eyes on mine and nodded as if he were listening intently and expected me to continue. I did. "Obviously, you believe in God or you wouldn't be here. I just don't know how you hold up under the pressure."

He tilted his head with perplexed concern. "Pressure?"

"That omnipotent, omnipresent, supreme-being idea freaks me out. I don't know how to cope with the scrutiny, a judge hanging over me all the time, handing out endless punishments and rewards. There's just too much, I don't know, too much right and wrong, too much heaven and hell."

Pastor James didn't try to correct me or justify those impressions. He continued nodding his head slowly and waited for me to go on.

After thinking some more, I told him that if I was going to believe in God, then it would have to be something that didn't include judgment. "I've never liked it when people say, 'God The Father.' It makes God sound too human when they do that. If anything, my belief in God comes from questions like, How did all of this get started: Earth, the galaxies, and the entire universe? When did it start, and what was going on before? How big is it? How small? Where does it end, and then what's beyond that? I guess I think of God as the engine of evolution. A mystery great enough to drive all of creation is worthy of the name God, I suppose. But even if that is God, I don't know what it has to do with me and my life."

"Ah, yes, faith is baffling, but it's good to question one's faith; it's a quest worth taking."

I wasn't sure what to say next; it was as though my fount of ideas had dried up. I felt myself shutting down and struggled to suppress a yawn.

"Kelly, you know, service this Sunday is at ten o'clock. Maybe you would like to come. My sermon this week will be about trust — trust in self, trust in others, and trust in God. You might find it interesting."

In my head I was thinking both "yes, that sounded interesting" and "no, you've got to be kidding me." My body language might have suggested something, because he also pulled out his wallet and handed me a business card with his full name, phone number and e-mail address on it. "Or, Kelly Tremblake, you can contact me whenever you want."

As he was reaching around to find the pocket to return his wallet to, he asked, "Kelly, would it be alright if I prayed for you? You know I do have faith, and it is my feeling that a little prayer doesn't hurt, and…who knows… it might possibly help."

Assent was the least I could do, although saying, "O.K." felt odd. I had never had anybody pray for me before. I wasn't sure what to do with myself as he put his hands together and bowed his head. I closed my eyes and just listened. I had told him nothing of my circumstance, so what was he going to pray for? I had to figure he knew what he was doing and conceded it wasn't going to kill me to let the guy do his thing.

"Dear God, Today I am here with Kelly in humble prayer. I ask that you help guide her during her time of challenge and reflection. Give her strength, courage, patience and wisdom so that she might face each day with peace in her heart. I pray that she be allowed to overcome her obstacles and shed her sorrows. Help her know that she is never alone, and that you are there in mercy not judgment. In Your infinite love, dear God, carry Kelly and keep her safe. Amen."

When he was done, he inhaled deeply then let his breath out slowly. He remained sitting at my side, seemingly content to wait me out. He must have been waiting for me to go next, but I couldn't imagine what would be appropriate. I didn't think I should take up any more of his time; surely he didn't have all day to sit with me. After more awkward seconds lapsed with nothing being said between us, I finally thanked him for his prayer and got up to leave. I offered to shake hands as a parting gesture, and he stood up to walk me to the outer lobby door.

At the door he reminded me, "Sunday, ten o'clock, and you've got my card." I raised my hand for one last, uncertain wave goodbye. The A A meeting had ended and the parking lot was almost empty except for a couple of cars. Pastor James was a nice man, but I didn't know about going to church.

Walking my last half-mile home, I mulled over the encounter, but it already seemed to be evaporating. I was hot, tired, and hungry. I had Mitchell to face. I had my life to face. Lofty notions of God faded into the ether, like air.

Chapter Seven

At the end of the week, Mitchell asked if we could go to the cemetery. I had placed his breakfast tray on the patio table and turned to go back in the house as was my routine, but Mitchell was approaching the table and called out, "Aunt K," just as I reached for the door handle. I was rummy with morning blahs, but turned to focus on him.

"Aunt Kelly, do you have to hurry back inside?"

"I'm not hurrying anywhere," I corrected.

"I just wondered if you would sit with me."

I was puffy-faced and bleary-eyed, my hair was matted to my head, and Grayson's clothes, which I had bonded to, were rumpled and wrinkled on me. I was not keen to sit across from him but figured he was going to tell me he would be leaving, and that I was keen on. I was expecting a short stay, and was willing to hear his departure speech. I squirmed a bit, but with guarded hesitancy, I sat down.

"Were they all here?"

I knew what he meant. He was referring to the funeral.

I answered him without much elaboration, "Yah, they were." Then after another moment's thought, I added, "Aunt Margaret and Aunt Clair came down from Ashland, and your grandfather came out from Florida, but your mother didn't make it."

"Figures," he said. "Did they ask about me?"

"Margaret tracked Cheryl down and told her what was happening and tried to find out how to get ahold of you, but…but nothing came of it."

Cheryl said she would be at the service, but she wasn't. I don't think anyone really expected her to come.

I had lost track of my thought with Mitchell because I was reminded of Margaret's encounter with Cheryl, who lives about an hour north on the Russian River. Clair had refused to go to her younger sister's house, so Margaret went by herself. Three hours later when she returned, she came in the house carrying a potted something. When she set it on the dining table Clair and I could see it was topiary in the shape of a teddy bear. It didn't take much imagination to see that the "gift" had been plucked from somewhere in Cheryl's junkie yard, half-dead and mud-splattered; those were the kind of "gifts" Cheryl would bestow: used, broken, useless. The chicken wire framework of the bear was crumpled on one side where the pot had a chunk cracked off, indicating that it had fallen over at some point. I probably should have seen it as, "It's the thought that counts," but I didn't. I thought it was pathetic looking. I took the underwhelming gift from Margaret and said thank you with as much sincerity as I could muster. I carried it to the kitchen sink where I could have my back to the two sisters while I washed mud off its red, glazed pot. It looked to have been something from Christmas time. In one of the bear's outstretched paws was the wiry remnant of a Christmas ornament. I removed it and pulled some of the brown leaves off, but that didn't help its appearance any; I just exposed its metal mesh form. I gave up working on the sucker after a sharp wire cut me.

I was wringing my eyes, rubbing sleep crust from my eyelids, and mildly perturbed to be getting into those details.

"So what did you do?" he asked.

"What, about Cheryl? I don't give a damn what she does. If she can't pull herself together for her own brother's funeral, then that's her baloney, not mine."

"Actually, I meant about Uncle Gray. Did you do like with Gram?"

Slightly chagrined over my venom for his mother, I gathered a more civil tone and let him know that, yes, I had Grayson's body cremated and the ashes were buried next to Helen's, Mitchell's grandmother.

"Could we go out there?"

His question hung in the air. I put my elbows up on the table and hid my face in my hands. The boy had astounding nerve. Couldn't he tell he was an unwanted intruder? It was all I could do to tolerate him within a few hundred feet of me; crammed in a vehicle was a ghastly prospect. I supposed, "No, that won't work for me," could have been my reply, but it wasn't that simple. I wanted him to act like a grown-up, and he was trying. It was reasonable and proper for him to want to go to the gravesite. He owed his uncle that much at least. The problem was that I didn't want to be stuck in a car with him for the hour it took to drive out and the hour back.

When I looked through my fingers at Mitchell, I could tell he was all but holding his breath while waiting for my reply. He wanted to take the trip. The more I thought about it the more I realized how much I preferred to go west where my mother-in-law and husband were buried. A wave of tears came up and I tried to rub them away, but they kept coming. An already used ball of Kleenex had dried in the breast pocket of the Pendleton shirt I was wearing. I pulled it out and separated the sheets again to mop up my face. My crying did not dissuade Mitchell. He did not offer to forget his request. I found it interesting that he had not schemed to "borrow" one of the vehicles to go by himself. He was good at coming up with virtuous reasons to do wrong. I had to decide, and before I over-thought the subject, I cleared my throat and agreed, "O.K., we can go. Do you still have a driver's license?"

"Yes, Officer, I sure do."

His droll response repeated sarcastically in my mind and probably caused my lip to sneer while I commanded, "Then you'll drive?"

"Sure, awesome."

Reckless as Mitchell was, I had little concern about his driving abilities. Grayson had taught him not only how to drive, but how to master driving. When Mitchell was just learning, on rainy days, the two of them would go out of town to an abandoned parking lot and practice car control: how to do spins, how to use the brakes and accelerator to control the vehicle's momentum, how to slalom through and avoid orange cones that they would set out. If Mitchell had turned out to be the hellion kid killed in a car accident, it was not going to be because he didn't know how to respect the road, Grayson vowed. We worried about stuff like that when he was growing up — him getting killed performing, or being involved with, some insane stunt. As I got up from the table I put aside those years of worry and I said, "In an hour," as both a question and a statement.

"Sure thing."

"Oh, and the driver's license? I'll want to see it," I called over my shoulder as I passed back into the house. Inside, I washed my hair, scrubbed my face, put on makeup and a pretty cotton dress. I inserted the earrings Gray had given me as an anniversary gift. It was as if I were dressing for a first date. I wanted to look nice for my husband, crazy as that might sound.

When I went outside to gather my nephew, he made a wolf whistle at the switch in my appearance. I didn't take it well. I controlled an impulse to swing my purse across his face, but shut him up with the iciest of glares. I lifted my hand and arm in a blocking gesture to signal that I wasn't flattered. "Give it a rest, would you?" I said in an arctic tone.

"Be that way then. I was just going to say…"

"Save it!" I almost shouted, and thrust my arm again in the blocking motion.

I was incapable of explaining to him why his attention bothered me so. It felt like something that was meant for Grayson was being stolen, or certainly cheapened. I wasn't some flirty chick swinging her hips down the boulevard. He wouldn't have whistled if his uncle had been standing there. No doubt he thought he was paying me a compliment. His intentions were probably harmless, but his intentions didn't matter. As far as I was concerned, he had not earned the right to have an intention, flattering or otherwise.

"Where's the driver's license?"

He produced a frayed, army-green, canvas wallet and flashed it open, and was about to flip it shut again when I reached out to take a closer look. He rolled his head and sucked a bothered sound against his teeth but turned over the wallet all the same. The protective window was no longer clear but worn dull; a corner was peeled up and crushed flat, and gummy bits of dark crud stuck to both sides of the plastic film. I had to pull the card out to read it clearly, and it all seemed to be legitimate and current. Not to be rushed, I took my time reinserting the driver's license into its sticky hold, remembering that I could back out of the whole plan if

I needed to. But without a word, I handed the wallet and the keys to Grayson's truck to my nephew. Spending any length of time with Mitchell was never going to be easy, so I figured that I might as well get it over with sooner rather than later.

Mr. Finch and Mr. Ritell, from their post across the street, watched Mitchell and me get inside my husband's truck. The engine turned over without the slightest hesitancy. The two men smiled and lifted their hands in unison to wave. Except for a few directional statements — left here, right there — I was a silent passenger just as I had been on the previous Sunday. Grayson's father had arranged a limousine to drive him, his two daughters and me to the cemetery before dawn. I had insisted on a private, sunrise interment of Grayson's ashes, and they obliged when I said I would go out with a shovel by myself if they were unwilling to get out of bed so early. I reminded them that the big memorial service was scheduled for later that afternoon in town; perhaps they would find it more convenient. Grayson loved sunrises, and I wanted to give him that. It was a mission that helped keep me focused, helped keep me sane.

In pre-dawn darkness I rode in the limousine rigid with determination, clinging to the urn of dust that my husband's beautiful body had been turned into. With Mitchell driving, I fixated on the picturesque scenery, the passing vineyards and dairy farms. The road to the coast curves around gently sloping grassy hills, shaded here and there by clusters of giant old oaks, bay laurels, eucalyptus, pines, and sycamores. My passenger-side window was lowered slightly and I could feel the air temperature drop as we got closer to the Pacific Ocean. At sea level we skirted along the edge of Tomales Bay. Seagulls in flight searched above the waters while sandpipers scurried along the muddy, lapping shore.

Groups of people were milling around the front doors of roadside seafood joints, waiting for tables, waiting for shrimp cocktails and Crab Louie, chowder and oysters, fresh San Francisco sourdough slathered with chilled sweet butter.

We turned onto the dirt driveway leading to the Cypress Cemetery parking lot; a dusty wake engulfed the truck when we stopped. I felt a sudden impulse to burst from the vehicle and run to my husband's grave and claw at the dirt to pull his urn from the soil and rock it once again in my lap. The futility of such an effort pierced my heart. He was gone; no digging would ever bring him back. Little surprise, the tears came and would not stop. Mitchell asked if he should go in by himself, and I shook my head, no. I took a few deep shuddering breaths and reached for my husband's wedding band for strength, then signaled with a nod that I was ready.

As we passed through the creaking wrought-iron gate, Mitchell seemed to be thinking back just as I had been, except his thoughts went back five years.

"Gram found this place, didn't she?"

"Yes, she did."

A few steps later, he seemed quite puzzled. "I wonder how."

It was a good question that I couldn't answer. Cypress is so far off the beaten path that it was odd that she had located it. I was never in the position to ask her about her arrangements. While she was sick, she made it clear to all of her children that her final wishes had been addressed with her friend and attorney, and we were not to worry, so we didn't discuss afterlife stuff, not with her. Two days before Helen's ashes were to be buried, Gray and I drove to the cemetery to see how it was. Upon finding it, we instantly understood why she had picked the spot; it's unique, and, above all, Helen was unique. Shortly after Helen was buried, Gray and I braved what seemed like a vastly remote prospect, and purchased the parcel next to hers for ourselves.

It helped to think about my mother-in-law. She was independent, open-minded, a brilliant artist, funny, and fun-loving. I could imagine her being satisfied with the cemetery. There are no lawns, and no landscapers. The plots vary in size and are mostly delineated by low and narrow concrete, curb-like borders. Each personalized parcel is decorated, or should I say adorned, by the friends and families of the people buried there. From the sky it would look like a big — say five-acre — quilt, each small patch a different color and texture, each patch holding its own story. Leave it to Helen to find a cemetery with character.

Almost intuitively, without guidance from me, Mitchell found his way to his grandmother's grave site. Helen's plot is adorned in an Asian theme. Her headstone is an engraved boulder. Two smaller boulders flank it for balance. There are small, smooth, black pebbles that meander from the boulder cluster to the opposite corner, evocative of a river. A miniature, oriental-style red bridge arches over the stones. There is mossy ground cover, a dwarf Japanese maple, and a couple of low-growing evergreens pruned to suggest bonsai. Her epitaph reads, "Out of sight, but never out of mind." "Out of sight" had been one of Helen's favorite phrases, and her children believed she would have enjoyed the play on words.

Adjacent to Helen's patch was the parcel of freshly turned earth that held Grayson's ashes. It had yet to be adorned; only his bronze marker was there. A few feet below the surface was an urn-shaped vessel made of biodegradable cardboard. In time, Grayson's ashes would melt into the same earth as his mother's, and, also in time, my ashes would join theirs.

Pearls my Mother Wore

When Mitchell faced the two plots squarely, he paled and leaned back against a nearby retaining wall. "Whoa," was all he said as his eyes moved between the two names of his family members, his grandmother and his uncle. A hand-holding or a hug may have been called for, but I couldn't do it. I couldn't comfort myself, so I would be damned if I would try to comfort him. I walked on and left him to sort out whatever it was he was thinking.

Ever since Helen's death, I have had a number of occasions to somberly stroll the cemetery grounds. Grayson and I would come out on her birthday and around Christmas, and then a couple of times in between. The oldest monuments are in the center of the property, and the newer, more colorful gravesites, such as Helen's, radiate off that aged core. I walked a spoke path that led straight to the heart of the cemetery. I passed a towering marble obelisk. It is for a man Grayson and I referred to as "The Captain." Captain Everett, it says. His first name is one of those old-fashioned names that I can never seem to remember — Ezekiel, Jerediah, Josiah, something like that. Many of the names in that old section are from bygone eras: Samuel, Matilda, Gertrude, Abel, and there is a Winifred. Some of the crypts date back to the early 1900's. They're lichen and moss-covered. The family names are proudly etched into the doorway lintels. They make me think of people with money: mansions and butlers, dressing for dinner, and Duesenbergs parked around circular, cobblestone drives. Many of the names, dates, and epitaphs are weathered smooth away from decades of bleaching summer sun and soaking winter rains. Dozens of wooden markers show nothing but their dark silvery, patina, and eventually will splinter away to nothing at all. In many parts of the cemetery, the earth has heaved and settled over time and the headstones are no longer perpendicular to the ground.

Circling out to the newer graves, I conjure up a fuller, more contemporary sense of the people honored in the little plots by the way they are maintained. One spot has a small bench seat on it. The bench is painted purple and has tiny, yellow handprints on it. Written diagonally across one end, in child's script, words read, "We love you daddy." Packs of cigarettes, liquor bottles, rolling papers and hash pipes are left on some of the sites. There are whirligigs, wind chimes, Buddha and Goddess figurines, animal fetishes, and lots of candles, especially the tall glass ones that have Jesus or the Virgin of Guadalupe depicted on them. One grave has a laminated photograph of a broad-shouldered young man wearing a football jersey on it. The picture is one of those close-up professional shots where he is kneeling on one knee and resting his helmet on the other. On a couple of occasions I have seen guys hanging out visiting the football player, maybe his teammates.

As I moved around the rolling terrain, closer to Mitchell, I could hear he was playing a harmonica. Bluesy hobo tones floated through the surrounding cypress trees making me think of Louisiana and the Mississippi River. He was seated on the ground, his back against the retaining wall; eyes were closed, his face turned up towards the sun. He stopped playing when he heard the dried-leaf-and-gravel crunch of my steps.

"A harmonica?" I questioned.

He looked down and blinked several times to adjust to the light before squinting up at me.

He wasn't answering me, so I asked more specifically, "Where did that come from?"

"Over there," he said as he signaled lazily with his head.

"You stole a harmonica off of one of the graves?"

"I didn't steal it."

"No? Did the owner crawl out of the grave and give it to you as a gift?"

"Stop it. I didn't steal it. It's there to be played, so I played it. Now leave me alone. I'll put it back." He crooked his head to look away from me with a pout on his face.

I hovered over him wondering what to think. Ignoring me, he used the hem of the tee-shirt he was wearing to polish the chrome skin of the instrument. The music had sounded hauntingly beautiful, and the harmonica owner surely would have appreciated it, as would have Grayson and Helen. I stepped closer to my nephew and squatted down directly in front of him. "Truce," I said, and I waited until he would look me in the eye and give an acceptance before I got back up. A slight smile briefly crossed both of our expressions.

I stood next to Mitch in quiet meditation. The sun-drenched retaining wall was warm against my back. Crisp, white-edged, cotton-ball clouds floated against a baby-blue sky. In a field adjacent to the cemetery parking lot, a cow was mooing. Black crows squawked at each other. A flash of my stoic father-in-law, in his loafers, pressing a shovel into the yielding soil entered my thoughts and I tried to push it aside. Clair and Margaret had several bouquets of multicolored flowers; they pulled the petals off of each stem to line the dirt hole, just as we had done with Helen. I had been sitting in exactly the same spot that Mitchell was in, rocking my precious urn. White light backlit the gray fog at the horizon. The sun was rising. It was time. I folded myself over the container, shielding it, wishing I could convert myself into it, wishing somehow my cells could penetrate his and breathe life back into his dust. Richard helped me to my feet and helped me let go of the urn. Tears and perspiration were streaming down his face.

I broke off where my meditation was going and asked Mitchell if I could have a few minutes by myself before we headed back home.

"Are you sure?" he wanted to know, and for some reason that question made me laugh. I wasn't afraid of cemeteries. My nerves did not quake with thoughts of restless spirits, hobgoblins and black cats. "Yes, I'm sure."

As he was walking away from me, he tossed the harmonica back onto the grave where he had found it.

Mitchell and I had been the only ones on the property, and with him now back in the truck, I allowed myself to release a spasm of grief that I had been holding in because I couldn't have borne its being witnessed. My leg muscles twitched from having walked the undulating terrain and buckled gladly so I could sit in the lumpy soil next to Grayson's burnished bronze nameplate. A gush of pressure pulsed at my temples. He wasn't the dirt and he wasn't the carefully placed nameplate; he wasn't the cardboard urn just a few feet below the surface. He wasn't there waiting for me as I had somehow allowed myself to secretly imagine. I cried for the life he wasn't living; I cried for myself, and I cried for crying, soaking tissue after tissue. I had to resist the temptation to dig deep into the soil and retrieve his remains.

Perhaps five minutes passed before I became aware of the sounds around me and was lifted out of that place of deep sorrow. The cows were randomly mooing in neighboring fields. A flock of honking geese flew overhead so low I could hear their wings flapping. A breeze rustled through the thick, wind-defying cypresses that had been planted along a nearby fence line. I heard a rustling and slowly opened my eyes to see a fluffy-tailed gray squirrel snooping within a few feet of me. As I focused and turned my head even more, the creature stared back with alert, full, brown eyes. As I reached up to wipe my blurring tears away, it scampered off. I remembered how Helen used to call Grayson "Squirrel" as a pet name.

A small lizard was scaling the side of Helen's boulder. Her plot looked good. The coastal fog and winter rains had fed the plants well. The mossy ground cover and bonsai were emerald green; the dwarf maple was putting out delicate new leaves on fine, scarlet-red branches. There were not many ants, beetles, flies, or spiders, but there were a few.

"Helen, are you taking good care of him for me? I miss you both," I said in a low voice, and again my vision blurred with tears.

It was like a one-sided telephone conversation; I couldn't see or hear them, but I spoke anyway.

"Honey, what's it like where you are? Have you met all of our neighbors out here? Who's this man on the other side of Helen? Have you met my mom? I wish I were there with you. So Mitchell's with me; I guess you already knew that. I'm sorry I haven't been very nice to him, but he seems comfortable enough in the backyard. Do you like what I have on? I wore your favorite perfume."

I played with the dirt as I spoke: lifting it and then letting it sift through my fingers, patting it smooth, poking my finger into it to write "Kelly loves Grayson." Wisps of cool fog were drifting overhead, and the denser mass of moisture was heading my way. It approached like an immense ocean wave moving in super-slow motion, as if it could knock me over if I stood in its way.

Had I been by myself, I might have stayed longer. A part of me wanted to set up house and never leave.

"I'll be back soon, honey, I promise. I love you."

I kissed my dirty fingertips and touched his raised name on the bronze plaque. Before standing up, I gathered a handful of the soil to bring home with me. I gave Helen's big boulder a pat and returned to the truck.

Mitchell's Adam's apple protruded sharply as his neck arched back to reach the headrest; he was asleep on the driver's side of the truck. He jumped when I opened the passenger-side door. The interior of the vehicle was warm from the greenhouse effect of its windows. I found an envelope in my purse to put my handful of dirt in, and a bin on the back bench-seat held paper towels to wipe my hands. The bin also had a bottle of water in it, which I opened to moisten the paper towel. I took a long drink from the bottle before handing it to Mitchell. "Finish it," I said, and that was all the permission he needed to drain the bottle in a couple of gulps. Roused for the drive home, he started the truck without paying much attention to me, my dirty hands or my red face, swollen from crying.

Mitchell seemed relaxed at the wheel. We weren't talking but not because of any current hard feelings. "Everybody has a story," I had thought as I was walking around the uniquely arranged cemetery plots. I wanted to know what Mitchell's story was. I debated in my mind whether the drive home would provide a good opportunity to hear Mitchell tell me what he had been doing with himself during the previous years. I had begun to wonder if I might be harboring a fugitive or something. I couldn't understand why he continued to hang around.

"Mitchell, can I ask you something?"

A sickened look came over his face, but after some hesitation, he said, "Sure."

I shifted slightly in my seat so that I could look at him more comfortably. "Mitch, what's going on with you?"

He took his eyes off the road and shot me a sour, questioning look.

"Are you in any kind of trouble? If you are, you need to come clean with me about it. Why are you still…I don't know…hanging out?"

He swallowed hard and adjusted his grip on the steering wheel to one that looked less at ease. When he spoke, because I was looking at him and was expecting an answer, he said, "Are you serious?"

"Yes, I am absolutely serious. I need you to talk to me. It's been almost a week and I want to know what your plans are. I don't know what's going on, but you've got some kind of secret you're holding on to, and I want to know what it is. If you can't tell me what you've been up to, then you need to think about moving on."

The ultimatum didn't sit well with him. He sighed deeply with air whistling through his nostrils. His lips twisted and pressed in against his teeth, and his eyes darted around the road and to the fleeting vistas. Again and again he glanced my way to see if I would let him off the hook.

I waited as he squirmed, determined to either hear his story or hear him tell me to go to hell. One way or the other, I wasn't going to let him get away with silence.

"What do you mean? Nothing is going on with me."

"Why are you here? You were doing one thing and now you are here doing another. What happened? What changed?

"Ah, man. You're serious, aren't you? You really want to hear this?"

"Yes."

His shoulders dropped; I hadn't realized they were hiking up. He sighed again and resumed a more casual grip on the wheel.

"Ah, man."

I blinked but kept an expectant look on my face.

The mesmerizing roadway lent itself to Mitchell's exposition.

"O.K. This is what happened. I mean. O.K. Let's see, how do I say this? O.K. You know I was strung out on meth, right? Oh yah, of course you do, that's dumb, I don't have to say that part; you already know that part."

The rest of what he had to say came out that way. He was speaking out loud, and I was his audience, but he was also speaking to himself. He edited his words as he went along and could barely get through a thought before he was criticizing himself and adjusting what he was trying to say.

"So I had this homey, Daryl. I mean he wasn't really my home boy. You know what I mean, 'home boy'? I mean he was a friend. Not really a friend-friend, he was just this dude I hung with. You know? I mean he was cool. He was a good guy and all, but he was off. You know? Not normal."

"No, I'm not sure I do know. What wasn't normal?" I asked.

"See, he had a bad accident a long time ago. I think he said he was like eighteen or something when a car he was working on fell off one of its jack stands and nearly crushed him to death. When his dad found him he was barely breathing and shit. I don't mean 'and shit,' I just mean he was seriously messed up, almost dead. My man, Daryl, he was in the hospital for months. His skull was crushed, ribs crushed, his lungs collapsed and his heart even stopped for a while, and since his brain didn't get enough oxygen, he was majorly fuc…screwed. But for some reason, he didn't die.

After all of that shit happened to him he had to learn how to do everything all over again, walk and talk. The dude had to be taught all over again how to get a damn fork to his mouth. He even had to learn how to take a shit all over again. I'm sorry, that's rude, but that's what went down. 'Scuse my language, but I would have killed my ass, one bullet in the head, done.

But anyway, by the time I met him, he was really doin' pretty good; that stuff all happened a long time ago, like twenty years ago. He still talked different and stuff, but I could understand him. He could make me laugh like hell. I mean, sometimes he'd get on my nerves because he would get nervous and start stuttering and shit, I mean and stuff, so I would have to tell him to shut the fuck up. But he was all right. He was cool."

For the next half hour, Mitchell told me about his escapades with his older handicapped friend, Daryl. He didn't look at me but fixed his eyes on the highway. The two met hitchhiking. Mitchell wanted to get down to Los Angeles to meet up with a girl he had met, and Daryl was going to visit his sister. The driver who picked them up was happy for the company and quickly offered up a marijuana joint. The three had a nice little bonding experience as they drove down the state.

It turned out that the girl was underage and her parents told Mitchell to take a hike or they would have him arrested.

Mitchell left Los Angeles as a roadie in a punk-rock band, "Psycho Stink or PS for short." By the time the group reached San Francisco, Mitchell was tired of hefting their gear around and not being paid for it, so he "bailed on that shit," as he put it. Then, as fate would have it, Mitchell ran into and reconnected with Daryl.

Daryl sounded like an affable fellow, a good listener and easy to please. "All he needed was a pint of 80-proof and he was happy," Mitchell said.

Mitchell also said he wouldn't let Daryl "smoke the pipe" because he went into convulsions the one time he had tried. "He was cool with a little Jane, but ice, no way."

I had to ask him what that meant. He found my question amusing; Jane is marijuana and ice is crystal methamphetamine, he informed me. Then he almost couldn't continue for laughing when I commented incredulously, "Wow, I've never heard of pipe tobacco giving someone convulsions."

It took a minute for him to quit snickering, and then he corrected me, "No, Aunt Kelly, it was the crystal meth in the pipe, not tobacco."

"Oh," was all I said, but I was extremely chagrined by my exposed naïveté.

Mitchell was protective of Daryl and the people around them knew it. Daryl had been beaten and robbed once after cashing a government-assistance check. Mitchell took the attack as a personal call to arms and vowed to "kick the shit out of..." boy bravado blah, blah, blah.

I could see through Mitch's chivalry; he was bent out of shape because Daryl provided a place for the two of them to stay, a room in a residence hotel in the Tenderloin, and Mitchell didn't want to lose that. He was concerned that social services might place Daryl closer to his sister in Southern California, an area Mitchell didn't care to return to. Mitchell felt justified in what he took from his disabled companion because in return he provided a level of security to his physically challenged friend.

"The street will eat a man up. He'd a never made it on his own," was Mitchell's take on the arrangement, but I wondered what Daryl had been doing before meeting Mitch. He hadn't been eaten up yet. Mitchell wasn't doing the guy any favors presuming to be his bodyguard. He simply welcomed the government stipend and a righteous excuse for a good brawl every once in awhile.

Daryl's disability checks went part of the way toward funding their combined drug and alcohol use. They also stole from unlocked cars, or if they saw something they wanted in a locked car they would smash one of its windows and pawn what they took: leather coats, laptops, tools, CD players, cell phones. One time, Mitchell bragged, they took a gun from a glove box and got two hundred dollars for it from some guy who bought and sold guns from the trunk of his car. For their daily necessities, food and drink, they regularly stole from liquor stores, convenience stores, and grocery stores. For cash, they picked wallets, plucked cash out of unattended tip jars, and cashed in shopping carts full of collected bottles and cans at the recycling center.

Mitchell got Daryl kicked out of the residence hotel after he, Mitchell, was high on crack cocaine and became belligerent and destructive. All of this Mitchell conveyed with an odd quality of pride, street pride. Together they lived for months on the streets and in the parks throughout San Francisco, sleeping in bushes, boxes and abandoned unlocked cars. Daryl told Mitch he didn't like being cramped up in the hotel anyway. "We told ourselves we were camping, not homeless," Mitchell told me. The rent money they saved was put to "better" use — getting loaded. He used his fingers to make quotation marks in the air when he said the word "better."

Daryl's alcohol consumption escalated, and he was less inclined to buy alcohol for both of them. He would turn over his food stamps to Mitchell to sell on the street because Mitchell was a more adept wheeler-dealer. But then Mitchell would secretly pocket some of the cash for his own needs, justifying the action by calling it a "seller's fee." Hyped up on drugs, Mitchell took more and more risks with his thieving, apparently breaking into houses when the occupants were sleeping inside, and on one occasion he held up a corner market, pretending he had a gun in his pocket. He expressed halfhearted remorse for these crimes, but in the end, still saw it as what he had to do to survive. This was not the time to interrupt him for a debate, so I remained silent and listened.

The guys would snatch fresh clothes from unattended driers in public Laundromats. They'd panhandle for spare change. Free hot meals and snack bags could be had; they knew where to go for such freebees. When it was cold and wet, if they were lucky, they could get a shower and a cot at a rescue mission or armory.

Mitchell's voice started to waver and it lost the matter-of-factness it had as he was explaining his lifestyle and its catalog of offenses. Beads of perspiration were forming on his upper lip. He hesitated and took a moment to push his hair away from his face. He tilted his head from side to side until his neck made chiropractic pops. "Oh, man," he said out loud, but also to himself as he struggled to maintain his composure.

He returned to his story, apparently determined to finish it. Daryl, it turns out, had found a fifty-dollar bill on the ground. It was folded into a small triangle.

"Folded like they do flags, the last edge tucked in, you know?" Mitch explained.

Daryl snatched the bill up so quickly that Mitchell didn't get a chance to see what it was. Daryl was thrilled by his find. "He was dancing in circles and shit, like he just scored a touchdown in the end zone. The dude was stoked."

Mitchell demonstrated at me how Daryl had shaken his closed grip in Mitchell's face. He imitated Daryl's taunting, his accident-compromised speech: "I got it. I got it. It's mine. You can't have it."

Initially, Mitchell assumed Daryl had found a large cigarette butt and told him to keep it; he didn't want it. But when he discovered it was cash he was stunned.

"I swear, nobody was around and it was right there in the gutter just waitin' to be picked up. My blind ass missed it completely."

Mitchell told me how irritated he became at Daryl's good fortune, how he suddenly wanted to slam Daryl's face into a brick wall as they walked past one industrial building after another in the South of Market area. He wanted that money. He tried to think of a way to get the fifty-dollar bill away from Daryl and sulked as he schemed. Daryl realized Mitchell wasn't talking and began to feel guilty. "Let's get shit-faced," Daryl offered eventually. Initially, even that offer didn't satisfy Mitchell; he wanted all of the cash for himself; he remained silent even though he knew they were headed for the Liquor Emporium.

Mitchell waited outside of the store. I didn't have to ask him to explain why, because after he took a moment to catch his breath, he volunteered that he had been caught stealing in it too many times and was told not to come around anymore. Mitchell simply said, "Rum and Coke," as Daryl headed for the store entrance. Waiting outside, Mitchell was still plotting how he would rob his friend of the leftover change. When Daryl came out of the store with two big grocery bags Mitchell momentarily forgot all about the change. Inside the bags were two cheaper-by-the-half-gallon jugs of rum, one for each of them, two liter bottles of cola, a six-pack of beer, a large bag of chips, bean dip and a couple of sticks of beef jerky.

The beer was the appetizer course they enjoyed as they made their way to China Basin. That area in the city is beginning to be built up; Pac Bell Park is there, but there are still huge, abandoned fields that were once train yards, and that is where they headed.

At the bay water's edge there are numerous dilapidated shacks and boat piers. Mitchell described a place he called "base camp," a nest of sorts in an unattended dirt lot with plenty of hiding places among the overgrown grass and brush. It was the place where they kept their "stuff." Stuff? I imagined shopping carts overflowing with unusable stolen and found junk. I wondered if their base camp referred to freebase camp, but I didn't say anything. I didn't want to embarrass myself again in case I was wrong.

That night they drank themselves senseless. "We were fucked up," Mitchell joylessly reminisced, clearly envisioning the scene. He paused in his description, swallowed hard, and then coughed an unproductive cough that was obviously a stalling tactic.

The next day when Mitchell woke up, he said, he discovered that Daryl had asphyxiated on his own vomit in the night. Even before Mitchell opened his eyes he could smell his friend, and threw up himself.

"It was rank. He had pissed and shit himself. Brown puke was all over his face. The dude was gray. I touched his hand quick; it was cold, just like they say."

Mitchell scrambled out of the bush cave and went to a nearby shopping center to call for help. He didn't know how to describe the location of the camp and so had to wait at the sandwich shop he was calling from for the police to arrive. The shop owner told him to wait outside. When the patrol car pulled up, nobody was in a hurry. Mitchell got in the backseat and they drove as close as possible to where Daryl lay dead in the bushes, on the dirt. More officers were called in and Mitchell was asked to wait in the police vehicle.

He was also asked his name, to which he responded, "Kevin Mitchell." The last thing he wanted was to "get popped" for an outstanding warrant from the hotel vandalism incident, so giving his true name was out of the question. He told the officers his wallet had just been stolen and he hadn't had a chance to replace his driver's license. In the end, it didn't seem to matter. He also lied to the officers when he said he didn't know the dead person but just found him there while he was hunting around that notorious area for his wallet. The officers must hear so much nonsense out of guys who look like Mitchell that they didn't flinch at the looking-for-his-lost-wallet routine.

To save his own tail, Mitchell had turned his back on the only companion he had. By denying any previous knowledge of Daryl, Mitchell spared himself a more in-depth police interrogation, but he hated himself for the denial. Mitchell used the words lame, loser, and messed-up to describe how he was feeling about himself. He had fallen below his own code of conduct, as peculiar as it was, and that was all that mattered to him. That was his turning point.

Several of the transients who camped in the same general area surfaced to see what was happening. While he was waiting in the patrol car, passersby gawked at Mitchell, and at first he stared back defiantly. "Trapped inside that car cage, I wanted to kill those stupid bastards," he said. But then he said something inside of himself broke; he saw himself as they must have seen him. He imagined himself looking crazed, a wild man, desperate, frightened and frightening. His eyes teared up as he described sitting in that backseat, frantic to run away, but still feeling responsible in some way to his friend. He told me that all of a sudden he started crying and couldn't stop himself. He hid his face from the onlookers by pulling his collar up to his forehead. He hadn't caused the death, but he hadn't prevented it, either. He could not get the image of Daryl's pained, vomit smeared face from his mind. Mitchell swore he hadn't heard a sound; he was out cold, probably less asleep than truly unconscious from the guzzled rum.

Watching the officers, Mitchell could see the blend of disgust and resignation in their faces; this was not the first time they had arrived at such a scene. One of the officers was a young man, a peer in age, and that bothered Mitchell. He commented that the cop was "nothing but a lucky bastard whose father probably got him the job." It wasn't the time to argue, but I disagreed that luck alone could get a person hired onto the SFPD. It takes hard work, something Mitch had always refused to do.

Mitchell told me how relieved he became when he saw them holding Daryl's ID and the familiar, tattered business card of Daryl's social worker. The system would kick in for Daryl and, Mitchell believed, his sister would be contacted, and she would take care of her brother one more time.

A hazardous-materials team arrived at the site and cordoned off the encampment with yellow caution tape. He referred to them as "the marshmallow dudes" because of their white, haz-mat jumpsuits. The teams of city workers had no reason to preserve the shielding walls of tall grass, and they trampled it down as they moved around the area. Mitchell watched from inside the police vehicle and through openings in the twigs and underbrush as men wearing full protective gear and respirators combed through his and Daryl's belongings. He hoped that there would be nothing to identify him among the "stuff": blankets, clothes, burnt pans and Sterno cans, toilet paper, liquor bottles, drug paraphernalia and porn magazines, which he called "chick mags."

He said how, until then, he didn't really care when people called him a fuckup or an asshole. It meant he wasn't playing by anybody's rules. He said he would almost feel proud when somebody called him a son-of-a-bitch. But watching that day, all he could think was that he was a "serious loser." And he made a vow to himself to change.

When the officers released Mitchell (Kevin Mitchell), they asked if he had someplace to go. He said yes, even though he knew he didn't. He didn't have a home to go to, no job, no friends, and at that time, he didn't consider he had family to go to either. He was pensive for a moment and then, heavy on the melodrama, said, "Destination Nowhere, that's me." He told me that at the time, he couldn't think of anything to do, where to go or why to go there, but he started walking anyway.

His friend Daryl had died on the same day my Grayson died.

Mitchell said that for the next several days he crisscrossed San Francisco without being under the influence of drugs or alcohol. He wanted nothing to do with his old haunts, gathering places where trouble was bound to find him—China Basin, the Mission, the Tenderloin, Justin Herman Plaza. At a drop-in center he was able to get a free box lunch and a clean blanket that he covered himself with at night.

One of his first concerns was whether he could get through a night without being "buzzed." To his relief, he could. Wandering around Golden Gate Park, he found secret hiding places off the trails and paths, where he could burrow under a bush for shelter from the cold, damp, and wind. The nights were cold, but he was surprised to learn they weren't as unbearable as he thought they would be. He couldn't remember a night when he had fallen asleep rather than passed out. It was a relief to know that he could wake up if he needed to, that if someone tried to mess with him, he could respond, and that was new.

He was amazed by the strangeness of not being loaded, not being chemically altered. Streets he had walked a hundred times appeared to him as if he had never seen them before. Instead of being on guard for trouble or looking to score drugs, he saw ladies holding children's hands, walking them to school. He saw gardeners tending yards. Grass seemed greener, flowers seemed brighter, and instead of seeing trees in a general way, he noticed the interesting shapes of cypress, eucalyptus, and oak trees. He said there were times when he had to just sit down and wait, that, "being clean was, like, seriously hallucinogenic."

He was up and about early enough to observe people dressed in work clothes getting into cars or waiting for public transit — going to their jobs. Instead of seeing them as suckers, he envied them. He got excited as he was telling me of his observations and punctuated each sighting with a "and shit" and a "you know?" For example, he said, "I was checking out all the twisted cypress trees and eucalyptus trees and shit. You know? I mean it was a trip and I wasn't even trippin'."

For the first time, rather than skirt around San Francisco State University, he walked onto the campus. He said he had no interest in ever sitting at a desk, but just being at the school made him "feel smarter and shit. You know?" In his exploration of the campus he noticed an abundance of sculptural art pieces displayed all over the landscaped grounds. He made the comment that spotting the art pieces was "like an Easter egg hunt" — some of it was tucked into flowerbeds or around a corner so that he had to look to find it. The art made him think of his grandmother; he wanted to walk the campus with Helen to see what she would have thought of it.

From S.F. State Mitchell made his way out to the Great Highway; it runs along the Pacific Ocean. The cool, salty mist that came off the surging Pacific made him "feel awake and shit. You know?" He roamed the hilly streets instinctively, turning right at one corner or left at another, checking out some neighborhoods and avoiding others. He meandered through Golden Gate Park and Presidio Heights. He stayed to himself, and tried not to attract any unwanted attention. He said he had numerous opportunities to buy drugs or alcohol, and every time one came up, out of habit, he wanted to go for it, but he just didn't do it.

"I wanted to be high, damn I wanted to get high. But I also wanted out of that shit. I just didn't cop. And one day when I thought I would, I started walking and sweating instead and forgot about it for awhile. Later when I started thinking about using again, I realized I wanted to be clean just a flea shit more than I wanted to use, and that saved me. That sounds so lame, but that's it. Like there was a scale with clean on one side and high on the other; that flea turd tipped the scale towards clean."

He didn't care how worn out he was, he just kept marching from one location to another; all he wanted was to keep moving; he didn't want to be "a stationary target."

With each passing day he felt a degree of health return to his abused body. He said he didn't realize how bad he was feeling until he started feeling better. He described swiping a fresh orange from a piled-high display outside a corner market, eating it as if the fruit were some exotic delicacy, delicious beyond description. Despite the incremental return of health and appetite, he remained afraid that if he sat still for too long he'd "lose it."

As he was finishing up his accounting for the past four years, he probably expected me to congratulate him, but I wasn't as impressed with his abstinence as he seemed to be. "Welcome to my world, Sunshine," I thought. "You don't see me smoking this, that and the other thing just to feel good, to escape. You don't see me sloshed. I could go to any doctor and tell them what I have been through recently and they wouldn't hesitate to give me a prescription, something to help me sleep, something to help me feel better." Ugh. Talk about throwing kerosene on the fire. If I had a bottle of feel-good pills, I'd have taken the whole lot in one gulp. There was nothing out there that could remedy what was hurting me.

Again I had to force myself to pay attention to Mitchell. He worked his way to the previous Monday, when he showed up on my front porch. He had caught a bus on the north side of the Golden Gate Bridge, first crossing the famous span on foot. Midway, he considered hurdling the railing and ending it all, but said he didn't have the nerve. Looking over the edge made him weak in the knees. He looked out to Alcatraz Island and tried to imagine being imprisoned there. "Maybe it wouldn't be so bad, prime real estate and all." He had walked the Golden Gate on one of those stunning fogless mornings when the deep blue water, whitecaps and boats, and all the surrounding cities sparkle like a giant treasure chest of precious jewels. He used the word "awesome" several times and said he was sorry he had never walked across the bridge before. He thought Daryl would have dug it.

We were getting close to home and Mitchell sat up in his seat and twisted himself into more chiropractic pops. He was ready to stop talking about himself. Transitioning from reflection on his past to the present, he asked me if it was still alright for him to stay, "until I get on my feet." Before I could say a word, he explained that he intended to get a job and start paying his own way. He made a pitch for painting the entire house, said he could do it all if I bought the paint "and shit." But I didn't want to think about such a project; I didn't want to think about the future. I wanted to think about what he had been telling me. He interjected, "It's been thirteen days since I've done any dope or anything. Anything! Not even cigarettes."

I felt like he was trying to switch subjects so that I wouldn't make any comments about all he had revealed.

We were parking in front of the house, but I wasn't ready to park what I had started. With the numbing drone and vibration of the truck engine silenced, I said, "Mitch, thank you for telling me all that you have. It took courage and I respect that. You don't have a lot to be proud of, but I can see you are trying to turn things around, and that's good. But having said that, you need to know I am still taking this on a day-by-day basis."

He was offended by my lack of loving support. His tone sharpened and he sneered, "What is your problem?" He swore he had told me the truth and asserted that his uncle would have helped him out, being clean and all. The guilt card was the wrong one to play; it instantly brought out the bitch in me and I snapped back, "You're uncle isn't here."

Mitchell went silent for a moment but then asked that most juvenile of questions: "Why do you hate me?"

Oh, brother.

"I don't hate you, Mitchell; I just don't trust you. I believe you have told me the truth, but what have you left out? Humm? What haven't you told me?"

He countered with, "What? What do you mean? I don't understand what you want."

"That's fine. We'll leave it on a day-by-day then."

I stared at him and watched as his face contracted into a surly pout. He glanced at me a couple of times and then looked away.

"Fuck! God damn fuck! Shit! Alright then, there is one other thing but it's fucked! I took all of Daryl's money before I went to get help. I rolled him over to get the cash from his wallet in his back pocket and I took the coins that fell out of his front pockets. There, are you satisfied?"

He was furious, but I was satisfied. By avoidance, denial, or design, he had omitted the important piece, the part I instinctively knew was in there. I know about selective autobiographies, and he had just given me one. Until the final theft detail came out, he had just been chronicling events. There is the story we tell the world, and then there is the truth. I wanted the truth. I wanted the piece that hurt to talk about, and I got it.

A tiny piece of my heart did go out to him. As he had tried to say "satisfied" his voice cracked and went an octave higher. He wrapped his arms around the steering wheel and leaned forward, knocking his chest against it. His shoulders curled around as he tried with all his might to stifle his crying shame. He had a lot to deal with and I wondered if he would. I suspected that he would straighten up for awhile and then reward himself with a big drug and alcohol blowout. I had seen my mother do that over and over again. She never described her sobriety as being clean; she'd say she was on "a diet." He could find himself in the exact same on-again, off-again cycle. It killed her. I could see where, given the chance, it would eventually get him too.

I asked, "Do you remember how Helen would say, 'Keeping secrets hurts you more than it hurts me'? You're lurking around here with the weight of the world on your shoulders, and you're not fooling anybody. You don't have to tell everybody your business, but you've got to tell somebody, and looking around, I don't see who else you have. Nothing is going to get any better buried inside you. If you are going to get clean, then you need to come clean."

He had stopped heaving, but stayed slumped over. I reached across and pulled the keys out of the ignition. "I'm going in. I'll bring you a dinner tray in a few minutes." Maybe he was going to continue hanging around, maybe he wasn't. It wouldn't have broken my heart if he gathered some things and struck out for friendlier grounds, but he didn't.

The first thing I did when I got in the house was to change out of the dress I was wearing and get back into the soothing comfort of Grayson's sweat suit. I brewed a fresh pot of coffee and enjoyed a few sips before I called through the door to Mitchell and asked if he wanted any that late in the day. "Definitely," he answered. He was at the table when I came out with a plate piled with the last portions of the assorted foods still in the refrigerator from before he had arrived. Frankly, the international mounds of Italian, Mexican, and American comfort foods nearly turned my stomach, but the young man saw nothing objectionable and dug into the warmed array. "Thank you," he mumbled into his lap. I said good night and stepped back through the blanket-draped doorway into my dark house.

I had my own secrets. The hypocrisy had not escaped me. I was preaching one thing while practicing another. I wasn't going to allow Mitch to hide, but I would be damned if I would let him in on my world. He would never ask, and I would never tell. He had no idea. Hypocrite, secrets, oh well.

Chapter Eight

A second week of Mitchell's residence, and my enervated attendance to him, brought us to Mother's Day Sunday. I had not missed one visit to my mother's grave on that Hallmark holiday, and all week I had been mulling over my ability to handle it. Just the day before I had made up my mind that I could go, and I should go. I feared that breaking with my traditional pilgrimage would bring on unclear but nevertheless frightening consequences. Except for Mitchell's meals that I had been serving out on the patio, I had not been outside all week. The drive would do me good.

The day began with a familiar mix of duty, dread, and delusion. I had always been unwilling to be sidelined or made to feel irrelevant on that occasion simply because I had no living mother to heap affection upon. Undaunted by facts, as her daughter, I leaned into my annual ritual of delivering flowers to her grave as one leans into a headwind. This year was different from the previous thirty when I could float on the prevailing bullshit sentiments of the day: that mother always knows best, that she is always there, that there is no greater love. To strengthen my resolve, I focused on continuity. It was not the time for a break with tradition. To ignore the responsibility to my mother's memory, a responsibility I had tended to for almost three decades, was impossible. It would have been more disturbing not to go than to go. I would buy the yellow and white roses she had insisted on while alive. The one year I had attempted a surprise of red roses, she immediately threw them in the garbage, disgusted because they were the color of blood. Over subsequent years I stuck with the formula that worked, ever mindful of her rebuke, even from the grave.

At breakfast, Mitchell seemed agitated. He lumbered toward the patio table with his head down; everything about him seemed to look down. As he got closer, his eyes rolled wearily up from their downward cast to see why I was still standing there after having set down my tray. I produced a smile. I wasn't eager to drive over the hill to Napa and put flowers on my mother's grave, so to procrastinate, I offered, "Hey, Mitchell, do you think you would like me to trim your hair this morning?" I was about to retract the offer, he so hesitated before saying, "Yah, if you want."

"If I want? This would be for your benefit, not mine," I responded snippily.

"Alright."

"Alright what?"

He threw himself into the chair with a sulking pout. Everything was always so difficult with him. "Mitchell. What's up with you?"

He shrugged in irritation and turned away. Clearly he was bent out of shape about something, but it didn't make sense that this display was related to the haircut or anything else that had gone on between us. He was about to glass over completely and shut me out when I spoke his name with stronger force, "Mitchell," and then I waited for him to come around, growing less and less patient by the second.

"There ain't no more toilet paper," he finally explained.

I had to do a double take. "Is that what this is about? Jesus, Mitchell. We've got plenty of t.p."

"No," he raised his voice and looked straight at me, "You have plenty, I don't have squat."

It was my turn to go silent. He was right in a way. Materially, I certainly had heaps more than he could lay claim to. The pathetic state of his affairs made me want to apologize, but for what? I hadn't derailed his life, he had. After a moment of sympathy, I rebounded. "Don't look at me as if you expect an apology for the condition you find yourself in. I'm not going to say 'Sorry' for staying home and playing by the rules while you did whatever you wanted out on the streets. Sure, I have toilet paper, but I don't have Grayson. If staying here this week hasn't meant 'squat' to you, then be my guest, leave."

"Dang. That's not what I was saying."

"No?"

"Hell no. I'm just pissed. I can't even buy my own fucking toilet paper."

"Listen, could we just start over? Do you want a haircut today or no?"

He grabbed his ponytail and inspected the ends. Before letting it go, he wrapped the hair around his neck as if it were a noose, and with fake-strangled vocal cords he said, "Yes, please."

I very nearly laughed, but caught the smile and turned it into a smirk. "I'll get some t.p.," I said as I blinked and shook my head, dismissive of his comic turn.

An hour later, I returned yet again to the patio, this time with a pair of haircutting shears, a comb, and a plastic drape. In our previous life together, I had been Mitchell's barber without question. After a brief request to keep his hair long, he submitted to the drape and clippings as if in a trance, relaxing under the petting comb. I inspected his scalp and hair for lice and was relieved not to find any signs of the bugs.

Pearls my Mother Wore

While I was snipping away, I casually asked my nephew if he knew it was Mother's Day. My attempt at offhand conversation came out sounding staged. His response was that he had been hearing it advertised on the radio, "every five-fuckin' minutes." There came that edge in his voice, and I wondered if he thought I was going to suggest he go make nice with his own mother. That was honestly the furthest thing from my mind, but it was the only thing I could think of that would account for the scowl on his face and the vibe he was giving me to shut up. Either that or he thought I was fishing for some kind of acknowledgement for myself, which I certainly wasn't.

I told him I was going to drive to my mother's cemetery in Napa, half hoping he would ask to come along, but he didn't respond. He knew nothing about her except that she had died long before he was born. Perhaps he thought I was trying to rub it in, trying to show how much my mother meant to me, how much his theft had hurt me. For all he knew, I revered my mother; it was an assumption I let people have; it was easier that way. It is one thing to have a kooky mother. It is another thing altogether to have one with a diagnosis. In my case, I had found it was best to leave folks to their own imaginations.

After the haircut, I wrapped up a peanut butter sandwich for Mitchell to eat while I was gone. I didn't bother changing out of Grayson's sweats; nobody was going to be looking that closely at me anyway. I added the blue Pendleton as a jacket and didn't give my appearance another thought. I wasn't expecting a warm and fuzzy Mother's Day outing. I was going to complete my mission and return home as soon as possible.

The florist near the cemetery gave me a sideways look when I came in to purchase the roses. Instantly, I could see how the chopped hem at my slippered feet was strange, and then I remembered that I hadn't looked in a mirror before leaving the house. My unwashed face and uncombed hair were probably a sight as well. When I set the roses down, the gentleman at the counter said, "We only accept cash." Fortunately, I keep a spare hundred-dollar bill hidden in my wallet. The cold clerk watched as I produced the money. I didn't like his attitude, so I wasn't very polite when I instructed him to cut the stems to ten inches, the size that fit into the permanent vase at her headstone. Normally I would have couched such a request in a bunch of nice phrases such as, could you please, if it wouldn't be too much trouble, and thank you so very much, but the man got none of that from me.

Driving through the pillared gate was like returning to a familiar dream, one that has repeated itself so many times that the dreamer accepts it as a dream even while it's happening. Although it was May, I could see the drizzling day in February when I was driven through the gate for the first time. Following that day, I would ride my bicycle out and sit for hours at her grave wondering what was going to happen to me. I have a visceral memory of standing up on the pedals, straining to get up the slight incline just inside the gate, anticipating my destination, her grave.

JP became my legal guardian. I had just turned fifteen a few months before she died; I was too young to go off on my own. It was either JP or foster care. He was as unhinged by her absence as I was, but we more or less functioned. He continued to take jobs that kept him away from home for days and sometimes weeks. I took care of the house as if it were my own, but it wasn't my own, and sometimes when JP was drunk, he'd mumble and grumble about it. "I pay the bills around here and don't you forget it, or you can get out. Do you hear me? Get out." It was impossible to predict how he would act once he started drinking; he might fall asleep or he might start pacing the floor or kicking and punching the walls. I had never seen him naked, but one night he was walking around the house stark naked. That was shocking and scared me into hiding for days — so much hair and those yucky things hanging at his crotch. Another time he took a pair of scissors to my mother's nightgowns and cut them to pieces.

Every month I received a Social Security death benefit check which I squirreled away in a bank account until I could afford an escape. There were nights when I would pretend to be asleep. He would open my bedroom door and just stand at it, breathing heavily, sometimes snarling comments about my absent father, bastard child, momma's girl, prissy bitch. I didn't know what he was going to do to me. He had hit my mother and threatened to hit me, but, to her credit, she was convincing when she said, "You touch her and you won't live to tell about it." He never did lay a hand on me, but a full-grown, drunken man growling foul remarks at my bedroom door in the middle of the night was petrifying.

I lived in that minefield for two years after my mother died. During that time I took drivers' training at school. Everybody wanted to get their license as soon as possible, and I felt the same way. I had saved the Social Security money, and my bank account was bulking up quickly. I wanted to buy a car, but then didn't have to. One day I came home and a used Capri was parked in front of the house. JP dangled the key in front of himself when I walked in. We weren't big on greeting each other when we entered the house. It wasn't like he would say, "Hello Kelly. How was school?" It wasn't like I would say, "Hi JP. How was your day? What would you like for dinner?" It's not that we didn't speak a single word to each other. He'd tell me that dinner was good, and I'd ask if he'd gotten enough to eat. He'd tell me when he was going to be away at a job for a couple of days, and I would tell him when I had a field trip with school. But generally, we had little to say to one another, and that was just the way it was. So when he handed me the key, it wasn't so strange that all he said was, "Don't hit anything."

The thing is, it was always clear that conversation made him uncomfortable. It was almost the case that not speaking to him was a sign of respect, not disrespect. I didn't want to cause trouble, or get kicked out with no place to go. Leaving him alone was the way I showed my gratitude for not being sent to foster care.

I planned my escape secretly and carefully. I was still under eighteen years of age, and I was afraid he would try to stop me if I asked for permission to leave. I wanted to get away because I didn't trust him. I couldn't exactly use the truth to explain my plans. Since he was oblivious to just about everything I did, I was able to secure a job fifty miles away, in Santa Rosa, as a live-in babysitter, without him ever knowing. I lied through my teeth to get the job because it included room and board, with days and weekends off.

My employer was a single mom and nurse who worked nights. I conducted myself well during the interview — yes, I could help her seven-year-old, Ariel, with her schoolwork and play games with her; yes, I understood no visitors; yes, I understood no television except on the weekends; yes, I could cook and clean. I gave Roxanne made-up names and phone numbers for references, and fortunately she never called any of them. Back then, pedophiles, abductions, and infanticide reports didn't pepper the news the way they do now. At the end of her questioning she wanted to know how soon I could start. I had told her I was nineteen and that my parents had been killed in a car accident when I was seventeen. I said I lived with my mother's sister, but that it wasn't working out so well and

I could start the following week. Without so much as a note saying goodbye, that summer, I drove to Santa Rosa and didn't look back. It was from that time forward that I reserved Mother's Day as the only day I would visit Napa and my mother's grave.

Roxanne needed me to be home with Ariel on nights when she was at work. With my days free, I enrolled at the Santa Rosa Beauty College through an adult education program. The tuition was almost nonexistent, a fraction of what it costs today. I forged every parental consent signature needed. I sent in a change-of-address card to the Social Security office. I got a second job working weekends at a place called Sammy's Sandwich Factory for additional cash, and whoosh, all at once I was living a completely different life. JP never tracked me down through Social Security, and I never saw him again, thank God. He may have done a few nice things for me, but he was no savior. I was lucky to get away from him with as little damage as I did.

Driving through the gates of the cemetery instead of riding my bike reminded me that I had become an adult; in fact, at forty-three, I was a year older than my mother had been when she died. Her cemetery is massive compared to the Tomales Bay cemetery where Grayson and Helen are. Mom's has one-lane roads that crisscross the grounds. I parked next to a couple of other cars at a wide gravel turnaround at the end of her road. A small group of people were standing nearby and talking. They each looked at me as I pulled up, but out of respect, didn't stare. A second group of three was scattered but together, walking the rows looking for a particular plot. All of the markers were flush with the ground. A six-foot-wide green tractor lawnmower was parked in the shady corner of the field. As I was walking across the squishy, over-watered grass, I heard one of the three call out, "Here it is." My mother's grave is in a part of the cemetery that was filled up many years earlier, so it wasn't likely that I would see anyone newly distraught. The people buried in that area had been gone a long time.

I had never felt raw and distraught over her death. It wouldn't have been real. Even at fifteen, I judged her life not worth living, and when it was over, I didn't question it too much. I understood she was done with living, even though I didn't see it coming. I don't think of myself as old, but when I was fifteen and she was forty-two, I thought she was an old woman. It wasn't until that afternoon, standing there with my stiff, plastic wrapped flowers from a corner florist, that I realized how young she had been, how young JP had been, how young I had been.

I removed the clear plastic shield and rubber band from around the bouquet and loosened the flowers before bending over to place them in the imbedded cup that was sunk into the soil next to her marker. I stood over her marker, a burgundy-colored polished stone with grape clusters etched in its corners. "Hum, homage to wine, that fits," I thought. I hadn't questioned the grapes before. JP must have been responsible for picking out that marker; the grapes must have appealed to him, and he must have thought they would have appealed to her, too.

Etched within the grapes were three perfectly centered lines: Irene Marie Perkins, Born November 11, 1934, Died February 9, 1977.

I went to school on February 10,[th]1977, and said nothing to any of my teachers or classmates about my mother having just died. Later that day I fixed dinner, as usual. I carried on as if nothing had happened. There was a funeral, but very few people were in the chapel, and I didn't recognize any of them. I remember that the closed casket had some kind of contact-paper veneer on it, burgundy-colored, with a raised, velvety, paisley pattern. A priest read a numbing eulogy that I couldn't follow, except that it condemned suicide. Afterwards, JP and I drove home alone. That was it, and it was over; nothing more was said about Irene Marie O'Donnell-Perkins.

"Are you happy now?" I wondered, standing at her grave as a grown woman. That thought started out with a genuine wish for her eternal happiness, a release from the heap of unhappiness I believed her life to be. But my gentle concern didn't hold. It turned into, "Are you happy now?" the accusation, as in, "are you happy now, look what you've done." In that flash instant, I was furious at her.

In my thoughts I demanded, "Where are you? I am too God damned young for you not to be here. Didn't you care what was going to happen to me? Right now, right now I need you to take care of me. I need you to make me a cup of hot cocoa, to brush my hair and rub my shoulders. I need you to read to me until I fall asleep, bring me home a little present. I need you to kiss me on the forehead and tell me you love me. Why did you ever have me in the first place? Hadn't you ever heard of birth control, condoms, ovulation? He was married, for crying out loud. Was I conceived in an act of sex or an act of love? Were you sober or drunk? You've missed everything. You've missed Grayson. You've missed Helen. You've missed my pretty little house. You've missed my career. You missed it all."

I actually stomped my foot and threw my fists to my sides. "It's not fair!" I wanted to whine out loud. The three people several rows away were startled by my childish antic and watched for a moment to make sure I was alright. I squatted back down and fussed with the yellow and white roses to hide my embarrassment. My unanswered questions and accusations hung in the air around me, slowly drifting away like a child's lost grip on a bunch of helium balloons.

"I'm sorry," I whispered to the flowers. I also whispered, "Rest in peace, Mommy. I love you. Happy Mother's Day." It was time to go. I wanted to get back into the safety of my car, where a box of Kleenex could sop up the tears I hadn't expected to shed.

Chapter Nine

The next morning I awoke from a bizarre dream about my mother. In it, my ears were ringing from a piercing doorbell sound. It was not the usual two-note chime of my home bell, but the steady buzzer that rang at JP's house. The coarse noise was impossible to ignore. Staggering against the painful volume, I stumbled down the hallway, pressing my fingers to my ears. I opened the front door without stopping to sort out the logic of what I was hearing. A gust caught the heavy oak door and pushed it wide. Bright yellow daylight poured in around me, the sun having just crested the eastern hills.

My mother was silhouetted against the radiant solar glare. Even after the door was open, she took her time in releasing the buzzer; the sharp point of her frosty-orange polished fingernail kept depressing the button. Filament fibers from her angora sweater blurred her form; her physical boundary blended into the atomic glow of the sun.

Dumbstruck, all I could manage to say was, "Mom."

"Baby Girl," she addressed me as she breezed into the house. Her cheek was a chill of wind as it brushed against mine for a greeting.

I stuck my head out the front door to see if anybody or anything else was out there. When I turned back to her, I was not at all sure what to say.

"Not bad, Baby Girl," she said, looking around, reaching up to adjust Helen's painting that hung in the entryway and was slightly off-kilter.

Agog, I watched as she glided effortlessly on her white, V-toed stilettos into my living room. She picked up an empty, hand-blown glass candy dish that sits on the coffee table and turned it over to inspect the quality and maker's mark on the bottom. She materialized a silver cigarette case and withdrew a Pall Mall. Along with the case was a slender silver lighter. She raked her thumb across its tiny flint wheel and tilted her head slightly as she put the cigarette to her lips to light it.

"Oh, Mom, I don't let people smoke inside the house."

That statement had no effect on her. She flicked the lighter cap closed with a snap and blew the drag of smoke toward the ceiling.

"For cryin' out loud, Baby Girl, don't be such a bore. Look at you. Your face is all scrunched up like you're gutting fish. Aren't you happy to see me?"

"Well, yes, I am. It's just that I wasn't expecting..." and then my thought evaporated mid-sentence.

She continued to peruse the living room, looking but not commenting. On every flat surface was a vase or two of wilted flowers. She took an edge of one of the wool blankets that covered the sliding glass door. I became afraid that she would look and see Mitchell sprawled out on the chaise lounge. That would require entirely too much explaining. I tried to divert her attention by offering to make us some coffee. She hesitated before stepping away from the tacky blankets and rubbed the material between her fingers, "Polyester?"

I wanted to respond, but couldn't find the right comeback. To correct her would make me sound desperate to impress, and foolish. To say nothing also left me feeling foolish.

She strolled over to where I was standing. As she got closer and closer, I wondered what she was going to do. She picked up my left hand. My wedding ring and band caught the light from the opened front door; the delicate diamond glinted as she inspected it closely.

She let go of my hand and jutted her own right hand away from us. The smoldering cigarette was pinched between her slender fingers, and a luminous four-strand pearl bracelet clasped with intricate gold fretwork was around her wrist.

"My mother's," she said. "Goes with the necklace and earrings. I want them."

My expression must have gone from fishmonger to speared fish: eyes bulging, mouth gasping for air.

She stopped admiring her adorned wrist and pulled away from me. With a condemning squint in her eyes, she turned up her palm. "I want them."

"Mom, I don't have the necklace and earrings anymore."

"Yes you do, and I want you to give them to me right now."

"Mom, they were stolen several years ago. I'm sorry. They're gone."

"You've lost them?" She spoke accusingly, raising and sharpening the pitch of her voice.

"No, they were stolen. It's not my fault."

Pausing between each word, she insisted, "Those were not yours to lose."

In anger, she stubbed out her cigarette in the dirt of the teddy bear topiary. I didn't know what to do. There would be no making the situation right. She would never forgive me, no matter how many times I said I was sorry.

Her voice could be smooth and melodic, but when she was disturbed her enunciation was clear and cutting: "Where is my coffee? Or have you lost that too?"

Quickly I moved to the coffeemaker and proceeded to make a mess, scattering grounds across the countertop; water sloshed over the reservoir, compounding my ineptitude.

"Do you still take it black, Mom?" I asked with a high squeaking strain in my voice.

There was no reply. I turned back toward the room. "Mom?" But she was gone. Vanished. "Mother?" I called out louder. I think I woke myself with my own voice, moaning out, "Mother." The top of my ear was bent over on the pillow, causing pain that I related to the hurtful buzzing in the dream.

As the morning wore on, with growing urgency I drank several cups of coffee and nibbled at buttered toast. I picked at my fingernails and scratched at the last stubborn flecks of nail polish, waiting for Mitchell to start moving around in the backyard. The specter of my mother and her demand for the pearls repeated over and over in my thoughts. He knew where they were. I had to get them back. I gathered a tray for Mitchell's breakfast. He was in the shower when I put down the thermos of coffee, mug, spoon and large bowl of cereal and small pitcher of milk at the patio table. I noticed he had swept the patio and wiped the table and other wrought-iron furniture clean.

In a few hours, Mitchell would have been with me for two full weeks. I wasn't sure how much longer he would stick around. I took the morning's sleep apparition as a call to action. The more I thought about it, the more filled with anticipation I became. I couldn't squander this opportunity to confront Mitchell about my mother's pearls. If he had sold them to somebody, I would gladly double the price to get them back, triple, it didn't matter. He knew where they were and I had to find them. I was on the verge of panic that I hadn't come to this sooner. Every minute I wasted trying to ready myself for the day was a minute that he might get away, and the whereabouts of my mother's jewelry would get away with him.

I had to shower and get out of Gray's hacked-up Pendleton and green sweats in order to go out and retrieve what rightfully belonged to me. But Grayson's clothes had felt like protection. I needed him close to me, and his clothes were the only way I could think of to achieve that sense of courage, confidence, and security. So I went in search of a combination of his clothing that was street-appropriate. I found one of his tee shirts that had a bison on the front; we had bought it while visiting Yellowstone National Park. Then I added a pair of his long shorts. The shorts were held up and the tee was cinched in by one of my own cloth belts. I didn't look good, but it would do.

I waited until Mitchell was finishing the last of his cereal before I went out and sat next to him at the table. Because I wasn't picking up the tray, and because I was somewhat dressed in street clothes, he could see this was not going to be a typical day.

"Hey," he said casually, nodding his head as if to give me permission to sit and speak to him.

I had imagined a number of scenarios. A Mitchell blow-up was always a possibility, and that would be the worst-case scenario—hollering obscenities, fist smashing, stomping around kicking things, storming off never to be seen again. Amnesia would also be difficult to combat; he might tell me he was high and couldn't remember anything about ripping us off or what he did with the booty. The best scenario would be that he took the black-velvet-covered case holding my mother's luminous, creamy pearls to his mother's house and they were hidden in a drawer or special hiding place that only he knew about.

My nephew held the rim of the table, bracing himself for whatever I was about to ask.

"Just out of curiosity, when we let you live with us four years ago, and you left without saying goodbye, what exactly did you do with the pearl earrings and necklace that you took?" My bluntness did very little to get the ball rolling.

"What are you talking about?"

"Mitchell, don't even play that, 'I don't know what you're talking about,' crap with me. You know what I'm talking about, and you owe me an answer. Now, what did you do with the pearl set? I want to know right now."

He turned his head away from me and looked off into the distance. After a hard swallow, he did answer me. He said, "I gave them to a chick."

"A chick? You didn't sell them?"

"No. She was a babe I wanted to impress."

"A babe," I repeated. "Does this 'babe' have a name?"

"Yeah, she has a name," he responded coyly.

"So what's her name?" I pried with feigned light interest.

"She was the only chick that ever dumped me."

"So what's her name?"

Mitchell didn't want to say, but couldn't avoid smiling when he did. "Gina Bennett," he said, while shaking his head from side to side at the memories of old times.

That was the first time I heard her name. Obviously, she hadn't been a bring-home-to -meet-the-family kind of gal. I remembered Tammie, Sonja, and Star, but not Gina. Mitchell wasn't prepared for where my thoughts were going.

"This Miss Gina Bennett, do you know where she is? Where she lives?"

He stopped musing over the past and looked at me with trepidation.

"That's right, Mitch, I want to know if the girl still has my mother's jewelry. Where does she live?"

"I don't know where she lives."

"Then where did she live?"

His brow furrowed into a scowl, "With her parents," he said flatly.

"And where was that, exactly?"

More pinched-face scowling. "In Livermore."

"Livermore, huh? That's not far from here."

"Livermore? Yes it is," he contested.

"Livermore is only about an hour's drive from here. Let's go. Let's go for a drive right now," I said, not allowing, "no thanks" for an answer. I immediately began gathering his dishes onto the tray.

"Ah Mannnnnn. Those people hate me," he whined.

"That doesn't matter. I'll talk to them. Get whatever you need, but we're going to see what we can find."

"You're crazy. We're not going to find her, and even if we do, what if she doesn't have the stuff anymore?"

"Quit weaseling. You made this situation, now you've got to try and clean it up. I really need you to help me with this, Mitch. I've got to try. You don't know what those pearls mean to me."

He folded himself over the table and covered his head with his napkin and arms. "This ain't fair."

"You'll live," I said and snatched the cloth napkin off of his head.

"We'll take the Volvo this time," I instructed.

From a voice buried under his arms, a muffled, "alright" could be heard.

Slowly he lifted himself from the table and walked hangdog across the lawn to the cottage, where his shoes were. I washed and dried the dishes in less time than it took Mitchell to put on his shoes. I raised my voice and called across the yard, "Mitchell, let's go." He appeared in the doorway, shoes on, shirt tucked in; he had shaved the few whiskers he had on his face, and his hair was combed back into a smooth braid. I could smell a fresh layer of deodorant.

After a slight hesitation, the Volvo engine turned over. Mitchell pulled the wiper lever several times to wash and remove the yellow acacia tree pollen that had settled on the windshield since the day before when he had washed the entire vehicle. We pulled away from the curb. I had a momentary scare; I couldn't remember if I had turned off the water at the kitchen sink or locked the doors.

"What is it?" Mitchell asked.

I wasn't aware of making any sound or movement, but he had noticed something. "It's nothing. Let's keep going."

"Do you have any money? He asked. "This thing's gonna need gas."

I leaned over to look at the gas gauge. I thought he was stalling, but he was right. We had to stop and I huffed because the delay was irritating. "Hey! Don't get pissed at me. This is your idea, not mine."

"Just drive, alright?"

Up the road he used my credit card to fill the car with gas. He lifted the hood and pulled out the dipstick to check the oil level. More stalling.

We pretty much drove the rest of the way ignoring each other. He turned on the radio, and I turned down the volume. The drive to Livermore took close to an hour and a half; it was farther than I had remembered. We arrived at the Bennetts' house after making one wrong left-hand turn.

Gina's mother answered the door. The woman appeared to be many years older than I. She looked old enough to be my grandmother; there was no way she had given birth to the girl I was looking for. The woman was either a relative or Gina had been adopted. Mrs. Bennett opened the door cautiously. "Can I help you?" she asked, her little voice tremulous. She reminded me of Nancy Reagan, a tiny little woman with friendly eyes looking out of dark, hollow lidded sockets. Not wanting to frighten the woman, I spoke slowly and introduced myself. Mitch had warned me that Gina's parents didn't like him, so I told the lady that I was a friend of Gina's, hoping that she would not question the age disparity. I said that I was only in town for the day and hoped to see her. The timid woman didn't blink once while I was talking, and may not have taken a breath either. When I finished, she didn't say a word but continued to fixate on my face, glassy-eyed, as if in a trance. "So Mrs. Bennett? Is Gina here or do you know where she is?"

Mrs. Bennett didn't answer me but turned away, leaving the door ajar. I wasn't sure if she wanted me to follow her or not. I looked out to the car and Mitchell was watching me; he swooshed his hand like he thought I should go in. I shook my head no. I couldn't see much of the inside of the house, but I could hear her trying to discreetly explain who was at the door. I could hear a man's voice but it was garbled, as if he were speaking out of only half of his mouth. What I could see through the door was the foot end of a recliner; his feet were covered with a pale pink crocheted blanket. When the woman returned, with a palsied hand, she held out an envelope to me. The other hand clutched a traditional looking greeting card to her breast.

"We don't see Gina much anymore, but she sends me little notes sometimes. Maybe she lives where this one came from. She moves so much, you know, I can't keep track." And then she giggled and covered her mouth with the card.

I thanked her for the envelope and was eager to get the hell out of there. When I got back to the Volvo, I hopped in and said, "O.K. That was creepy."

I asked Mitchell, "Are you sure those were her parents and not her great-grandparents?"

"She called them Mom and Dad. Was her old man there? He was a mean son-of-a-bitch."

"I think he's a mean stroke victim now. Some man was in there with her."

The envelope had a Fremont return address on it. Fremont is about another forty-five minutes south of Livermore. We were getting farther away from Sonoma, but I wasn't about to quit the hunt. I had to exhaust every possibility of finding Gina and the pearls. Fremont was too close not to try. My heart wanted to race at the possibility that my mother's pearls could be back in my hands within the hour. It was entirely possible that this Gina had them squirreled away in a sock drawer or something. Mitch had said that she dumped him, but perhaps she just wanted him to grow up and then return to her. I knew girls tended to fall hard for him. I imagined Gina looking at the black box and its lovely contents from time to time, pining away, remembering the day he gave her the extraordinary gift.

According to the envelope, Gina Bennett lived on Mission Boulevard. Mission runs for miles and miles. Having only the vaguest idea where we were going, we exited the freeway when it indicated the historic Mission San Jose Chapel and Museum. Unfortunately, that turned out to be the south and opposite end of where we wanted. Initially, we found ourselves going yet further in the wrong direction judging by the descending street numbers. We pulled a U-turn and headed north. The addresses were way off, but at least we were going in the ascending direction. It took another half an hour to get across the sprawling metropolis of Fremont, through the district called Niles, until we were almost in Union City.

179558 Mission Boulevard could have been easily missed. I wouldn't have expected a residence on the commercial route we were traveling along. The house was tucked back from the road, a run-down clapboard bungalow sandwiched between two used-car dealerships. Several junker vehicles were parked in the narrow yet deep front yard, some on blocks, some with flat tires, all of them smashed in one way or another and encrusted with years of dust. The shrubbery around the house was massively overgrown, a natural bulwark of climbing rose, wisteria, ivy and blackberries knitted across mature redwood, palm, and pepper trees. It was only from the driveway opening that we could see into the property. The place was very intimidating. A black Doberman was barking and growling at our idling vehicle — lunging against the chain it was tethered to.

A hard-looking young woman about Mitchell's age came out. She had a toddler on her hip. She squinted at us as she jerked the dog's chain. My face must have filled the passenger-side window of our vehicle. Tightening her squint to see if she recognized me, she was clearly perturbed that I was gawking at her. She gave the rabid beast a strangling tug at the collar; "Butcher," she asserted, and the dog whimpered and settled down. I turned to look at Mitchell; his head was resting back on the headrest and his eyes were closed.

"I don't know nothin about no babies," he answered before I asked.

He turned off the car's engine. "I'll go talk to her," he said as he was opening the driver's side door.

Once he stepped from around our car that was blocking her driveway, her demeanor shifted dramatically. She recognized Mitchell instantly, and dropped her jaw in utter amazement. She put down the little boy and gave her ex a full body hug, jiggling up and down with excitement. The rush of cars on Mission Boulevard made hearing what they were saying to each other impossible. I could tell she was asking what he was doing there, and he was telling her I was his aunt. She brightened more and more with every thing he said. A pretty smile crossed her face, something I wouldn't have guessed possible by the way she had frowned only moments earlier. She gave me a friendly wave and seemed to be asking if I wanted to come in. He was answering for me, no, I didn't want to go inside. They both looked back at me; she picked up the toddler, and Mitchell followed them into the house.

I waited. I waited and waited, and my nerves were getting the better of me. He wouldn't have taken that long to ask if she still had the gift. If she still had my mother's pearls, he would have come right out and given them to me. My heart was sinking; in fact I believed it was a lost cause. When he did come out, she was leading the way, the baby straddling her hip. I retracted the window all the way down and she came straight to it and looked in at me, "I feel terrible. I can't believe this. I'm so sorry." Those phrases were familiar to me because so many people had used them about Grayson. My face flushed red with heat, and my thoughts galloped in a dozen different directions. She was referring to the pearls my mother wore, not Grayson.

"I'm afraid I pawned your jewelry two years ago, in Las Vegas. I had no idea they had been stolen from someone," she said and then back-handed Mitchell's shoulder. "Dane was only about a month old, and we really needed money. I had no choice; it was my kid. I thought I would be able to get them back, but by the time I had enough money the pawn ticket had expired, and somebody else had bought them. We can pay you back. They gave me three hundred dollars."

I looked at the young mother. Her eyebrows were shaved off and then drawn back on in smooth, jet-black pencil strokes. Her eyes and lips were also lined with the same crisp black edge. Inside the black lip liner was grape colored lipstick. Her brunette hair was slicked with a polished sheen into a solid knot at the back of her head. She was a tall, broad-shouldered girl. Her black tank top had something in gold glitter pictured across the front of it; the design stretched across her ample breasts. Purple bra straps paralleled the shirt straps.

She reminded me of something poisonous, tropical, and exotic. She was young, too young to understand why I bristled at the suggestion of repayment. My mother's large, iridescent pearl-and-gold filigree set could have easily fetched five times what she got for them, but that was hardly the issue. What was gone had nothing to do with monetary value; to me it was a sentimental loss. My mother wore those pearls on special occasions, and she had so few of them, special occasions. The pearls represented happy times. No amount of cash could take their place.

My disappointment was almost more than I could comprehend in that immediate moment. Over the previous four years I had assumed the pearls had been used for drug money. Gina was telling me that the pearls had helped pay for her son's survival, but I wasn't sure I believed her. I had my doubts about the crowd Mitchell hung out with in those earlier days. I pegged Gina as a doper too. And so I pried, "Gina, can I ask you a question?

"Sure, anything."

"Can you tell me if you used any of the Las Vegas money to get loaded?" I had to know; I had to ask, even though I might not trust her answer.

"No. I swear it. I'm not into all that mess." She looked straight at me as if it was just as important to her as it was to me that I believe her. "Dane's father was killed in a motorcycle accident when I was five months pregnant. We weren't married, and my dad disowned me when he found out I was going to keep the baby. My son's father was half black, and my dad is a pig-headed racist."

I looked at the child again and noticed his amber coloring and curly golden locks. He was a mixed-race baby. He had large, pale-green eyes with thick, curly eyelashes. At that moment, he was twisted over sideways off his mother's hip, reaching for Mitchell. Gina cooed at her son, "What are you doing little boy? Are you playing?" He pulled himself up and plowed his face into her arm: suddenly he was bashful. "Silly boy. Are you being a silly boy?" she cooed some more.

I gave Mitchell a look and a nod as an indication that we should leave; my business there was done. He put his arm around the girl's shoulder, "Hey Gina, we's gots ta go. I'll call you." She raised her face to him and they kissed on the lips.

Mitchell gave the little boy's hand a shake, "Hey, little man." The child buried his face back into his mother's chest.

Mitchell came around and slipped back into the driver's seat. I was irritated with myself for having such optimistic hopes. Gina could see it on my face; I felt gutted.

"Mrs. Tremblake, I'm so, so sorry."

"So am I."

I didn't need to know her whole life story to see that she was still living on an edge. Leaving her and the innocent little boy at that ramshackle house pulled at my heartstrings. I could feel tears beginning to well up in my eyes. "I'm glad to have met you, Gina."

"I'm glad to have met you, too." She took a few steps back and used her son's hand to wave goodbye. "Say bye-bye."

"Bye-bye," he started repeating.

Mitchell had just started the car when a dark-metallic-blue, low-rider Monte Carlo pulled up behind us. Gina gave an exasperated groan when the driver of that vehicle gunned the engine. I looked back over my shoulder. I hoped the young man behind the wheel would see that I was nobody he needed to be threatened by. I could see his hair was towhead blond, compressed under the heavy webbing of a black hair net.

"Later Gin," Mitchell called across me, and we accelerated into traffic, leaving the capable young woman to tell Hairnet what ever she pleased.

The drive home was a somber one. I rolled up one of Grayson's jackets that was still on the backseat and propped it against the window where I could rest the side of my head. We got on the freeway in Union City and took a different route home, a route that took us past the towns of my youth—Hayward, San Lorenzo, San Leandro. I looked out the window and watched as we passed the steady stream of homes, shopping centers, business parks and industrial buildings. In Oakland were high-rise buildings. The landmark Tribune Tower, built in the 1920s, appeared dwarfed and quaint against all of the newer structures. We continued north through Berkeley toward Marin, crossing over the San Francisco Bay when the sun was lowering behind majestic Mt. Tamalpais.

I had only worn my mother's pearls once, on my wedding day. I wasn't looking to get them back because I wanted to wear them; I didn't want them to wear. I wanted them to remind me of my mother's beauty. So much of what I recalled about her was in fact ugly. And so the black velvet box that held her perfectly spherical pearls, their radiance nestled against rich folds of black satin, reminded me of her wit, smile, and sophistication. My mother was not just the booze, and her pearls helped me remember that.

As if the theft were occurring all over again, I grappled with what to do next. With Mitchell driving us home, one angry thought pushed against another, a mosh pit of resentment, fury, disappointment and regret. If I had only kept the pearls in a safety deposit box instead of a jewelry box, I still would have them. My mother was right; I had lost them. That Gina, if she had only made better choices, she would never have had to go to a pawnbroker in the first place. Mitchell, it was all his fault. How dare he feel entitled to sneak off with our belongings! He was not stupid; he knew what he took from me was special. How dare he recognize the value of our belongings and take them anyway! None of this would be happening if Grayson was still alive. I wanted to take a baseball bat to Mitchell's head and bash it until it cracked open and the pearls fell out.

In town, Mitchell broke the silence.

"Aunt K? Can we get some drive-thru?"

We hadn't eaten since breakfast and fast food was better than me attempting to pull something together in my own kitchen. The temptation to season his food with rat poison was too great. I straightened up in my seat and got the credit card from my purse as my answer; that yes, we could stop.

He studied the backlit menu board and pulled forward to order.

"Do you know what you want?" he asked.

"Yes, I want my mother's God damned jewelry back."

He rested his head on the steering wheel. "Aunt Kelly, I'm sorry, alright? What do you want me to do? Just tell me and I'll do it. Do you want me to leave? If that's what you want then just say so."

"Sure, run and hide again. That will fix everything."

A male voice from the speaker said, "Can I take your order?"

Mitch looked at me as if to ask, Are we ordering or not?

"I'll have whatever you're having. Just order two of everything. I don't care."

Four heavy bags of fast food were passed my way—large chocolate shakes, jumbo fries, onion rings, half-pound hamburgers, breaded chicken bits, deep-fried apple pies. I spent the remainder of the ride home separating out the bags so that we would each have two bags of our own. At the curb in front of the house, he went his way to the back gate, and I went mine. Once inside the house I slipped back into Grayson's sweat clothes again. Over the next several hours, in front of the numbing television, I slowly munched my way through the pile of junk food.

Chapter Ten

The next morning I got out of bed feeling like a cat trapped in a hot drier. I had to get out of the house, put some space between my nephew and myself. I needed to shake Mitchell, Gina Bennett, Mitchell's handicapped friend Daryl, my mother, and even pastor James from my thoughts. I used groceries as an excuse to leave. I had spent a good part of the night crying. My face was puffy and swollen; my nose was raw from so many tissues. Tissues, I remembered: Add that to the grocery list, that and aspirin. I planned to drive to Santa Rosa to do the shopping, a place where I could feel fairly anonymous. Thirty miles from home, I could get away with my red face and odd clothing. With a pair of running shoes and a baseball cap I looked like I had come from the gym; nobody would know the difference.

I had thought a trip to the grocery store would do me good. It would feel normal. I should have known better, however, because I detest grocery shopping, always have. Circling the parking lot for a parking space reminded me of my long-held distaste for the chore. I walked through the automatic retractable doors with a bad attitude and left my dark sunglasses on to prove it.

It's disturbing to be so grumpy inside a grocery store. It's like being grumpy at an amusement park or inside a casino. The stores try so hard to be fun, energizing, and upbeat. I guess studies show happy people spend more money, and that's why the supermarkets go to such lengths to be entertaining. I guess I am not a typical customer; that's what my problem is.

The first department inside the store was the bakery department where wax replicas of happy-birthday cakes and multi-tiered wedding cakes just made you want to celebrate, unless you preferred to be, oh, I might as well say it, dead. Helium balloons in the shapes of hearts, butterflies, fish, and cartoon characters jumped for joy in the breeze of the store's chill-factor air conditioning. Interactive displays were surely intended to make one's shopping experience engaging as well as informative. There was actually a squeeze-and-sniff display at the baby diapers; one had a choice between the "Awakening" fragrance or the "Calming" fragrance in their disposable diapers. On every shelf of every aisle coupon dispensers with perpetually blinking lights jutted out, gladly extending a "Take Me" offer. Musical hits from the '80s played over the intercom and were repeatedly interrupted by a pleasant female voice.

"Visit our deli department today for appetizers and party trays. We have decorations and gift wrap. Don't forget desserts. Shop with us for all your needs... We're here to make your life easier."

Oh, if that were only possible.

When the cashier, eager to please and overly enthusiastic, said in the most chipper voice, "Hello, how are you this morning?" I was ready to scream. Before he hit the total key on his register, he asked if I found everything I wanted. I told him yes, because I didn't believe my husband was on any of the shelves. "Have you found everything?" is just as useless as "How are you?" They don't mean anything; they're just empty phrases, noise to fill up the air. It's all fake. Nicey, Nicey. Yuk.

I left the store with an extreme case of the malserks. Malserk is a word I made up after a day of mall shopping. It is a combination of malaise and berserk, and it describes how I can get to feeling when I have too many choices and none of them particularly satisfying. It is like being bored and agitated at the same time. It feels like being hungry but not knowing exactly what for. Add to that a sprinkle of road rage. I wanted to ram my grocery cart into a pyramid of Budweiser twelve-packs outside the market's front door. But I didn't. Instead, I seethed irrationally for several miles along the drive back home.

Mitchell offered to help me carry the groceries inside, but I barked at him to leave them be, that I could take care of the bags on my own. At that, he walked across the street to visit with Mr. Finch and Mr. Ritell, and that infuriated me too. What had gotten under my skin was the new fact that Gray wasn't going to meet me at the car to help carry the bags in. He wasn't going to help unpack the bags in search of the snacks he loved. He wasn't going to toss paper towel rolls through an imaginary basketball hoop. He wasn't going to avoid touching the box of tampons. He wasn't going to ask if I needed any cash to pay for what I had bought, or suggest what we should have for dinner. He wasn't going to hug, kiss, and thank me for doing all the shopping.

I made room for the newly purchased necessities by purging everything in the refrigerator except the basic condiments — mayonnaise, mustard, ketchup, and relish. Capers, hoisin sauce, mint jelly and mango chutney, and a dozen other bottles and jars were relegated to a heavy-duty garbage bag along with an assortment of foil and plastic-wrapped plates, platters, cartons, and bowls, as well as Tupperware containers and Ziploc bags. I didn't even have to think twice; it felt good to have all of that funeral food gone. I tied off the loaded bag and tugged it over to a corner in the kitchen.

On the emptied shelves I put newly purchased sandwich meats, sliced cheese, three loaves of bread, peanut butter and jelly, two heads of lettuce, butter, two gallons of milk, two dozen eggs, hot dogs, a bag of apples, and a chocolate cake.

From time to time, as I worked at putting away the groceries, I could hear the guys across the street laughing. I stopped what I was doing and pulled aside the café curtain a fraction to see what was going on. Mitchell had been given his own folding chair. While I couldn't discern what they were saying, I could see they were relaxed and enjoying each other's company. Mitchell did not appear in the least bit self-conscious that he was wearing my husband's clothes, that one of his teeth was missing, that he had nothing to his name, or that his pals were probably sixty years older than he.

Mitchell was showing my neighbors his tattoos. Mr. Ritell's short sleeve was rolled up, exposing his tattoo on the side of his flaccid bicep. Mr. Finch said something, probably something bawdy, and they all laughed. Mitchell hung his head and shook it as if he was embarrassed by what the old guy had said. Even from across the street I noticed Mitchell's complexion and color had improved with regular food and sleep.

I heard more laughter. When I looked out again, I thought I caught a glimpse of Mr. Finch nodding his head towards my house. I decided the new best friends were having a good laugh at my expense. Mitchell must have told them I was making him sleep outside. The old guys would think that was terrible. They would wonder just what kind of woman was I. I fretted that the men may invite Mitchell to live with them. My nephew could then get good and comfortable and never leave. The backyard was a temporary arrangement; I fully expected Mitchell to be moving on soon. With more thought and self-doubt, I concluded that Mitchell would convince the neighbors that I should go and he should stay.

Of course Mr. Finch and Mr. Ritell would prefer another male for a neighbor over me. I wasn't a strong young buck. Mitchell could help clean their gutters, trim their trees, and haul junk to the dump. Of course they would want a strapping young fellow to visit with and talk to. They could discuss sports scores and statistics, the price of gas, and what cars were good or bad on the market. I realized that the old guys had been pleasant to me out of respect for Grayson. Gray was the one who would chew the fat with them. Most of the time, I had thought a wave from a pretty girl was good enough, but in light of that day, I could see I was of no use to them whatsoever. My smiles and waves were nothing compared to good old male bonding.

I had to talk myself down from my silly insecurities. Despite my efforts, there was still a part of me that remained suspicious of the camaraderie that was developing across the street.

I let go of the curtain and returned to my grocery items. The remaining five bags held canned foods, frozen dinners and vegetables, and dry goods — boxed cereal, cookies and crackers, potato chips, and candy bars. I had to make room in the cupboards for so many weeks' worth of food. Since I wasn't planning on doing any baking any time soon, I decided to move the large bags of sugar and flour to the empty top shelf. I dragged one of the dining chairs over to use as a ladder. Stupid. The chair swiveled and was hardly suitable. My stepladder was still in the living room; I hadn't bothered to put it back in the garage after nailing blankets to the wall. I should have just gone the twenty feet to get it instead of using the chair.

While stretching to push the flour and sugar to the farthest back corner of the top shelf, it happened. A siren was approaching from the highway; its red scream got louder and louder. I knew they were not trying to find their way to my house, as had been the case only too recently. When I was waiting for them to arrive, I could hear every corner and stop sign where they hesitated and blew their horns, but still they had not arrived fast enough. Listening to the wailing fire engine distracted me from wedging the heavy flour sack into place. I lost my footing, the chair flipped, and I tumbled to the floor, the side of my head cracking against the countertop on my way down.

Reflexively, I reached for my head, tensing every muscle against the stinging pain, the siren noise receding into the distance. I rolled onto my back and off my right hip that had connected with the floor. My right foot and ankle also throbbed from the wrenching twist they had done before leaving the seat. I didn't have enough hands to cup all of the places that hurt— my knee, thigh, rib cage, elbow. Stunned and in disbelief, I rolled over to my other side and waited for the pain to subside enough that I could get up and get some ice. Even if I could have managed to drag myself across the kitchen and to the front door, the last thing I would have done was yell for Mitchell's help. He was indebted to me, not vise versa; nursing bruises, regardless of their severity, was not the retribution I was looking for.

I broke out in perspiration from the trauma, and the cold from the linoleum floor seeped a chill into my damp flesh. I was shivering and tried to stand up, but my head spun and I immediately felt nauseous and faint. I gave myself a few more minutes to recover before I tried to move again. What had I let happen? I didn't think anything was broken, but I was hurt; there was no denying that. I held still and tried not to twitch. Lumps and bruises were rapidly forming on my flesh. I cradled the good side of my head in one hand and used the other to apply light pressure on the goose egg that was growing above my ear.

As I lay sprawled out on the kitchen floor, the siren sent my woozy thoughts to the Sunday before last.

I had dialed 911. Within minutes, half a dozen, then a dozen men were marching through the house, busily crowding around Grayson who was motionless on the bedroom floor. I knew Grayson was gone the moment I found him, but I really believed he could be brought back to life. Now, I wish I had never dialed that 911 number because it put into motion a series of responses that I couldn't control. But I had to dial it. I had to call for help even though it meant I was going to be in the way from the moment they arrived until the time they rolled his body away. I had to step aside to give the crew of emergency personnel room to fix my emergency. "They will turn this around, they are the heroes, they save people, that is why they suit up everyday," I told myself as they worked on him with purpose and determination, but one by one I could see this was going to go into their reports as D.O.A.—Dead On Arrival.

Several of the paramedics and officers were younger than me, I realized when they referred to me as Mrs. Tremblake.

"Mrs. Tremblake," one of them said, trying to get my attention, "We'll have to wait for the coroner to come and take possession of Mr. Tremblake's body."

I might have buckled at the knees except the young man ushered me to a nearby chair.

It was not long before a suit-and-tie-wearing deputy coroner and his assistant joined the dizzying cast who were in command of the situation. "Deputy" sounds young, but he wasn't. He was a mature man in his late fifties, formidable, barrel-chested, well over six feet tall. His face was darkly tanned, like the face of a man who does a lot of boating or golf. The red veins in his slightly bulging eyes made me think he could put away a pint of gin with no adverse effects. He looked like he had seen it all and nothing would ever surprise him. He eased me out of the bedroom and into the kitchen where he said he needed me to answer some questions.

In his deep, resonant voice, he asked, "Kelly, how do you spell your last name?"

I took a breath and tried to focus as I spelled out the letters of my last name.

"And was it Greg or Gregory?"

"My husband's name is Grayson. G-r-a-y-s-o-n."

He tilted his head and looked down at me, over the half-frame reading glasses he had put on. "Sorry," he said with a mixture of procedural sensitivity and a need to keep the upper hand.

He asked me if Grayson was under the care of a doctor, which the EMTs had also asked. He asked me if Grayson used any drugs, legal or illegal, in the same tone as the previous innocuous questions.

"No, absolutely not."

"How do you know your husband didn't use drugs?"

"How do I know? I just know. There's no way."

He thought for a moment and wrote a few tiny notes to himself on his small, spiral-bound note pad. He slipped the tablet and pen back into the inside breast pocket of his dark brown suit coat.

"If your husband was taking drugs of any kind, would you say so?"

"Yes, but he wasn't. You can ask anybody who knows him. This isn't a drug overdose."

A metal gurney was being rolled down our hallway to the bedroom where Grayson was. I heard its sturdy parts clang and collapse next to him.

The official was speaking to me. I was looking at him and nodding my head as though I understood everything he was saying, but few of his words penetrated my hearing. I remember he said something about an autopsy, and "Please sign here." I complied.

In the bedroom one of the men prompted, "O.K.," right before I heard the heavy thuds and rustle of the men transferring my husband's body from the floor to their gurney. They were covering Grayson with a standard-issue pale green sheet when I rushed into the room. I couldn't let them take him away. I tried to think of how I could stall them.

"No. Wait. Wait. Wait. Can you just leave him here a little bit longer? I'll stay with him. Please, can't you just come back tomorrow? Wait."

I laid my head on Grayson's chest, willing with all my might that he would wrap his arms around me like always before. But it was happening. He was gone and soon his body would be too. I took his dead left hand and slipped off his wedding band.

It was happening. My guy, he was property under legal jurisdiction.

The coroner cleared his throat and said, "We'll determine cause of death. Once the autopsy is complete you can have your funeral director recover the body."

Tracking my thoughts was like trying to focus on a single spark in a Fourth of July parade. That the official, a wall of a man, referred to Grayson as "the body" was just an instant in a shower of flashes.

"How long will it take for you to do what you have to do?" I managed to ask.

His succinct answer: "One to three days."

"Can I go with you?"

"No. That would be impossible. I'm sorry."

I shouldn't have let them take him. I should have put up more of a fight. Who would I have had to be to get them to go do something else for a few hours and come back when I was ready? Could I have become ready? I should have asked them what an autopsy was. The word, "autopsy" banged around in my head. How utterly inept I was. I had thought autopsies were done with needles, probing biopsies; I didn't know at the time that they were total eviscerations. I should have been able to save him. I should have noticed something was wrong. I should have gone looking for him sooner. Maybe if I had suggested going to the beach that day instead of repairing the fence then the whole day would have turned out differently. My mind was imploding into a knot of constricting thoughts, making it nearly impossible for me to speak. A police officer had asked if there was anybody he could call. I don't remember any of this very clearly, but I must have given the young man Mike and Lindy Skilken's phone number because before the last of the uniformed men left, Grayson's boss and his wife stepped through the front door. I let the men leave without knowing what to say or do. I was mute, stunned, stiff, destroyed.

At some point, I must have asked Mike to call my father-in-law in Florida. There was no way I could have found the composure to inform Richard of what was happening, but he had to be told. Richard was at the top of the phone tree; one call to him would save me from having to contact the others, Gray's sisters. Richard and I were not close. I've not met with his approval and he has not met with mine. We tolerate each other, but I always hoped for better. I could never crack his businesslike shell, and I couldn't stand how cold and distant he was to me. Maybe if I was smarter he would like me more. Maybe if I had a wealthy professional father, a man he could relate to, he would be warmer. Maybe if I was funnier, prettier, or had a talent beyond hairdressing, he would find me worth talking to.

Shortly after the deputy coroner and his men took my whole life on their gurney, Lindy did her best to console me. I tried to speak, but my throat was closed. I was blank. I stood there looking at her, looking through her, looking at nothing at all. My eyes were open, but I wasn't seeing much of what was in front of me. The Skilkens stayed with me that night, answering the phone the couple of times when it rang. Lindy made a pot of coffee. We sat unspeaking at the kitchen table. I, like a naughty child at school, laid my head in the crook of my arm on the table, pressing Grayson's wedding ring to my cheek. After midnight, we acknowledged that we should lie down. Lindy saw to it that I was under covers before Mike moved through the house, turning out the lights and settling into the guest bedroom.

Again, the sirens were returning along the same route, on their way to the hospital, still in emergency mode. I slid the toppled chair out of my way and slowly pushed myself up off the kitchen floor. From the refrigerator door I released ice into three Ziploc plastic bags, one for my head, one for my ankle, and one for my hip. I hobbled to the couch, wedged my ice packs in place and flicked on the TV with the remote control.

The Alfred Hitchcock movie "The Birds" was on. I know the movie well, and faded out through most of it, staring more at the screen than actually following the story. What I noticed, however—and I had never realized it before despite the numerous times I have seen it—was that the women never get hysterical in the horror parts of that movie. The children scream, but the adults don't. The one woman who does lose it a bit, the mother in the diner, gets slapped across the face for her outburst.

The actors' voices filled the living room, and then the movie was ending; Mitch Brenner, his mother, sister, and Melanie Daniels were all in the little Aston Martin driving away from Bodega Bay; black crows were bidding them a somber farewell.

I needed to fix Mitchell his dinner. The sun was setting, and our routine had been established. I was sure he was waiting and wondering. I stood up too quickly and had to stop and steady myself before I could walk across the room; a wave of dizziness and nausea came over me. I pulled together some dinner for Mitchell, a can of hearty chicken soup and several slices of buttered toast, milk and some cookies. He seemed to eat anything I put in front of him. Still trembling, I delivered the meal at dusk.

At the patio table I had to sit down for fear of falling down. Mitch had been doing something in the shed but walked over when he saw me land in the chair. My vision was blurred, my ears were ringing, and I was damp with perspiration.

He spoke to me in a questioning tone. "Aunt K?" And when I didn't answer, he said it again, "Auntie K?"

I didn't want to cop to being hurt. My stomach was in my throat and I needed to get back into the house. I thought I was about to throw up.

"Whoa. I just got dizzy all of a sudden. I'm alright now," I said and staggered to the door.

"Are you sure?"

All I could do was bob my head yes. If I opened my mouth, I was afraid vomit would come out. He reached around me and helped slide the door open and then closed it after I had stepped inside. I had reached back to prevent him from following me any further. I made it to the bathroom. The up-close sight of the toilet bowl was all I needed to go full-tilt purge. Once that was over, I lay on the floor for several minutes.

At the bathroom sink, I splashed cold water onto my face

and then dunked my whole head under the faucet. The room had stopped spinning, but I was afraid to move. In slow motion I got myself to bed. I lay still, but my thoughts raced. How could I have been so stupid?

Chapter Eleven

When I served the next morning's breakfast, I was feeling bruised but not nearly as horrible as I had the night before. It amazed me how quickly my body was willing to heal. Mitchell inspected my delivery like a scientist at a scope. "How ya doin?" he asked for the first time in the weeks he had been with me.

"Better. I must have had a touch of the flu."

"Oh. That sucks."

"Thanks for asking," I commended before returning to the safety of my dark cocoon.

For much of the morning Mitchell went on a cleaning jag that I never would have guessed him capable of. With a broom and overturned bucket, he swept cobwebs from the eaves all the way around the house where he could reach, skipping the high, north-facing side. For a couple of hours I heard the bristles of his broom scratching at the walls, nearly driving me out of my mind. When he was finally done, I gasped with relief. A few minutes later he was washing the outside windows. Every few swipes with his wet rag would send out a squeaky-clean squeal. I should have been impressed by his sprucing efforts, but I couldn't stand the unpredictable zinging shrill that the rubbing caused.

I couldn't endure another minute and asked him to stop when it was lunchtime. When I went out, the portable radio was loud and he was bopping his head and rockin' out to the music as he worked. To the beat of the song he squealed his rag against the window glass like a club DJ scratches on a turntable. Bobby McFerrin style, he was popping and clicking his tongue and hissing his breath to match the staccato bass rhythms. Initially, he did not hear me call out his name; he was so into what he was doing. I practically had to scream to get his attention. When he looked over and saw me, he was surprised. I refrained from saying anything about him driving me up the wall. Instead, I tried to play it cool. "Hey Mitch, why don't you call it a day? You've done enough already."

"Nah. I'm good. Windows are my spez-eality."

Trying to sound like I had concern for his well-being, I said, "No, really Mitch, I would hate to see you get sunstroke. The sun is too intense out here. It will be easier if you wait until you're not fighting sun streaks anyway." It didn't take much persuading.

"Yeah, you're right." He stopped what he was doing and beatboxed his way back into the cottage shed. A little while later, when I peeked out the curtain, he had finished his sandwich and was asleep on the chaise in the sun, shirt off, magazines and newspapers scattered all around him. At dinner he asked if I could sharpen his pencil so he could do the crossword puzzles; later in the night I saw him sitting in the cottage apparently doing just that.

When I awoke the next morning something was amiss. It was about 9:00 a.m. when the nagging something-isn't-right impression caused me to pull aside the blanket curtains and look out to the backyard. I unlatched the door and stepped outside. Mitchell was gone. His blankets were roughly folded in a square at the foot of the chaise lounge. The radio was not emitting the usual morning chatter and popular rock, a constant noise I had become inured to.

Inside the cottage shed all was still. The laundry basket of folded tee shirts, jeans and underwear was atop the potting table where it normally was, several days worth of clean clothes waiting to be worn. The newspapers and magazines were in the recycle baskets. Nothing appeared to be missing except Mitchell. Even the portable radio was still sitting in its spot.

The bathroom door was open and empty within, empty of him, I mean. My quick glance was halted by something on top of the toilet tank. It was the collection of metal he studded his face and ears with. When had those come out? I thought to myself. I couldn't remember if he had been wearing them or not. Surely I would have noticed, but I honestly couldn't recall if he was or wasn't wearing the jewelry the night before. I recognized the pieces immediately, but I had no clear memory of him wearing the stuff except for the first day when he showed up at my front door. I couldn't imagine not noticing such a glaring feature of his appearance removed, and began to feel a little crazy about the oversight.

Perplexed, I sat in one of the patio chairs and began to question myself. Quickly my self-doubt turned to frustration, anger and then, in fact, sadness. I looked over the fence just in case he might be across the street with the old guys. "Damn him," I thought. "Not so much as a goodbye. As soon as I think the rift between us has a chance of shrinking, he goes and disappears." It was true that I had been little more than cold and blunt with him. I certainly could understand why he was sick and tired of me, and I honestly didn't blame him. "Your uncle isn't here, and don't you forget it," I had stabbed him with early on. I probed mercilessly about his friend Daryl. Nothing was ever easy and natural between us. He must have realized there really wasn't anything here that he was interested in. A place to sleep, clean clothes and regular food were hardly worth daily doses of me, the hag. Grayson's nephew let me know what he thought of my humorless, clipped comments. I had told him he literally stank that first day he arrived. How snide and insensitive I had been. It's my way or the highway, I warned, with what I thought was impunity.

Throughout the day I cried with such intensity I thought I'd burst. Losing Mitchell felt like losing one last morsel of Grayson, and I had caused it. I had pushed him away. I hated myself for being so unaccommodating, so uptight, and so un-hip. But he had wronged me by stealing my mother's pearls and I was going to punish him for as long as I cared to. I had punished him all right, punished him right out the door. Go team! What good is righteous indignation when the offending party up and vanishes? I hated him for getting in the last word; his silent exit was a voluble "F-off." I had wanted to show him who was boss, not the other way around. I had botched the whole thing. I ached for my husband to a degree I would never have believed was bearable.

It was after 5:30 when I heard the distinct rattle of a diesel engine truck idling out front. There were a few minutes of loud conversation over the vehicle noise. Mitchell was returning. My every nerve fell into a bloodless shiver; my extremities went cold and my face burned with heat. My thoughts ignited, irrational, uncontrollable, furious and frightened. Was I going to hug him or kill him? In that instant I was a child again, hearing my mother return home after a drinking bender. Would she be drunk or sober? Would she be mean or sheepish? Would she come through the door ready for a fight, or with gifts? What was going to happen?

The vehicle pulled away and I heard the side gate unlatch, open, and then spring shut. I peeped out the edge of my blanket curtain to see him appear and to witness his condition. There was a bounce in his step and a grin on his face.

"Hey Aunt K, I'm home," he called out with good cheer.

What in the world? I opened the door dumbstruck.

He lifted his hand in the air to give me a high-five while announcing he had gotten a job! I did not return the gesture but could only look agog at him. He let his unmet hand fall as he started to explain how he had gone downtown to find construction sites. He found one and asked for the foreman and then asked if they needed any help with cleanup, lifting and hauling. He told the guy, "I don't have tools, but I have muscles." The fellow turned him away. Undaunted, Mitchell continued to roam around until he found another job site. He was turned down a second time, but at that one whoever he talked to told him to go around the corner where a crew was painting an entire condominium complex. The guy said to ask for Ron, and as it turned out Mitchell had gone to high school with this Ron. It was Ron who had just dropped him off. Ron was going to come back in the morning to pick Mitchell up for another day of condo painting.

"Mitchell, don't you think you could have said something to me before you left?"

"I tapped on the door but you didn't answer. I thought maybe you still had some flu. I didn't want to wake you."

"So you just split?"

"I left a note."

"What? You left a note where? I haven't seen any note."

Mitchell walked over to the blankets at the foot of the chaise lounge and from within its folds he pulled a piece of paper with, "Gone job hunting. Be back later" was written on it.

"Oh, brother! Maybe next time when you leave a note you could put it somewhere where it can be seen."

"I didn't want it to blow away," he confessed with the enthusiasm in his voice completely deflated.

Suddenly I felt bad for raining on his parade. "Well, congratulations. You got a job. I'm happy for you. Really. It's just that I've spent the whole day thinking you'd abandoned ship."

I tried to smile, but I started crying instead. I stood there pathetically bawling. He was clearly elated by his day's employment, but I couldn't manage to shift gears fast enough to share in his success and exuberance. I should have been patting him on the shoulder; instead he had to pat me.

"I didn't mean to make you worry, Aunt Kell. I'm sorry."

Eventually I did manage a smile. It was embarrassing to be so emotional.

"I bet you're eager to clean up." My voice sounded weak but conciliatory. "How about I fix you some food and maybe you can tell me more about your day while you eat?"

"Yeah, that's cool."

In the kitchen I warmed a can of raviolis and a can of minestrone soup. To that I added a couple of slices of buttered toast. He was also given a thick slice of chocolate cake. I put the meal together, but I was wrung out. I moved around the kitchen zombie-like. I opened the refrigerator door and gazed in at nothing in particular. The cool air was soothing to my flushed and swollen face. I sat down at the dining table for a moment, slid down in the seat to rest my head and neck against the chair back and nearly dozed off. I revived myself by splashing tap water on my face. I wasn't in the best frame of mind to hear about his day, but I would try. A bit wobbly, I carried the tray out to the patio table where Mitchell was ready and waiting.

"So where were you? Where was this job?"

"Down the street from your beauty parlor. You know, where Top Ten Market used to be."

"Oh, of course, I know where you mean. That's a huge development. I think they're putting in over fifty condos."

I asked questions so it would seem like I was paying attention, but I was only half listening. Half of me was not listening at all. As he spoke, I repeatedly had to rein in my thoughts that wandered to no place in particular. I watched butterflies hover from one flower to the next. I noticed a roof tile on the house next door had dislodged and was at an angle away from the others in the row. A thread was unraveling at the collar of the tee-shirt Mitchell was wearing.

"Yeah. One of Ron's guys crashed on his dirt bike and is off for the rest of the week. I get to fill in. For once in my life I had good timing. He's going to give me a hundred dollars a day. Under the table," he added with conspiratorial glee.

Mitchell seemed satisfied, if not pleased, with the pay, but I didn't think it sounded so great. It's hard physical work, that painting. I held my tongue about the chintzy wage.

In between slurps of soup and mouth loads of raviolis he told me what a great painter he was, far superior to any of the other more experienced crewmembers. It was his opinion that he could paint faster and neater than any of the other guys he saw working. His prideful boasts were backed up with examples of mistakes the others were making, how they stood around talking more than anything else, how they would cut in trim with the wrong brush, or load too much paint onto their rollers so that it flung drips everywhere.

"You should have seen this one dude, he had more paint on his face and shit than he did on the walls."

His excited demeanor settled as his dinner digested. He began to yawn with a halfhearted attempt at covering his silver filling-filled mouth. He arched his back and rolled his bony shoulders. He stretched his tattooed, taut, bulk-less arms out wide and then reached with the right and the left up to the sky for an additional stretch. He cracked his knuckles and twisted his neck from side to side until it too popped. He was full of self-satisfaction. I remembered to notice his face; it was free of the metal bits; only a modest silver hoop remained in one earlobe. The snake tattoo slithering up his neck still gave me the creeps, but he looked much, much better without all that hardware hanging off his face. He looked more like an average, everyday kind of young person instead of an inductee to the Hannibal Lecter society. I didn't say anything about the jewelry, if you can call it that. I was afraid he might reinsert it if reminded.

We were running out of things to say. I had asked as many questions as I could think to ask: What did he know about Ron? Not much; he was a stoner in school, but now had a wife and two kids. Mitch said Ron didn't "party" anymore, which I was glad to hear. How many guys worked for him? Seven. Did Mitchell mind the paint fumes? Was I kidding? he asked. After all the cocaine, speed and heroin he had inhaled? "Paint fumes. What paint fumes?" he joked.

Mitchell was getting tan, his complexion was clearing, he had put on a much-needed pound or two, and he now had a small temporary job. I stopped hearing what he was saying and started worrying about what would be next. Future tripping, I could see that soon there would be more work and money, girls, cars, parties, staying out late or all night, lies and trumped-up alibis. With money in his pocket, his surly mood would return and he would be impossible to tolerate. Four years earlier when he lived with us, he was a foul-mouthed, ill-mannered, inconsiderate, intimidating s.o.b. If that personality resurfaced in him, I didn't know what I would do. There was nobody to protect me, nobody to hide behind. It occurred to me that I had made a big fat mistake letting him hang around. He might just disappear again with who knows what of my things in his bags, or he might make the rest of my life miserable and never leave.

"So what do you think?"

"What?" He caught me not paying attention.

"Lunch."

"Oh. I can do that. I'll um, I'll pack you something and bring it out with breakfast tomorrow morning. You know, I think I'm getting tired, so I'm going to say goodnight. Congratulations about the job."

"Yeah, thanks. No, I mean it Aunt Kelly, thanks for everything."

Chapter Twelve

Ron arrived at 8:30 the next morning to pick up Mitchell for another round with the paintbrushes. Mitchell had set the alarm on the portable radio and actually responded to it when it went off. In my mind it was a test. If he slept through the alarm then that was going to be his problem. Sure, I could have gone out there and given his arm a tug and woken him up, but I didn't want that to become my responsibility. He passed the test; time would tell how long his discipline would last. I supplied him with breakfast at 8:00 and gave him a lunch bag. He thanked me because that was our agreement, but clearly his mind was elsewhere. He was edgy with anticipation of the day ahead. His hands were shaking as he pulled the bowl of frosted-flake cereal from the tray.

"Kick butt out there today. I know you'll do great," I said with as much encouragement in my voice as I could muster. He nodded in acknowledgement while chewing a spoonful of cereal, milk slightly escaping out of the corners of his mouth. It was early and the fog had not yet burned off, so even though it was exciting to send him off to his first full day of work, I thought the morning seemed gloomy and sad. I left him to finish his breakfast and I was sitting in the kitchen staring off into space when I heard the diesel engine drive up the street.

Mitchell gave a quick rap on the glass door and raised his voice to say goodbye.

"Later Aunt Kelly, I'm out of here," he called in a cavalier tone that I doubted he fully possessed.

I gathered his dishes and began a day of waiting for his return. I wanted to busy myself somehow so that I wouldn't think about how he was doing. I wanted him to find his way, but I didn't have much confidence in his ability. I wouldn't have been surprised if he returned with a black eye and said he got in a fight with one of the crew. He could be so petulant. There had been times in the past when he would go bananas over the slightest provocation. One time he got in a fight because somebody parked too close to his car, not touching it, just getting close. He liked to punch holes in the walls at his mother's house, lucky to get sheet rock and never a 2x4 when he did it. I wondered if he would be able to control his anger, if he could figure out how to think before he reacted. Even though he had been exceptionally tame recently, I didn't trust him. I was waiting for the explosion, waiting to see what drama would supply the perfect excuse for him to relapse.

In passing my day, I tried to read a book but couldn't do it. I couldn't retain what I had just read, and twice went back to the beginning. I couldn't get any further than a couple of words into a sentence before I lost the point and had to start over. Reading, I decided, was out. Daytime television was most definitely out. Soap operas and talk shows are filled with such absurd characters that the thought of them made my stomach ache. I don't care what those people's issues are, and I don't care if they get them resolved. They don't care about me; I don't care about them.

I fell asleep on the couch and woke up when I heard the radio going in the backyard. It was just after 6:00. Mitchell was home from work and apparently showering. I was seriously unsettled by the hour; I had slept almost the entire day. I did my best to shake the dopey, too-much-sleep feeling that made waking up difficult. I dunked my head under the kitchen faucet and slicked my wet hair back into a tight clip.

Mitchell didn't appear to have any scrapes or bruises, no bloodied nose or fat lip. I went out with a tall glass of ice for one of the sodas that was still left in the cooler, and I asked him how the day went. He responded that he was beat.

"Damn, they're killin' me. My back. I'm really out of shape. I feel like I'm fifty," he said, as if fifty was really old.

I asked Mitchell if he was hungry and he said, "Starving."

"Did I give you enough in your lunch bag?"

"Oh yeah man, it was awesome. The guys all wait in a line at the truck and shit, but I was cool. Thanks."

Talking to Mitchell could be a challenge. I almost always understood what he was meaning to say, but sometimes it was a stretch. He was lazy with his enunciation; clear diction was clearly un-hip. And so when he said "truck," as in the ubiquitous catering truck that shows up at job sites, I thought he said "trough." For a minute I got confused and thought he was saying something gross about a urinal trough and shitting. "Truck and shit" sounded like trough and shit. I didn't want to give it away that I was lost, and after that quick lapse I did catch his meaning. I didn't particularly relish asking him to repeat himself. It is so annoying to keep having to ask, What? What did you say? Especially because I didn't particularly care what he had to say anyway. Our laconic exchanges were just enough to keep the peace.

Finding ways to busy myself while Mitchell was at work was a chore. I did his laundry, I paid some bills from the mountain of mail scattered over the dining table, but beyond that I found myself living in my head most of the time. Staring blankly off into space became a major pastime. I also began talking to myself. I would talk my way through the small tasks I was doing.

"Here is a sock, now where is the match to it? Oh, there it is. This shoulder goes to that shoulder, fold once, fold twice, and fold again. This basket goes to the cottage, these go in this drawer…"

When washing the dishes I would count the number of forks, spoons, knives, the number of cups and glasses. I would count how many wipes it would take to get them clean or how many wipes it would take to get them dry. I would count the number of times I would stir a pot, or bowl. I counted like on a rosary the number of links in the chain around my neck that held Grayson's wedding band, my most cherished possession. I was not reciting the Hail Mary or the Lord's Prayer, but going around and around the gold links, counting. When I had nothing to count, I would numb myself out by reciting the numbers one, two, three, one, two, three, over and over. Eventually, the recitation would put me to sleep.

It was during this time that I began pulling my hair out, literally. It started with me sitting at my reading chair in the living room, splitting my split ends. I would delicately get hold of one frayed end and then pull it apart until one side would sever off of the main strand. Because the main strand was then weakened, I deemed it unfit and expendable. I would work my fingers down to the base of that compromised strand and, careful not to get more than one hair, I would pluck it right out of my scalp. I laid the strand across the arm of my chair when I was done handling it and then went after another. Initially it was just an absent-minded activity. I wouldn't pull that many hairs out at one time, but after several episodes the arms of the chair were developing webs of long, blonde fibers. Before the webs got too thick, I was counting the hairs and rearranging them from the left arm of the chair and then on to the right, fixating on the evenness of the spacing between each blonde hair.

While I was doing all of this it didn't bother me that I was crossing a line. It was like telling myself I shouldn't eat a second dish of ice cream, but then doing it anyway. I knew it wasn't a good idea, but I didn't think I was putting myself in any danger. I felt like I had complete control over my neurotic indulgences. At no time did I think my behavior was beyond control. I could stop it any time I wanted, I just didn't want to, I told myself. I wasn't seeing little green men in the rafters. I wasn't banging my head against the wall. I knew my name, my address, and if not the exact date, I knew the month and the year. I wanted to think about my life with Grayson every minute of the day: vacations we had taken, sporting events we had gone to, movies we had seen. As much as I longed for and meditated on the memories of my beloved, it tore me up, and the little compulsive behaviors I adopted simply put space between the next fantasy of my better life and the truth of my present state.

Mitchell completed all three days of work and was pleased to report that Ron had told him he would be in touch when more work came up. Saturday morning I was serving Mitchell a breakfast tray as usual, but this time I included a recent issue of Car and Driver, one of Grayson's magazines I found in the jumble of mail I had tried to weed through. Mitchell was in the cottage when I came out with my load. I could have just left it on the patio table, but I called out to him, was he interested in the magazine? He looked out the opened door. Not quite hearing me, he put his hand to his ear, but before I could repeat myself he was trotting barefoot across the dewy lawn.

"Say what?" he asked as he got closer.

I didn't have to repeat myself because right away he caught sight of the magazine and seized upon it.

"Whoa, Car and Driver. Can I see that? Are you leaving it here? Awesome."

"Sure, knock yourself out," I replied, amused that he was so elated. It didn't hurt anything to give him a magazine that I found absolutely uninteresting.

The morning was overcast and breezy; it looked like a spring shower was on its way.

"You may need to build a fire in the cottage. It's probably going to rain this afternoon. If it does, you can move things around and pull the chaise inside. O.K.?"

"Oh, really?" He looked to the sky seeming not to have noticed the dark clouds gathering.

"Maybe," I said, not wanting to sound like a know-it-all. But I was thinking to myself, "Definitely." There was no way he couldn't have noticed the change in the weather. Rain was coming; it was obvious. His, "Oh, really" was not a question. He was being cynical, and I fell for it. Chagrined, I returned to the house. Had he teased me? Maybe not. He wasn't much of a planner. He was more of a reactor. Maybe he really wasn't aware of the impending rain showers, and would only react once the rain started coming down on him.

By lunchtime, it was raining. Again he trotted across the lawn when he saw me appear with the lunch tray. I also had an old army-green flak jacket that Grayson never wore draped over my arm.

"Hey, Aunt Kelly, do you think I could borrow some drawing paper, I feel like doing some sketching." My mouth said, "Yeah sure," but the rest of me said, "Can't you see I'm giving you a nice warm jacket? You ingrate! He doesn't deserve any of this." I tossed the jacket onto a patio chair, confirming in my mind that the world is made up of givers and takers, and he, most definitely, was a taker.

He saw that I was annoyed.

"Oh, wait. Is, is that for me? I didn't see it. I mean, thanks. Hey, you don't have to give me the paper. It's cool."

"Oh please, I've got paper, if you'll just wait a minute. Can you just wait a minute?" I was mumbling as I was going back inside.

"No. Don't bother. I don't need it. I don't want it anymore," he was trying to say. After rooting through a desk draw I found a folder of unlined drawing paper and a few sharpened pencils. He didn't want to take them from me. "Take it. It's fine. Really," I tried to assure him, and myself. I didn't need him to feel bad about using the coat or the art supplies. It really was fine. I don't know what my problem was.

By dinnertime, Mitchell had started a fire in the wood stove. I could spy through the guest bedroom curtain and see that he was comfortable in one of the two wicker chairs next to the black iron potbelly, its small door open and revealing robust flames. Drizzling rain streaked down our respective windows. His stocking feet were up on the second chair and he was engrossed in his art creation. A cozy sight indeed.

In the middle of the night, I was pulled from a deep sleep by the fright of a nightmare. It was a struggle to rally out of it. I was in that strange twilight blend where asleep and awake overlap, not entirely out of the dream world, and not fully awake. I lay there terrified and somewhat helpless until I came to. I needed to recover my conscious intellect before I could gain a little perspective, but it came slowly.

There was nothing new for me about having nightmares, but not having Grayson to tell it to, not having him there to assure me that I was safe, felt horrible — lonely and horrible. I was going to have to sooth myself from bad dreams from now on. I was going to have to act like the mature adult that I was and shake it off. Even if I wanted to think about the significance of the dream, its sequence of events and the symbolism that appeared, I first had to stop being frightened.

In the dream I found myself inside the hollow stump of an enormous decaying tree. The encircling walls of the stump were several feet higher then my head. Looking up, all I saw was brilliant blue sky. The interior in which I was trapped was pulpy, unstable, sandy, and sawdust-like. I tried to scale up one area to get out of the tall stump, but it broke free, crumbling around me. That broken-away piece exposed and agitated zillions of ants, termites, and maggots. They poured out of their newly exposed crevices into the open stump that I was standing in. I didn't call out "Help! Help!" I cried out, "Is anybody there? Is anybody there?" The volume of my voice triggered an avalanche inside the dead tree, and I woke just at the point where I was about to be smothered in crawling decay.

That dream set my mood for the day. I stayed away from conversations with my nephew and let him spend his Sunday as a rest day if he so chose.

The phone rang and it was Margaret. I hadn't picked up the receiver, and listened to her leave a message. She was checking up on me, and wanted to make sure I was doing alright. She said nothing about the family silver; she wouldn't be so crass as to bring it up for a second time on an answering machine. The call nevertheless reminded me of the subject.

Not long after hearing her voice, I decided to tackle the job of polishing the silver, but before doing that, I pulled everything out of the hall closet to reorganize it. I started out with the thought that I was using my time productively, but I don't know how productive I actually was. The closet was over-stuffed with everything from pantry items—bulk flour, sugar, oatmeal, bottled water, canned food, paper products, etc.—to coats and sweaters, vacuum, cleaning products, Frisbees and board games. I could have held an entire yard sale with the contents of that closet alone. I dragged every box, broom, and hanger out of it, then took a coffee and donut break. When I returned to the closet I became panicked by the magnitude of the job. Up one side of the hallway and down the other was years of accumulation; it flowed into the living room and across the couch. I scanned the mess I had created and wondered how I could possibly get everything back into place. I managed to shove a pathway through the hastily created disorder and found my way to the bedroom for a quick nap. I then had to will myself out of that sleep-induced stupor. Just opening my eyes was a struggle. When I finally sat up and tossed my legs over the side of the bed, I stood up like a rusty robot. I made an ice-coffee with extra heaping spoonfuls of sugar to give myself energy.

Among the scattered contents of the closet was an old wicker hamper. Inside it, buried under old towels and sheets, was a Tremblake family heirloom, the Tiffany silver. Richard had given the set to Grayson and me on our wedding day. It had belonged to his grandmother originally, Vivian Orlean Tremblake. She must have been a dignified woman of impeccable taste. The pattern is graceful and sophisticated; it's named Faneuil-Engraved after Faneuil Hall in Boston. Her initials are classically etched onto each of the 180 pieces. All of it is stored in an amazing walnut box with many pale-blue satin-lined drawers and compartments. The box is so sumptuous that it was a shame to store it out of sight, but I was glad we did. Mitchell surely would have included it in his booty years earlier if he had known where it was.

Ignoring my earlier hall-closet-clearing project, I pulled the impressive Tiffany box out of its hiding place and set it at one of the only empty spots left in the house, the middle of the kitchen floor, where I could spread each piece out in front of me. With a ragbag and polishing compound, I settled myself next to it and started carefully shining each piece, methodically counting each rub.

I polished with the thought that I would send it all to Margaret. As Richard's oldest daughter, she had always seemed to be the rightful heir to it. The silver was given to Richard and Helen when they were married and then he kept it after the divorce. I think Margaret was rather stunned to learn that it had gone to me. The polishing chore took me, on and off, several hours to complete. It was relaxing to rub the soft, torn, tee-shirt cloth and petroleum-smelling cleaner over the amber-colored tarnish. The silver luster returned with dazzling brightness. When I was done, I put all the cleaned flatware back in its box. It was dinnertime when I returned the polished box and silver to the vacant hall closet. The box's walnut radiance was not diminished as it rested on the freshly wiped cedar floor of the forlorn closet; it glowed as if lit from within by the gleaming silver. I closed the door to protect it from a casual glance, in the event that Mitchell did somehow get inside the house. Everything else, all of the hodgepodge I had pulled from the closet, I left where it was. I felt certain I would put things right at another time.

At the end of the day, I retrieved something else I had extracted from the hall closet earlier, an old-style, hard-sided brown leather suitcase. In a melancholy mood, I walked the heavy suitcase to my bedroom and heaved it up onto the unmade bed. It was heavy because of its built-to-last construction, not because of the contents it stored. The piece of vintage luggage had brass latches that sprang open with the slide of a button. Inside it were the few hastily gathered tokens from my youth, the memories I wanted to hang onto when I ran away from JP's custody.

My mother's pearls left JP's house in that luggage. She strictly forbade me to touch her things without permission, but on the day I left his house, permission was not possible, and I wasn't going to leave them behind. I remember, in my heart I asked her if I could have them, and in my heart I believe she approved. I remember how carefully I lifted from her jewelry box the black velvet case holding her necklace and earring set, and I remember how carefully I secured them in my own little jewelry box. JP was not home and the house was silent when I made the transfer. I remember how I was startled when the tinkling music began after I lifted the lid of my own box, the tiny ballerina inside unbending from her bow as she began to twirl. That was the little box Mitchell had discovered when he riffled through my dresser drawers four years earlier.

With the suitcase opened for the first time in many, many years, the first item I pulled out from the jumble of mementos was my sock monkey, Juju. Its facial expression looked surprised, high arched eyebrows and full, round, button eyes. Small moth holes had frayed its yarn in spots and muslin-colored cotton batting poked through. Also in the suitcase were several 1970 and '71 issues of Tiger Beat magazine. Their covers were a colorful collage of male and female heartthrobs of the day — David Cassidy and Susan Day, Donny and Marie Osmond, the Monkees, and the boys and girls in "The Brady Bunch," bubble-gum cute pop stars. Long Beatle bangs were still in, squeaky-clean hair that was parted on the side and swept low across the forehead. Wide-collared shirts with suede vests were also the rage, although Bobby Sherman was extra dreamy and shirtless on one of the covers. The articles, contests, and quizzes were on brittle newspaper pages with faded black ink.

A small lockable diary was in my suitcase; the cover was designed with pink daisies and blue butterflies. Only a couple of pages have entries; they are written in colored ink — hot pink, purple, and lime green. The journal starts with January first, but on none of the pages had I identified the year. Stating the year I was writing in must have seemed as unnecessary as stating the planet Earth I was writing from. What I had to say on that New Year's Day of the unknown year was disturbing, so I didn't read much. My handwriting was scratchy and unrefined, the letters were uneven in size and the sentences strayed lopsided off the printed lines. Many of the words were phonetically misspelled and grammatically incorrect. "Today mommy has a bad hert on her side. I rapt her ribs with a ace bandag. Mommy wont see a docter. I had choklat cake for brekfast. It was good."

An assortment of birthday cards were banded together with a bright orange, fluffy piece of yarn, the kind girls wore in their hair as headbands, tied in a bow at top center or cocked to one side. I preferred mine top center. I unbanded the cards and read through each of them. Except for the one that had nine cartoon candles on it, I couldn't tell by looking at them what year they were for; they had not been dated either. There was a Snoopy and Woodstock one, a yellow smiley face one, another had a clown with balloons on it, and one with two turtles doing a patty-cake polka. All had printed birthday wishes for me, to which my mother had simply signed "Love, Mommy" to each. Emerald-colored glitter dislodged from the turtles dancing tutus and stuck to my fingers and then everything else I touched.

Next, I handled the First Holy Communion dress and veil that my mother had bought during her brief church phase. The garments were protected by nothing more than a dry cleaners' cellophane sheath. The two articles were folded together into a compact square, never to be worn again. I saved the ceremonial attire originally not because of the sacrament but because I was enraptured by its resemblance to a wedding dress. The whole thing, my brief exposure to the Catholic Church, was a farce anyway. We didn't go to church until Mom came up with it as a scheme to find herself a husband, to "meet a man of quality." My mother made superficial friendships with a few women in the church, but quickly she came to the conclusion that there was nothing in it for her, meaning no available men, so we quit going.

In the few catechism classes I attended, the nuns lost me at original sin. My spiritual education did not include debate, so I kept my skepticism to myself. I could accept an omnipresent deity, but the all-powerful part didn't make sense in the context of original sin. The way I saw it, even when I was seven or eight, was if God made Adam and Eve and included free will as part of the design, then, when free will didn't work out, it was God who was at fault, not the two prototypes. If God truly had the final say, then why didn't He fix the flaw at the beginning of time? Either God didn't think there was a flaw and therefore no original sin, or God was powerless to do anything about it, ergo, not omnipotent.

I pulled the fragile, yellowing lace garments from the cellophane bag and gave them a gentle shake. The fabric was breaking down and well on its way to crumbling apart; at each hard fold it was particularly vulnerable. A couple of green specks of glitter from the birthday card clung to the musty lace, and my careful attempts to pick them free caused more damage to the material. The small, mid-calf-length dress had a square neckline and an empire waist, and the veil still had, albeit misshapen, a white beaded wire band that had held it in place on my head. The rest of the ensemble—white gloves, anklets, and patent leather shoes—had never been saved. I have held onto the dress and veil because I thought I should. Seeing the little outfit in such decay, however, made me regret that I hadn't taken more precautions to preserve it.

Finally, I lifted a White Owl Brand cigar box from inside of the suit case. Some of the box's paper label had worn away, but the white owl perched on a smoldering cigar was intact, as was the price; the cigars sold for eight cents a piece or two for fifteen cents. The sturdy cardboard box had some heft to it. Inside were thirteen candles that had been on my birthday cake when I became a teenager, an opalescent glass bead rosary, an envelope with a lock of my corn-silk-blonde, baby-fine hair; "Kelly's first haircut" is written in my mother's perfect penmanship on the envelope. There was my original Social Security card and a blue Honorable Mention ribbon from the sixth grade science fair.

Also inside that cigar box is a picture of me right after I came into this world. It is the one the hospital took when I was born. A date stamp is on the back: October 3, 1961, under the Presbyterian Hospital crest. Unlike Grayson, I don't have any childhood pictures of myself. Cameras were not a part of my upbringing. I don't have any pictures of my mother. There are no pictures of the places we lived. I wasn't in any school clubs and I didn't play sports, so of course, no pictures. One time I brought a notice home about school pictures being taken, and my mother scoffed, "What a racket. Look in the mirror if you want to know what you look like." My timing was off. I knew she wasn't feeling well. I might have gotten the school pictures if I had approached her at a better time.

Why weren't there any pictures? Were school pictures really a waste of money? Or was it that there was nobody to send them to? Where were the pictures of her growing up? Where were her family photos? If she were alive today, I would ask her about that.

But what gave the cigar box most of its weight was my extensive swizzle-stick collection. I draped the rosary around my neck, the crucified Jesus dangled in my lap, and I scooped out the dozens of swizzle sticks and spread them across the bed in front of me — red, blue, black, green, yellow, white — crisscrossed like pick-up sticks. Mom would give them to me after "a night out on the town," as she put it. How I looked forward to those souvenirs; she had remembered me while out drinking and dancing. I treasured them for their colors and shapes. The word "swizzle" tickled my mouth as a kid. One of my favorites was gold glitter with a red-tipped king's crown on the end of it. Another stick had a Vargas-looking pinup girl around its shaft. There were ones with pineapples, palm trees, hula girls and Tiki faces on the ends. The plain ones that just had the names of the bars she had been in—The Circle, Blanky's El Rancho, The Viceroy Motor Hotel—were my least favorites.

One next to the other, I lined up those tiny wands that had stirred cocktail after cocktail. The pleasure at their sight was evaporating with each placement. Instead of party tokens, instead of glamour and adult sophistication, I saw them as talismans of doom, subtle and sinister, their glitz dressing up the elixir that would one day destroy her life. One by one, I began to snap the sticks in two. After they were all broken, I snapped the halves in two again.

Every satisfying crack punctuated a cruel question I wanted to launch at my mother. I wanted answers, answers that only she could give to me. I was tired of being reasonable. I had concocted justifications for the life we had led together, explanations that I had come up with on my own. I was ready for her side of the story. Why hadn't there been any pictures? Grayson took pictures of me all the time. Did she treasure Blanky's El Rancho more than she treasured me? Where did I fit in? Had I been her original sin? The source of her eternal shame? Who was my father? Give me a name, an address. I didn't care if he was married to some other woman and had children in his other family. I didn't care that he had a religion that prevented him from getting a divorce; I wanted a face-off. Who were my grandparents? Good, bad, or ugly, I wanted to know. She died before I was old enough to ask anything close to those questions. Over the years, entombed in my hard-walled suitcase of secrets, those questions had grown into monsters, ripe for the conditions that had me there looking in that moment.

If I could have pulverized the sticks, I would have. The smaller the pieces got, the more effort it took to break them in two. With frenzied determination I kept snapping. Each broken piece gave me a sense of control, the power to destroy. The sharp snapped-off edges cut into my gripping palms and fingers. Despite slippery drops of blood making it difficult to get leverage against the breaking point, I kept reaching for pieces to obliterate.

With one of the longer pieces, I began stabbing at the Communion dress, piercing it repeatedly, staining it with my red blood. The dress was all a part of what I wanted to destroy. If only I could rewrite the past and give it a happier ending. No sin, no shame. Grayson, Helen, and my mother would all be alive. My mother would treasure me as my husband and mother-in-law had. We would have adult conversations. I would know where I stood.

I wanted to scream but held back that last impulse. I still had enough wits about me to know that if I let loose with the primal howl inside me, Mitchell would hear me and come running. Our differences would vanish, and his protective instinct would kick in. He would throw a patio chair through the sliding glass door if need be, but he would come bounding in the house to address whatever was wrong. And I didn't want that. I wasn't being physically attacked. There was nobody for him to wrestle to the ground or chase away. I was being attacked by memories, intangible spooks from the past.

Disgusted with myself, I flung the dress one way, kicked the suitcase and whatever else I could reach on the bed the other. I stood on the mattress and ripped the coverlet up and sprayed the shards of multicolored plastic pieces across the room. That action sent the cigar box, diary, and birthday candles all crashing against the opposing wall. Teen magazines fluttered in flight. I fell to the bed and pounded my fists and kicked my feet into the mattress until I was out of breath and exhausted. Eventually I curled into the fetal position and cried myself to sleep.

At four in the morning I woke up, looked around at the mess I had created, then turned off the light. Somewhat amazed to find the rosary beads around my neck still intact, I fell back to sleep rubbing them. In a barely audible voice I repeated with each bead, "Forgive me, I know not what I've done."

Chapter Thirteen

The next morning when I set breakfast down, I got the sense that Mitchell was going to ask me something. Twice, I thought he gathered up his breath as if he was going speak, but all I got out of him was "Goomornin," and "Thankya." If he had something to say, he would have to spit it out. I didn't have the energy to coax him into a conversation. I left him to his thoughts half fearing he had somehow become aware of my bedroom episode the night before.

I gobbled a few bites of cereal myself and then sidestepped my way through the precarious piles of closet contents and bedroom shambles to get back into bed. A few hours later, I opened my eyes and lifted my head from the pillow. I looked over to the dresser and a clock that had 12:10 illuminated in red. Because of the drawn blackout curtains, I became alarmed that it could be 12:10 a.m., not twelve in the afternoon. I panicked that I had slept through an entire day. I hopped out of bed and looked down the hallway; there was daylight. I had been so entranced by sleeping, that I honesty wasn't sure what day it was.

I served up Mitchell's lunch, searching for a sign if anything was amiss. I set the tray down and acknowledged his obligatory "Thank you." He took a deep breath but again hesitated to say what was on his mind. His behavior was so suspicious. I ventured, "Do you need to say something?"

He hesitated and we locked eyes. Despite his relatively good behavior, anger seeped from his every pore, the squint of his eyes and the clinch of his jaw looked sinister somehow. I was alarmed by his expression and wondered what he was intending.

He stammered, "I. I um. I wanted to give you this."

He reached in his pocket and pulled out three hundred-dollar bills and handed them to me.

"What's this?" I asked as I spread the three bills between my fingers.

"Ron paid me in cash. This is like rent or something. I really appreciate you letting me crash here."

Once again, he managed to catch me completely off guard. I didn't know how to respond. I didn't want to let him see me cry, but a sudden urge came over me. I took the money initially, but then had second thoughts. So he was crashing in my backyard. Of course he was crashing at my place; he wasn't living with me. I wasn't creating a home life for him. He crashed into my life and had the nerve to call it just that. My cottage shed was the Taj Mahal of dog houses and he was one lucky dog, but dogs don't pay their own way. I wasn't used to him being responsible in any way, shape, or form, but this action resembled a responsible act. I certainly wasn't in need of the money, and I wasn't crying tears of gratitude. I just didn't expect the gesture, that was all. It kind of broke my heart, him handing over something he had so little of. The payment really touched me, but then inside I questioned my judgment. I couldn't shake my stubborn suspicions; I questioned his motives and wondered why he was trying to butter me up. On the flip side of that, I told myself to give him a break; take it at face value, he meant what he said; he wanted to pay some rent.

He was so tickled to be giving it to me; I could then see it was pride gleaming in his eyes, not malice.

"Mitch, this is a lot of money. Are you sure?"

"Money is not my friend, never has been. You'd be doin me a favor."

"Gosh, I don't know what to say. It's really sweet. Gosh, I don't even recognize you anymore; are you really Mitchell Camp?

He blinked and blushed at that and tried to subdue the big smile that wanted to surface.

I fanned myself with the dollars and tried to think what to do. I was sure his heart was in the right place, but something about it just didn't feel right.

"Listen, I can't take all of this. We need to open you a bank account with it, a savings account with limited check-writing built in. You can write your first personal check to me; we'll call that one rent. How does five dollars a day sound?" I tried to come across as positive and upbeat, but I was saying no to him, saying no to something he wanted to do. This time, I could truly see the cold steel of anger hardening on his face, the taut skin on his gaunt cheekbones tightening, the set of his jaw shifting into locked position. And his eyes didn't glaze over; he squinted as if focusing sharply from a place deep within himself.

"So what? My money's not good enough for you? I told you I don't want it. Shit, I try to do something right and look what happens. What's the fucking problem? Just take it."

"Whoa, whoa, whoa, Mitchell, stop right there. I am not your mother. You will not bully me and remain living here, no way, period."

I slammed the money on the table and glared right back at him with all of the fury that my mother used to glare at me with when she was angry. It was always an effective tactic. If he called my bluff, for I was bluffing at having the energy for a fight, if he challenged me in any way, then I was going to tell him to leave. I could not let him get the upper hand. Why should I? But I also knew I had nothing to hold the line with but my own intensity and faltering integrity. I didn't have it in me to get into a scrappy back-and-forth argument about his money or what he proposed to do with it. A row was where this confrontation had the potential of going, and I didn't have the strength. Our futures together paused in that critical exchange. My hand stung from slapping the paper bills to the glass tabletop. He looked at me, reading exactly how serious I was. It could have gone either way, but he reined in whatever temper flare had erupted and he blinked first.

"Damn, I am such a fuckup. I didn't mean it, you know? I didn't mean to go off on you like that. This has been working out real good for me; I don't want to mess it up. I'm sorry, O.K.?"

"Yeah, O.K. Mitchell." I waited a moment before I spoke again.

"I appreciate what you're trying to do, but you need to know there is something called financial security, and you won't ever have it unless you get right with the way money works. Giving it all to me isn't going to teach you much, a bank account will.

"Aw, man, do I have to? I don't trust banks. What if they lose it? What if they steal it?"

"Have you ever had a bank account?"

"No."

"Well, they're not going to lose or steal your money. If anything, you will lose it because you didn't put it in the bank. It will slip through your fingers and you won't know where it all went."

"Man, you got me there." He wrung his face with paint-flecked hands and gave himself a couple of light slaps. The look of wry amusement returned to his face. He stuck a finger in his ear and gave it an exaggerated couple of twists, as if to be clearing out old wax so he could hear.

"Say it again. Why do I need a bank account?"

I couldn't help but chuckle at him. I was relieved that the whole thing hadn't blown into a scene. He had a knack for physical comedy that reminded me of Grayson.

"It's the way society does business," I told him. "You want to get a life? Well, this is one of the things you will need to do that. Otherwise it is like buying penny-candy until your allowance runs out. You don't have many expenses right now, so a savings account will grow really quickly if you keep depositing into it."

"A bank account. I don't know. That sounds so grown-up."

I offered to take him to the bank, and after lunch, we did just that. I wore a blue bandana over my plucked hair, dark Jackie O sunglasses, and my winter coat over Grayson's sweat clothes. Mitchell scoffed when he saw me. "Is that what you're wearing?" I told him I didn't want anyone to recognize me because they would want to talk about Grayson. He gave me his best Valley Girl "Whatever" but then left me alone about how I looked.

Inside the bank I told him to go to one of the bankers at the desks, that the tellers don't open new accounts. He pretended to munch on his paint-encrusted fingernails. "Not the desks," he stammered in mock fear, "I hate desks; I always get in trouble at desks."

I waited for him in the small seating area. I wouldn't have been surprised if the surveillance cameras were focused on me in my trench coat get-up. I was dreaming to think I wasn't going to run into somebody who knew me. Sure enough, Mrs. Cole, a regular customer at Beau Tique, one of the incessant talkers, walked in and sat right next to me to fill out her deposit slip. I buried my face in the Travel magazine I had picked up as soon as I saw her come through the door. I must have been beet red when she sat next to me. I was repeating in my mind, "Please don't recognize me," when she cheerfully said, "Kelly, is that you, dear?"

I acted like I had been so engrossed in the magazine that I hadn't noticed her there. "Oh, hi Mrs. Cole."

She took my hand in her arthritic bony ones. "Dear, how are you, honey?" Before I could respond, she continued, paying no mind to anything about my appearance. "Gabriella told me about your loss. I am so sorry. You have been in my prayers every day. Dear Lord, I pray, take care of little Kelly. Your husband is with the Lord now. They are watching over us this very minute. I don't know what I would do if something ever happened to my Sam. He's out listening to the radio in the car; he drives me everywhere I need to go. God bless him. I don't know how to drive, never learned. When I was young it wasn't proper for a lady to drive. Today you girls just do everything. I don't know how you do it; you drive all over the place, don't you? And you all work so hard. My Sam never would have let me take to work. My place has always been at home with the babies, but now they're grown of course. Even the grandbabies are grown. They come to see us when they can, but they're always so busy, dear. The Lord did bless me and Sam, thank you, Jesus. Dear, just remember, the Lord has a plan. He would never give us more than we can handle. Don't you agree?"

Mitchell rescued me.

"Mrs. Cole, this is my nephew Mitchell. We've got to run, but it was nice talking to you." …Not.

"It's so good to see you, sweetheart. I'm coming in to Gabby on Friday. I'll see you then."

Under my breath I whispered to Mitchell as we were walking out the door, "She thinks she'll see me on Friday."

"Who was that?" he asked with his face pinched, clearly perceiving my annoyance.

"This town is too damned small. I knew I would see somebody. Why do those people always say that crap, 'The Lord has a plan. God is merciful. Lord Jesus is watching over you.' How the hell do they know? Because some preacher told them, hammered it into them. God doesn't give us more then we can handle? Don't those people watch the evening news? I think the guy who jumped off the Golden Gate Bridge may have gotten just a smidge more than he could handle. I think the psychotic who kills her kids might have found herself with a touch more than she could handle. The notorious despots of the world and their followers, hell-bent on killing entire societies of people, don't you think, maybe, just maybe they got just a bit too much of something they couldn't handle? I just don't buy it. God doesn't have anything to do with what we get or don't get. God doesn't give victories at sporting events; God doesn't give cures to diseases, doesn't sanctify marriages and doesn't bless one country over another. I don't know what God is, but I am sure-as-you-know-what that God is not some warped chess player in the sky who messes with people's lives to give them lessons or to work out some divine master scheme."

"O.K. O.K. O.K. Chill already. I came here to get a savings, not to be saved."

Chapter Fourteen

With the exception of regular meals that I served Mitchell, there was little to anchor my days, no blocks of time devoted to specific activities, no 7:00 A.M. aerobics class, no eight-hour workday, no appointments to keep, or places to be. I was awake and asleep at random hours of the day and night, so my life fell out of the normal context of twenty-four hour cycles. Time dissolved into an endless mass that I wasn't paying enough attention to.

My nephew hadn't gone looking for any more work, but seemed to be doing a fair amount around Mr. Finch and Mr. Ritell's house. I tried to focus on the colossal closet mess I had created, but couldn't get a handle on it. I wanted to get rid of much of what I had stored for years, but couldn't sort out what I wanted to keep from what I wanted to give away. The task was more challenging than I had imagined. Half of the time I thought I would give everything away, and a few hours later I couldn't understand why I would do such a thing. That irrational dilemma was a major setback, and nothing got accomplished.

At lunch, Mitchell bopped to the table as if he was working out some new dance moves. His animated gait caused me to pause suspiciously.

"Hey Aunt K, waz up?"

"Nothing. What's up with you?"

He smiled and did a Jackson Five pirouette. "Check it out. Know what today is?"

After inhaling in a way that suggested I wasn't enjoying this game, I shook my head no, I didn't know what today was.

"Thirty days man. I got me some dam thirty days," he said, pausing slightly between each word for dramatic effect.

I wasn't getting his drift, but rather than puzzle out his meaning, I cocked my head and wrinkled my nose, "Thirty days for what?"

"Thirty days of sobriety, dude." He raised his hand to initiate and receive a high-five.

While meeting his gesture, I said, "I'm not a dude."

Un-phased by my disinterest, and with unrestrained glee, he threw his head back and roared like a rabid fan at a rock concert. His exuberant display penetrated my lethargy and I found myself smiling for his joy; at least it felt like I was smiling. Whether a grin registered on my face or not, I couldn't say.

"You've been counting the days?" I questioned, forgetting that sobriety birthdays had been very important to one of the hairdressers that used to work at Beau Tique.

"Hell ya. If you think this is coming natural, you're crazy."

Pondering his fixation with fast drugs, fast girls, and fast living, I left him to his lunch nodding my head, appreciative of his shift. When I said, "Keep it up," it sounded more like and order than the encouragement I intended.

If Mitch had thirty days of sobriety, then Grayson had been gone for thirty days. A month had passed, which meant my bereavement leave of absence from Beau Tique was over. In the middle of the night, I called the shop. I waited until it was late enough in the evening that there was no chance of anybody picking up the line.

I left a message that I needed to take another month off, "to sort things out." I tried to sound sane, but doubted that I made much sense. I tried not to ramble, and knew while it was happening that I was going on too long about needing to have a garage sale because my sisters-in-law wanted me to give back the silver that my father-in-law had given to Grayson as a wedding gift, that it wasn't mine anymore because it was… "Well, it's a long story, but I won't be able to come back, O.K. Bye."

My fingers were shaking as I depressed the off button to hang up. A rush of adrenaline had me shaking from head to toe. To dissipate my nervousness I walked around in circles and paced back and forth in the kitchen; I did a few halfhearted jumping jacks, and shook my hands as if they were on fire. "You've done it now. You've really done it now," I thought. I questioned whether freedom from my job was worth the uncomfortable jittery sensations I was trying to shake off. I found myself shivering and perspiring at the same time, but I couldn't turn back. "Hey guys, just kidding!" No, that couldn't happen.

The next morning Kristy, the receptionist at Beau Tique, called and left a very concerned-sounding message. She wanted me to call her as soon as possible, but I didn't. I knew she just wanted to talk me into going back to work, but I couldn't. I wasn't ready.

Shortly after serving Mitchell his breakfast, I heard the distinct sound of Ron's truck idling out front. I heard the side gate slam and then I heard Mitchell talking to Ron out front. Next thing was Mitchell hurriedly rapping his knuckles on the back glass door. Ron needed him to pull a shift, and he was going to take off for the day. I asked if he wanted any lunch and he declined; he had to leave right away. And then the two fellows and truck were driving away from the neighborhood.

Inside the house I started shaking again. I couldn't say if it was nerves or cold, but I cut up a second of Gray's Pendleton shirts and added it to the layers I was wearing. The weight and warmth of the bulk helped me feel like I wasn't going to fly apart. Buried under my husband's heavy cotton and wool clothing, I paced from one end of the house, down the hallway of chaos, and back into the kitchen; I did that over and over again.

I found myself paddling in a sea of mystifying waters, getting further and further away from anything I recognized. Except for polishing the Tremblake silver, there was no place where I could look and see success, and I didn't exactly care. In big chunks, my life and my personality seemed to vanish as completely as my husband had. What bloomed on that morning was rage. I was furious at Mitchell; I was furious that he had stolen my mother's pearls, and I was furious at my mother for letting herself die. It was her suicide that caused me to hurt so bad. I couldn't forgive her for killing herself. I couldn't forgive her for leaving me. I raged at the church, my job, my unfeeling in-laws and acquaintances that seemed to disappear in the wake of Grayson's death. I couldn't be mad at Grayson; that loss was too raw.

But it was my mother, she was where it came to a boil. "What about me?" I screamed in my empty house. "Why didn't you hang on until JP got home? Why did you let go? What did you need that you didn't have? You were smart, and beautiful. How did you let it happen? What was I supposed to do? What am I supposed to do? I'm not so smart; I'm not beautiful. Me, I'm nice; isn't that rich? Remember when you used to say that, that something was rich. I remember everything you used to say. I remember the way you walked, how you would sit in a chair, every facial expression. I remember the clothes you wore. The pearls, where were they from?

You never told me. You never told me anything about who you were, and now I am left with this smear of a childhood that started with bastard and ended with suicide."

I heaved a cut crystal vase of dead funeral flowers against the wall, shattering it. The muck of fouled water streaked to the floor where brown lilies lay against heavy shards of glistening glass. The explosive sound of the crash jolted me out of the emotional maelstrom I was swept up in, and I stood stunned by what I had done. I blinked in disbelief at the sight. "What is happening to me?" I repeated over and over. "I must clean this up before somebody sees." I found a towel and smudged the putrid water stain wider across the white wall. In the towel I gathered the lifeless flowers off the floor. I picked up a large chunk of the vase, its base, and held it in my hand. The fragment's saw-toothed edge was sharper than any knife I possessed. I considered the shard just long enough to appreciate the damage it could do if I dragged it across the thin skin of my wrist. It would slice as effortlessly as a surgeon's scalpel, I imagined. My heart was racing. The towel would catch some of my blood. It would be quick. The carpet would have to be replaced.

I came that close.

Suicide had been her answer, I couldn't let it be mine; I couldn't. I released the glass blade, and to keep from hurting myself, I ran to the empty hall closet and closed myself in it. In the darkness I sank to the floor and rocked back and forth. I lifted the heavy walnut box of Tremblake silver into my lap, my hands stroking its smooth surface. "One, two, three. One, two, three. One, two, three," I repeated again and again in an attempt to clutter out those tormenting thoughts that were ready to pounce at the slightest beckoning.

The wood picked up heat from the friction of my hand. I let my mind travel into the wood grain and imagined being a part of the enormous walnut tree it had come from. I could feel its leaves soaking up sunshine, and I could feel its roots sucking moisture from the fertile soil. Thick branches stretched wide, ever reaching for more, more wind, more rain, and more sun.

I could feel the gripping claws of a black bird as it clutched one of the smaller branches. My mouth filled with the taste of walnut butter. The twig snapped under the crow's weight and we took flight over the walnut grove, domed treetops evenly spaced in tick-tack-toe rows. The bird's wings fanned cool air around us as we soared and dove along a course that took us over nearby farm houses. Rope swings, rocking horses, and old fashion, hand-crank washing machines were in the yards. Laundry fluttered on lines, white sheets billowed against the prevailing current. The bird came to rest on the stone sill of a stained-glass window at the local church. Inside, I could see the enervated body of Christ on the cross. His heavily lidded eyes gazed across the cathedral into my own. The black bird again lifted us into the air, banking sharply away from the jewel-colored window, gathering speed as it went. With the gush of wind at my ears, it came to me that Christ had not died for our sins; he died because of them, the mob mentality. It was all a cover-up, a spin.

After miles of flight over rolling hills, tree-lined roads, villages, and turreted estates we touched down in a stream. The swift crystalline flow carried me away from my ebony courier over rocky rapids that then fed into a placid lake. Floating like a leaf, I drifted to the shore where I sat up and admired the beauty around me. Tall, purple-and-white irises poked above green and golden shafts of grass in the surrounding meadow. A rabbit hopping along the opposing shore caught my eye, and I turned my head to follow its path. There, overhead I could see rapidly approaching thunderclouds. The storm was upon me faster than I could stand, and a ferocious wind picked me up and tumbled me through the turbulent sky until, finally, I landed back on another branch of the same old walnut tree.

At that point, I was rushed, in a gust of wind, through the entire journey all over again. But this time, instead of the vistas being vibrant with color and texture, everything hurried by, dull and in shades of gray.

I was given two ways of seeing the exact same event.

When the meditation stopped, I knew something inside me had changed. I wasn't as afraid as I had been. The two flights were in startling contrast. One was alive and one was dead. Dumbfounded, I saw there was a choice, and the choice was mine. Before me was life or a living death. I wasn't going to die any time soon; certainly not by my own hand. In the confines of the dark closet I pondered what I had just imagined, struggling to take it all in. What was I to do next? I stayed inside the ample closet where I felt safe.

In the darkness I curled into a ball, my arm wrapped around the walnut box as if it were my anchor. I drifted off to sleep. In my dream Vivian Orlean Tremblake appeared. She was wearing my mother's pearls. I wanted to ask her where she got the necklace and earrings, but I could not make my mouth work. She did not speak a word but looked at me with all-knowing kindness. Absorbed by her love, in dream logic, my question melted away. The last part that I remember is that she stepped forward, leaned down, and kissed me on the cheek.

Reluctantly, I emerged from the closet when I heard Ron's diesel truck pull into the neighborhood. Mitchell was home from work and would be expecting dinner before not too long. I was hungry myself. While heating up a couple of cans of soup, I believed I would take that remarkable day, that vision, to my eventual grave. The mental odyssey I had taken while self-sequestered was beyond description. I couldn't imagine trying to explain myself to anyone, and I wasn't sure I needed to. First, I had to figure out how to explain it to myself. Mitchell told me that he was going to work again the next day. I remained pensive the rest of the night.

Shortly after Mitch left for work, I went in search of art supplies with the intention of trying to capture the indelible meadow scene I had encountered during my extraordinary journey the day before, half sunbeams, half storm clouds. I caused a second closet upheaval getting at the materials, but the hunt was rewarding; I found Helen's paint board, sheets of deckled paper, watercolors, and brushes. I also retrieved Helen's tripod easel. The wood stand was speckled with the oil paints she would use. With Mitchell gone for the day, I drew the curtains in the guest bedroom and the room filled with light. I opened the window and fresh air rushed in. I unfolded a card table and set up a paint station for myself.

I'm no artist, but I enjoy painting. Sporadically over the years I had been motivated to take classes from Helen and other teachers, but I am just a dabbler. Despite the fact that I found it relaxing and gratifying, I never seemed to stick to it. Other demands on my time would develop and before long the painting would be half finished; the materials were in the way, and I'd pack it all back into the closet.

That morning I took my time getting started. I moistened a sheet of watercolor paper to prevent it from warping, taped it to the board, and then waited an hour for it to dry. While it was drying, I rearranged the room to give myself some space to work. In my art supplies was a folder of pictures I had cut out of magazines that I, one day, wanted to paint. The inspiration images were of flower gardens, snow-capped mountain peaks, ocean sunsets, Koi ponds, and fruit baskets, each one peaceful and serene. When the paper was dry enough for me to work with it, I sketched lightly with a pencil the impression in my mind.

I worked at it until late into the night, taking one break at dinnertime. I brushed on and wiped off water and watercolors, carefully building up layers of pigment. I started out tentatively and gained confidence as I went along. My hand moved slowly and unsteadily as I worked with the initial pale shades. The white paper came alive with a whisper at first. Late that night I mounted the board to Helen's easel and admired what I had created. I had not captured the exact impression; I'm not that great of an artist, but it was there for me just the same: blue-green lake water, golden grasses with dashes of flower colors, and the small brown rabbit in angled light. Dark storm clouds I placed on the distant horizon. The next day I started another watercolor, and after that another.

It was the following sunny Saturday morning when Mitchell asked if his old bike was still around and what condition it was in. I couldn't deny that it was in fact still hanging from hooks in the garage, but weakly I tried to dissuade his interest. I told him I thought the thing would be too small, too rusty, the tires would be flat, it would be too hard to get down off its hooks, but he wanted to see it anyway.

I hesitated at the thought of letting him into the garage; it felt like a risky border breach. I had succeeded in keeping him out of the house for over a month, and it seemed like the garage was also a part of my no-fly zone. But with further thought, I waffled. The garage isn't exactly the house, and I wasn't sure if it was too close for my comfort or not. One of my fears was that some urge might overpower my wayward nephew; all of those shiny tools and nifty gadgets could tempt him beyond his control. I also didn't like the fact that the kitchen door connecting the house to the garage was right there, and it didn't have a lock on it. It was irrational to worry that he would suddenly burst into the house because if he had wanted to, he could have at almost any time.

I wasn't quick enough to think up a tactful excuse to keep him away from the garage. Telling him that I still didn't have an ounce of trust as far as he was concerned was too bold for me to pull off. Then it occurred to me that if he left for the day on the bicycle, then I could pull the curtains in my painting room and enjoy another day of watercolors in the sun. That turned my thinking around and I was again able to feel in control of the situation. He would be doing me a favor, not the other way around. I further justified my decision to let him into Grayson's garage by acknowledging the fact that I would never be able to trust him as long as I kept temptations out of his reach. He had to show me that he was trustworthy by his own actions, not mine, and so I told him to meet me out front.

I pushed the interior switch that automatically opened the big garage door. As it was slowly lifting, Mitchell came around the corner and let out a "Holy shit" as the immaculate garage was revealed to him.

"I forgot what a neat-freak Uncle Gray was. This is awesome."

He took a step into the space and paused to look around. He had no trouble spotting a ladder or the bicycle. Without asking further permission, he got right to it.

I hoisted myself up on the dryer to watch every move he made. Despite my inclination to tell him I had changed my mind and wanted him out of there, I kept quiet and just observed. I used to love to watch Grayson work from the very same spot. He could repair anything I ever brought to him; a colander with a handle broken off, a bracelet that came apart, gardening tools. I loved to watch the muscles in his arms flex, and the broad curve of his back as he bent over a project. His hands were so strong with ability. Gray could build anything he set his mind to. Many years ago he had made his own bicycle frame, figuring out the geometry and welding it together. He attached the pedals, sprockets, brakes, and cables and was soon the owner of a custom mountain bike. We then purchased the two bikes that Mitchell and I used back when I still considered us a family.

Mitchell's bike was not in as bad a shape as I had tried to lead him to believe. He raised the seat and adjusted the handlebars. He used the air compressor to fill the tires, and oiled the chain. Mitchell respectfully put everything back where he found it, and was eager to give the bike a run. Telling, not asking, he informed me that he was going to ride out to the state park to "hit the dirt." I had him wait a second for me to fill the two water bottles mounted to the bike frame, and I grabbed a bag of peanuts and a candy bar for him. In the seat pack was a tire patch kit and some small bike repair tools. His gloves and helmet were still in a bin with the rest of our bike gear. He was all set. As he rode off into the distance, I called out, "Have fun." As the heavy garage door came down, I mumbled to myself, "Whatever that is."

Monday morning's mail dropped onto the unattended accumulation on the entryway floor. My quick acknowledging glance was halted by a 10 x 13-inch manila envelope from the Sonoma County Sheriff/Coroner's Office. I had little doubt that it was going to be the coroner's report, results of the autopsy they performed on Grayson's body. I handled the letter for a moment, unsure of whether I was ready to view its findings. I found a letter opener and sliced into the envelope. Again, I hesitated before pulling the form out.

The document looked similar to the death certificates I had received from the Department of Public Health—official blocks of information, organized and straightforward. The coroner's report had blocks for "Decedent's Personal Data," "Location Of Death," and "Last Seen Alive." Next to a box labeled "Classification" were four words: Normal, Accident, Homicide, Suicide. "Normal," was check-marked. I went back over that information a second time before continuing.

On Grayson's death certificate, "Cause of Death" had the word "Investigation" typed in. On the coroner's report in my hand, that same question read, "Myocardial infarction."

I reached under the layers of Grayson's shirts I was wearing to find his wedding band. It was long enough to keep close to my own heart, my own sore, broken heart. I untangled it from the rosary that was also around my neck. His thick gold band, crosshatched in design, was warm from my body heat. I lifted it to my lips and then pressed it and my hand against my cheek. The report made official what I already knew; my sweet, tender-hearted Grayson, had had a heart attack. I returned the document to its envelope with icy cold fingers and turned it face down in the pile of letters on the kitchen table that I had classified as important.

I went to gather the remaining mail that was still scattered on the entryway floor. What sat at the top of the pile was a small pink, envelope, face down. It was a personal letter. Curious, I turned it over to see the sender's name. It was from Gina Bennett, addressed to Mrs. Kelly Tremblake.

Chapter Fifteen

Dear Mrs. Tremblake,

I feel so bad about the mistake I made. I know that there is nothing I can say or do that will ever undo what has happened. My only defense is that I was desperate to provide for my baby. I needed money fast. Ever since you were here last month, I have searched everywhere for this expired pawn ticket. I knew I saved it. Mitch was a good friend to me when I needed one. His gift was obviously special, but I didn't know what I had. I am forwarding this ticket to you because of what it represents. I don't mean it to substitute for what I owe you, but I hope you'll understand that your mother's great taste saved my life and my son's life.

Gina

With a second look inside the pink envelope, I found a folded slip of green paper. In carbon, the details of the transaction were recorded: the insulting amount of money that was given, the expiration date, and most importantly, the name of the pawnshop — Royal Flush Antiques Broker and Pawn Dealer. That was all I needed. It was the last thing Mitchell wanted.

Pearls my Mother Wore

That morning I removed the shelter-in-place clothing I had wrapped myself in during the previous several weeks. I had never been to Las Vegas, but as soon as I saw the pawn ticket, I was going, and I couldn't exactly get away with wearing three layers of my husband's clothing in the desert. The green receipt from the Royal Flush provided a morsel of hope, and as long as there was that, I had to try. Without dwelling in the mirror, I took off the bandana that hid my unwashed, plucked-thin, dark-rooted blonde hair. In the shower I washed my entire body clean, scrubbing with sweet-scented soap and washcloth. I changed into some of my own clothes — cargo pants and a sleeveless shirt. I practically felt naked without being bundled in Grayson's cotton sweats and two Pendleton shirts. To assuage my protective-clothing withdrawals, I cut a square patch out of the forest green sweat suit sleeve and pushed it into my pants pocket. I told myself that the swatch was a talisman against bad luck.

When I delivered Mitchell breakfast, he didn't look at the food, but looked me up and down, then made the comment, "Now that's better."

"What are you talking about?" He could tell I wasn't pleased by his crack.

"I'm just saying you look better now that you're not in that pajama get-up you've been walkin' around in. It was a compliment."

" 'That's better' is a compliment?"

"Well, you know, you were starting to look like some of the people I hung with down in the city."

I was aghast. "I don't care what you think I look like. Let's get that straight right now. You don't get to have an opinion about me.

Just because you're gettin' all squeaky clean, doesn't mean you get to judge me, not now, not ever."

"I'm not judging you."

"You are so, and how dare you? I took pity on you. You showed up here looking like a gutter rat and you have the nerve to judge my appearance?"

"Is that what you think I am, a gutter rat?"

"It doesn't matter what I think of you. I've given you a place to live, food, clean clothes, and this is the thanks I get, a cheap potshot. What else do you think I should do to make things 'better' for you?"

"Listen, I'm not judging you. But I'd appreciate it if you'd quit judging me. I was the one who took pity on you," he had the gall to say.

"What in the world are you talking about?"

"I felt sorry for you, being here all by yourself. I know losing it when I see it, and you, Aunt Kelly, are losing it."

"Oh, so now you're not only Mr. clean and sober, you're my savior? Give me a freaking break. So what now? I'm supposed to thank you?"

"You don't have to say it, but I wish you felt it once in awhile. I've been working hard around here."

"You are high on crack cocaine if you think I am going to pat you on the shoulder for anything. You haven't even begun to earn your keep around here. If you think I am going to forget your history, you've got another think coming."

"I knew it. Now you're going to throw the past in my face every chance you get. That's bullshit. You wouldn't be saying this shit if Uncle Gray was here."

"You're damn right I wouldn't. Bring him back Mr. savior and we can all live happily ever after."

Pearls my Mother Wore

Both of us were flushed red in the face, and paused for a second to gather ammunition for the next round; I had tears in my eyes. But that wasn't how I wanted the morning with him to go.

"Goddamn it, Mitchell, nothing is ever easy with you. Listen, the reason I've changed clothes is because I am going to Las Vegas. I got a letter in the mail this morning from Gina Bennett. She included an expired pawn ticket that she got from the dealer who took my mother's stuff. I've got to go see the place. I've got to see if there is any way I can track down whoever bought my mother's pearls. I've just got to go."

"Hell no. Las Vegas? You are not going to Las Vegas by yourself. I don't care what you wear. Wear a fucking tent if you want, but Uncle Gray would kill me if he knew I let you go out there by yourself. I'll take you. Aunt Kelly? I'll take you, alright?"

We had been driving for hours and still had hours to go. Mitchell knew the route to Las Vegas as if it had been his daily commute. Once we were beyond the familiarity of the San Francisco Bay Area, beyond the wind turbines of Altamont Pass, cruising the long straight line down the state, the urgency I had felt in the morning began to gently slip from my clinched grasp. With each passing mile my confidence grew: I would make it to my destination, I would find the Royal Flush and I would track down whoever had purchased my mother's pearls, and I would get them back. I could pay. Before leaving Sonoma we stopped at my bank; I had thirty-five one-hundred-dollar bills in my wallet. In Livermore, in Coalinga, in the Tehachapi Mountains and then again in Edwards Air Force Base, where we refilled the Volvo with gas, I checked my purse for the cash and the pawn ticket. Mitchell didn't know how much money I was carrying.

At the gas station, when we opened our respective car doors, we were both hit by the contrasting air temperature and groaned against the dry, oven-like heat. The station was a hub of activity, and the sudden bustle of automotive and human traffic was disorienting after so many hours of open road and sparse populations. A bank across the intersection had a running marquee that displayed 4:00 p.m. – 112 degrees. The heat threatened to suck every drop of moisture out of me as I made my way across the radiant pavement to the air-conditioned mart. Mitchell, with measured exertion, attended to the gas pump and windshield. Edwards is a mid-sized civilization cluster inside the bounds of the Mojave Desert. The filling station offered the standard fare, gas, toilets, and mystery food stuffs. The short aisles were crammed with a variety of long-shelf-life food substitutes—stuff that looked like sandwiches, nachos, and pastries, but could have survived unblemished into the next ice age.

The stop left me feeling mildly uneasy, as in we're-not-in-Kansas uneasy. I couldn't say exactly when we had crossed the line, but at some point, the farthest reaches of what looked familiar to me had ended. So little seemed to live on the scorched rock terrain we were speeding over. The topography was so different, arid, and intimidating, a land where only coyotes, scorpions, and rattlesnakes could survive naturally. What jumped out all seemed manmade and not very pretty: billboards, high-powered electrical towers, homes, cars, and businesses, many of which appeared either recently new, or long ago abandoned.

Acres of the Air Force base with its fighter planes parked in huge block formations were visible from the road and gave me pause. The aircraft were painted "Desert Storm" camouflage brown and tan. We drove through the town of Boron before the road opened up again. I don't know what to think about a town named Boron, a chemical element. A ton of it must have been around, and that much of anything made me wonder if I was safe. At the road's edge, the scenery whizzed by in a swift blur; directly ahead, the asphalt waved with hot vapors, but further out, at oblique angles, the barren landscape unfurled into a hazy, mesmerizing vanishing point. Mitchell drove in silence. His attention was focused on the next car to pass, the next semi-truck to draft, and the rear-view mirror for highway patrol. He was consistently driving over the speed limit.

We were nearing Las Vegas at sunset. Sunset does amazing things for the desert. What had seemed parched and forlorn came alive with pastel shades of rose and rust; hues of green emerged from dusty sage and occasional cacti. White limestone turned golden, and the blue sky seemed to shed its chalky veil. With the exception of the freeway, all around me was vast and untouched, dangerous and yet alluring. As I watched out the window, I massaged Grayson's wedding band, wishing he could see what I was seeing in that moment.

An approaching rest area sign prompted me to request a pit stop. Reluctantly, Mitchell pulled off; I was disturbing his road rhythm and E.T.A. His argument was that Las Vegas was only about a half-hour's distance away, as if that would make me eager to get there. Arranging a hotel stay for the night was a transaction that didn't thrill me nearly as much as the opportunity to stretch my legs in that distinctly peculiar land. There was a paved quarter-mile loop that went out from the facilities to the bank of an arroyo and back. Cracked sediment buckled in the dehydrated gulch. Despite the highway drone, there was silence on the path, a silence as big as the desert itself. I stared out to the empty south and wondered what was there. Eventually, Mitchell honked the horn for me to return to the car.

I had thought Edwards was a hive of activity in the somnambulant desert until I laid my eyes on Las Vegas for the first time. It was so much bigger than I expected. I had been to Reno and thought Vegas would be similar but with more. It wasn't similar, but it was more, much more. Merging freeways, exits and entrances, overpasses, and the city grid only just prepared me for the famous Las Vegas strip. All I could say when we got there was, "Oh, my God."

What I saw was a colossal theme park/carnival. Mitchell knew the names of each hotel casino. "That's New York, New York," he informed me when I gasped at the combination Manhattan-esque cityscape, Statue of Liberty replica, and Coney Island-ish roller coaster. Every time I craned my neck, he had the name: The Luxor was a giant black glass pyramid with a sphinx to enter through; the City of Paris had an Eiffel tower; Caesar's was flanked by Roman gods; The Mirage had a flame-throwing volcano. In bumper-to-bumper traffic we inched down the boulevard amongst monster trucks, trick low-riders, limousines, and hot rods. Loud music blasted from car stereos, boom boxes, valet stations, and mall entrances. Agog, I watched people of all ages and varieties shuffle shoulder-to-shoulder along the doublewide sidewalks in near colliding opposition. Many of the people were pink with sunburns. Some in the throng were clutching beer bottles and plastic cocktail cups.

"Get me out of here," I pleaded once we got to the end of the spectacle and the traffic thinned somewhat. "There's got to be a basic Holiday Inn or Best Western somewhere around here," and right on queue, Best Western appeared. "How do people live like this?" I marveled. Mitchell knew I had no idea what I was getting myself into when I told him I was going to Las Vegas. He had made it sound like a dangerous place to go by oneself, but I was sure he was trying to scare me because the trip involved the pearls he had stolen, a subject he preferred would disappear. He gloated over my adverse reaction to the gargantuan glitz. "I tried to tell you," he said with a self-satisfied grin.

"I told you so," I mocked back. "Just park the car, would ya?"

At the reception desk I requested two rooms for the one night.

"We have double doubles," the sweet young female said with a smile, revealing a mouth of perfectly aligned large white teeth. She had cheerleader/pep-squad eagerness in her delivery.

I looked to Mitchell to see if he had a clue as to what she was saying, but he gave me a don't-ask-me look back. After over nine hours of driving, I couldn't exactly fault his surfacing petulant demeanor, but it wasn't appreciated in that moment. Between the two contrasting young personalities, I got an instant headache.

"Excuse me?" I said to the wide-eyed girl.

"We have a whole bunch of rooms with two double beds in them. You'll save seventy-five dollars."

I had a ton of money in my purse and didn't want Mitch digging around in it when I wasn't looking; it was not the time for saving money. Mitchell threw himself into one of the lobby chairs while I continued at the front desk, declining the receptionist's cost-saving offer and restating my desire for two separate rooms. Bells, blings, and electronic voices came from a nearby flank of unoccupied slot machines.

Once we drove around to the door nearest to our rooms, I asked for the car keys. I had a strong hunch that Mitchell was yearning to get back to all of the action on the strip, but not with my car he wasn't. Before he worked himself into a surly fit, I offered to buy us dinner at the Mexican restaurant across the street from the hotel. During the meal I made a couple of attempts at conversation, but they fell flat, so I gave up and found a free real-estate weekly to peruse while I ate. Before returning to our hotel, I steered us towards a gas station where I could get a map of Las Vegas proper.

At our respective doors, I had had as much of Mitchell as I could stand for one day. I thanked him for his driving and said that I wanted to go find this pawnshop first thing in the morning. "There will be a buffet in the lobby for breakfast, O.K.? So let's plan on leaving by ten o'clock."

"No pawnshop in this town will be open before twelve," he said as if he was an authority.

"Twelve o'clock. Who opens at twelve o'clock? They may not be open at eight, but, if anything, I bet they open at ten."

"Suit yourself, but they won't be open."

"Have you been to this place?" I asked, shaking the newly purchased map.

"No."

"Well then I will suit myself. I'll be ready to go at ten."

"Suit yourself."

"Suit yourself," I parroted.

In my room I collapsed onto the bed as if I had been a long-distance runner just passing the finish line, struggling to take in deep breaths. I was physically exhausted. I reached for Grayson's wedding band and held on to it for strength and courage, imagining an alchemy that could turn the gold into the man. In the eerie ventilation hum of the sealed hotel room I began to spiral into the land of doubt. What was I doing? I had come so far but suddenly wanted to quit. I was afraid of this Las Vegas and I was afraid of who and what I would find at the Royal Flush pawnshop.

I wanted my mother's pearls back because they were an important piece of my ever disintegrating foundation. But this "sin city" reminded me of something I hated to acknowledge. It reminded me of how malformed my base had actually been. I tried to shake free of that train of thought, telling myself no, there were the pearls, the pearls were about the good times. There had been pearls, I was sure of it. I turned out O.K. There must have been some pearls. I wanted to go home, but without Grayson, I didn't want home either; there was no home anymore. And then, like the roar of a lion, coming from deep in my belly, constricted by modesty, the words "Damn him for dying" escaped my lips. And then, "Goddamn her for dying. Damn Mitchell and everybody else." Curled in on myself, I tried without success to rock those searing resentments away. Eventually, dreamless sleep wiped the slate clean for a few involuntary hours.

Before sunrise I was awake again. In the nightstand was a local telephone book. I pulled the pawn ticket from my purse and found the Royal Flush Dealer and Pawn listing. The address was 17759 Ace, at the corner of Ace and Roulette. The location was in quadrant G7 on my map, on the opposite side of town to the west. I returned to the stiff hotel bed and with the yellow pages for reading material my eyelids grew heavy, and once again I succumbed to unpredictable sleep theater.

Chapter Sixteen

With the driving instructions written out in my bold print and resting against the car radio, Mitchell and I pulled into a tacky strip mall at the corner of Ace and Roulette at ten-thirty in the morning. It was far from the buzz and excess of the main drag and hardly resembled the same town. There were very few cars in the parking lot, which made me squirm. Again, it was looking like Mitchell may have been right. The Royal Flush had iron bars across a large storefront window; the iron had been painted white. On display in the window was a collection of hanging guitars, a jewelry case, a mannequin wearing a fur coat, and an old jukebox. A "Sorry We're CLOSED" sign was propped upside-down against the window glass. On the front door hung another sign that looked like a clock with red hands. It said, "We'll be back at," and the red clock hands were together in the twelve-noon position. Also on the sign, in faded black magic marker, was the store's hours: Twelve to Eight – Daily.

"Closed!" I cried out in disbelief. I pressed my face against the glass to see inside the unlit store. It looked a little like a hardware store with an identity crisis, for the first things I laid my eyes on were tools: a chain saw was leaning against a table saw, a red Craftsman toolbox had its lid and drawers open displaying screwdrivers, wrenches and sockets; there was a leaf blower and a paint sprayer. Next to all of that was a rack of sequined women's evening gowns.

On the left side wall inside tall glass and metal-strapped cases were hunting rifles locked individually in place; a taxidermist's antlered elk head was mounted above the guns, as was an oil painting depicting pheasants in flight. Two sets of chrome wheel rims were lined up in a V formation with lamb's wool seat covers draped over them. A stack of shelves held several outdated models of car stereos, portable radios, VCRs, small televisions and turntables. Atop a zebra skin rug was a burgundy-colored velvet Victorian settee and small, round, marble-topped end table. The cash register was inside a peninsula of display cases; that's where the jewelry, wristwatches, small antiques and electronics were shown. Empty satin pillows indicated that the good stuff was removed to a safe when the shop was closed.

My morning was a non-start. We were stuck with no choice but to wait. Mitchell re-parked the car in a spot shaded by the building and a grouping of palm trees. He reclined his seat and closed his eyes to pass the time. I sat upright and scanned the unimpressive storefronts: a beauty supply store, a copy store, a dry cleaners, a donut shop, an insurance office, one vacancy, and the Royal Flush Antique Broker and Pawn Dealer.

At ten to twelve a middle-aged black woman with short curly braids all over her head approached the pawnshop and unlocked the door. She was put together in the Las Vegas style, lots of sparkle — studded jeans, strappy gold lamé high heels, extra-large bejeweled sunglasses and a floppy pink beaded handbag that was almost as big as a pillow case, lots of bangles and bracelets, necklaces and rings. A minute after she entered the store, the fluorescent lights flickered on. I waited until noon and then woke up Mitchell. "Hey. It's time," I said, and Mitchell opened his eyes and looked to the fully lit store.

At the pawnshop door I pushed even though it said pull. Then I pulled, but it was locked. The woman inside looked up at Mitchell and me with an appraising glance before reaching down to a button that buzzed us in.

"Hi folks, how y'all doin today?" she asked kindly enough. Mitchell immediately started looking at the musical instruments: guitars, harmonicas, a tambourine, an accordion, and a ruby-red metallic drum set. I wasn't sure how to say what I needed to say and felt my face turning pink as I walked up to the woman.

"Um. I have a question. Do you keep track of the people who buy stuff in here?" That sounded off. I suspected she could tell that I was prejudiced against her line of work. Aren't pawnshops a wink away from being fences for stolen goods?

Her face tightened, and she said, "Can I help you?"

I pulled out the pawn ticket from my purse and she warmed slightly.

"Hum, let's see what you have there?" she said as she took the green paper receipt from my unsteady hand. "I haven't used this style of ticket in almost two years. There's nothing in the store from back then," she said with just enough sympathy and concern in her voice that I ventured to keep trying.

I pushed wisps of hair away from my forehead. "Yes, but I'm trying to get back a very special pearl earrings and necklace set that was brought in, ah, ya, it could have been over two years ago. I already knew they wouldn't be here, but I was hoping you could help me track them down." I stopped looking at her face because it was contorting into pained disbelief. "They were old," I continued, "possibly Victorian. The necklace was a four-string choker and the earrings were big pearls that dangled on short, gold-filigreed rods. A tall girl brought them in, brunette, her name was Gina Bennett," I stated in a questioning way.

The woman didn't know what to make of me but then laughed as if she had just gotten the joke. "Do you know how many people come in here every year? Do you have any idea how much jewelry comes through this place? I couldn't tell you who was in here yesterday. Two years ago, phaaa, I'm sorry, we don't keep those kinds of records."

I felt tears welling up in my eyes. "It's just that they were my mother's, and she died when I was fifteen, and my husband died a month ago, and I need to get them back because, because…they weren't mine to lose," and then the flood gates opened and I was sobbing.

"Heaven have mercy," the woman said.

"I have two thousand dollars," I blurted out. "I would be willing to give whoever has my mother's pearls two thousand dollars in cash for the exchange. They could buy any pearls they wanted, and I would get mine back."

Mitchell was in the far end of the store and dropped whatever he was looking at, a musical clang hit the floor when I said I had two thousand dollars in cash.

"Please, can't you try to think back? They were beautiful, very unusual."

The woman was clearly annoyed. She began fluttering through papers scattered around her cash register. I coached myself not to apologize for disturbing her, to stay quiet, and see what might happen. She wasn't telling me to leave, but she wasn't addressing me either. She was stalling while she tried to figure something out. She marched off to the back of the store and rattled around behind a partition. When she returned she was carrying a compartmentalized tray with several jewelry items in it. "You have two thousand dollars sister? You can afford anything in this tray.

Hell, you can almost buy the whole damned thing. What would you like?"

Then it was my turn to twist my face into pained disbelief. "I don't want any of this. I want my mother's pearls back. That's all I want. We've driven here from Sonoma, California. I'm looking for something very specific; don't you understand? I'll pay more if I have to."

"More? How much more?"

"I could pay three thousand. Do you know anything? Please try to remember."

The woman half stood and half sat on a stool that was next to her cash register as if she was settling in for a negotiation. "Pearls, you said, a choker and matching earrings, three thousand dollars," she tallied the specifics out loud. With that, Mitchell was at my side taking a hold of my wrist, "Aunt Kelly, can I talk to you outside for a minute."

"No," I snapped, and easily tugged my wrist from his grip.

"Then what the fuck are you doing? Are you out of your mind?"

"Except for the fact that I wouldn't be in this position if it hadn't been for you, you have nothing to do with this. I want my mother's jewelry back. Now stay out of it," I scolded.

That verbal smack silenced him. He had been trying to help, but then only watched as I desperately addressed the pawnbroker. "What are you thinking? Do you think you know where they might be?" I asked with bated breath.

"A pearl choker," she said and closed her eyes as if to conjure its appearance in her mind. She scratched at the back of her hairline and twirled one of her spiraled braids.

"Ya, that's right. Wide with round white pearls." I put my fingers to my throat to demonstrate what I was describing as if she suddenly couldn't hear or spoke a different language.

"O.K., O.K., O.K.; I know what you're talking about. I know where they are. I kept them for a birthday gift to my sister."

"Aaaa!" I screamed, raising my fists in triumph. "I can't believe it. Oh, thank you. Thank you so much. Oh my god, thank you so much." I reached across the counter to squeeze the woman even though she was beyond my reach. I grabbed Mitchell's arms and shook them with glee. He wasn't smiling, and he wasn't enjoying my display, which brought me back down to earth. I turned to the pawnbroker with the next obvious question, "So how do I get them?"

"Now that's not going to be so easy," she said.

My heart sank, but nothing could be as impossible as finding them had seemed.

"What do you mean?"

"Kiki lives about a hundred miles up 95 outside of Beatty, near Death Valley. She don't leave her place except once a month for her mail and supplies. Her place is out on a mean ten mile dirt road, so she's not likely to make a special trip."

"Well that's no problem. We can go to her."

Mitchell moaned.

"I don't know. Her road is a bitch. What kind of car do you drive?"

"A Volvo. They're like tanks."

Mitchell moaned again.

I turned to Mitch and said, "It's new. It can make it."

Mitchell moaned for the third time and squirmed under his imposed silence.

"What?" I asked. What could possibly be wrong with telling a complete stranger that I was willing to drive my new-ish, forty thousand dollar car out to the middle of nowhere, to bring three thousand dollars in cash to somebody I had never met in exchange for my priceless family heirloom?

"Aunt K, I need to talk to you outside."

Knowing what he was going to say, I conceded, looked apologetically to the pawnbroker, and stepped outside.

"We're not doing this," he blurted out. "You're a fucking fool if you think some lady is gonna be waiting down a dirt road for us. What's to stop this woman from setting up an ambush? They've already got the jewels. I don't know who's out there. She could have her old man, brothers, and cousins waiting for us. If they don't kill us, the hike back to civilization when they steal the car will. It's two hundred degrees out there. Didn't you hear her, Death Valley."

"Oh, for God's sake. That's the most paranoid thing I have ever heard."

"It's not paranoid. You're insane."

After holding my face in my hands for a few minutes, I looked up at him and said, "I'm going. It's fine with me if you don't want to go, but I'm going. I'll drop you off in the nearest town, and if I don't come back to get you, you can call the police. If I'm killed in the process, I really don't care."

"Jesus Shit Christ."

I tapped on the door for the woman to let me back in. Mitchell followed. The woman was all smiles.

"Goodness, I just talked to Kiki and she's expecting you, and she will be expecting three thousand dollars in cash. No checks or credit cards. You understand."

"I'm ready."

"Here you go then," and she handed me the driving directions.

"Do you have a business card?" I asked. "And can you put your full name and hers on the back of it?"

Pearls my Mother Wore

We filled the car with gas before leaving glitz city. Mitchell huffed and sighed and nervously rapped his thumb against the steering wheel as he drove. It was not quite 3:00 when we reached Beatty. Before entering the city limits we had seen a billboard advertising Flinty's Burgers and Barbeque. I commented that that might be a good place for him to wait. He ignored me and kept his eyes on the road. It didn't take much to drive through the small town of Beatty. We rolled passed Flinty's. As the town receded behind us, I said to Mitchell that he didn't have to go, and I meant it. He pulled the car to a stop on the shoulder of the road.

"This sucks. What am I supposed to do in bum-fuck nowhere if something happens to you? No car, no money, no luck. The sheriff in that town ain't gonna take kindly to the likes of me; I can guarantee you that. Shit, if you go down, I might as well go down too. This just better be legit."

The business card the woman in Las Vegas gave me said her name was Regina Laws. Regina's map indicated that we should turn off Highway 95 a mile north of Beatty, onto Phoenix Road. At the end of Phoenix was the forewarned mean dirt road. Initially, the surface didn't seem so bad, and I thought Regina had exaggerated the challenge. A mile into it, ruts began to appear. Two miles in, the ruts became gullies. We were up against a saw-toothed mountain range; the flat desert quivered off in the distance as a mirage. We were climbing as we worked our way into a canyon. At one point the pebbly road had washed out and we tilted precariously to get beyond that spot.

"I hope we're on the right road," I said after the tires had lost grip and slipped us sideways in the gravel. There was no place to turn around. Mitchell was concentrating so intently on his driving that I didn't think he heard me. We were moving along at a mile or two an hour. The car bounced and slid; if we slowed too much we were engulfed in a backwash of dust, so we continued on. I understood why a person wouldn't want to drive this road any more than absolutely necessary, but I couldn't imagine how anyone could live in such an inaccessible place.

At four o'clock I became concerned that if I had somehow directed us to the wrong road then daylight would become a factor. There was only enough daylight to get to the sister's house, make the purchase, and get out. I didn't want us driving that goat trail in the dark.

The dips, swells, and bends in the road made it impossible to see more than a couple of hundred feet ahead. I became encouraged when the road leveled somewhat and we drove over a cattle grate. An old split-rail and rusty barbed wire fence extended in opposite directions, the posts leaning at all angles, the wire taut or slack depending. Next, we passed something that looked like a stone igloo, a domed kiva or covered well, an incinerator possibly. And finally, over the last hill, a quarter mile away in the valley below, sat a cinderblock house nestled in a grove of cottonwood trees. Its roof leaned in one direction facing the sun and was outfitted with several solar panels. Beyond the house was an enormous rickety barn. An animal pen adjacent to the barn had a few sheep in it. A nearby garden had rows of vegetables in raised beds: corn, tomatoes, squash, pole-beans. I saw a couple of compost piles with a wheelbarrow next to them.

My business card said the woman I was there to see was named Kiki Laws. I assumed it was she that I saw carrying a pail of something across from the barn. She stopped walking and watched our car and its wake of dust approach. She put down the pail and waved with one hand while the other rested at her waist. An ambush seemed unlikely. She was wearing a tunic-style apron over a sleeveless shirt and lightweight cotton, three-quarter-length pants. Worn boots that looked soft as gloves were on her feet. Her bushy hair erupted out the top of a colorful scarf that was wrapped several times around her head; a few silvery strands twinkled in the sunlight.

She was wiping her hands on a corner of the apron as we got out of the car. Her eyes danced with the friendly smile on her face. I was prepared to shake her hand and introduce myself when she initiated a hug.

"Girl, I know you need a hug. You drove *that* car out here. You must need more than a hug, you probably lookin' for a sedative," she laughed and embraced me with her big strong arms. "And you brought me just the young man I was looking for. You have just the muscles I need," and she gave Mitchell an equally warm embrace.

This come-on was so disarming, Mitchell blushed and smiled.

"That road is something else alright," I said.

She was so humored by my statement that she doubled over with laughter and slapped her knee. And Mitchell, relieved to be out of the car, began to laugh right along with her. I tried to chuckle but failed to see what was funny.

I hated to disappoint Kiki, but if she had designs to put Mitchell to work, I was going to have to set her straight. We didn't have enough time. I noticed her bucket contained a dozen or so light-brown eggs. She couldn't be more opposite to her sister in Las Vegas if she tried.

"Kiki? It's O.K. if I call you Kiki, isn't it? Kiki, we can't stay."

"Ah-oh. Girl, I'm getting ahead of myself. I have to tell you some good news and some bad news."

With my eyes as wide as they would go, I repeated her, "bad news."

"I tried to call Regina back in time, but was too late, ya'll had already left the store. Our auntie has your pearls. I forgot I had loaned um to her last December for the Christmas Jubilee at her church.

I spun away from Kiki Laws so that she couldn't see how horrified I was at this revelation.

"Please tell me that's the bad news," I said with my back turned to her, about to faint if there was more.

She came around to face me and put her heavy arm over my shoulder, "Aunt Essie will be here tomorrow is the good news. She was planning to come out anyway. I called her when I couldn't get a hold of ya'll. She's got your momma's pearls and she'll bring them with her. Now steady honey, it's gonna be alright," and she pulled me closer with a reassuring grip on my arms.

I was beside myself. I didn't know what to think. Here we had survived that goat trail of a road. My ears rang a wagon-train rattle after almost an hour of the car jockeying over its ruts and ravines. I was empty-handed, hot, coated in a film of dusty sweat, and I was hungry; we hadn't eaten since the hotel's breakfast spread. It all left me weak in the knees. I didn't like the sound of waiting another night in a Beatty hotel room for this Aunt Essie. And then the dread over three more trips out and back on that dirt road, if it didn't kill us, it may kill the car, I seriously worried. Maybe an ambush was coming.

Kiki draped her arm over my shoulders and gave me another encouraging shake. "Come on. Let's go inside. I just made some fresh lavender limeade. If you've never had it, you'll be amazed. It's gonna be just fine. You'll see. Son, can you grab those for me?" she indicated to the eggs. "I've got plenty of room for the two of you," she said, as we slowly made our way, arm-in-arm, to her front door.

I let her lead the way. Her kindness was persuasive, too persuasive for me to fight.

Inside, the house was cool and dark. It took a few minutes for my eyes to adjust. "Sit. Sit," Kiki insisted. Mitchell was happy to plant himself in one of two recliners in the living room. I followed Kiki into the adjacent kitchen and sat at her vintage 1950s dinner table. The house was loaded with knickknacks and antiques. It was a fun house, with so many things to look at. I began to get the impression that Kiki had been the recipient of many, many items that had made their way through the Royal Flush Pawnshop. Her hutches, baker's racks, rolling carts, bookcases, an upright piano, tables and end tables were all crammed with framed photos, fiesta dishware, McCoy pottery, dolls and toys, trophies, marbles, snow globes, candlesticks, antique glass and porcelain, iron skillets, embroidered linens, and so much more. Nothing was staged; it was a mishmash of everything from A to Z.

Mitchell asked if he could look through her record album collection. She had a turntable console to play the albums on, and he was in audiophile heaven. *The Best Of Sam Cooke* was the first album he played. A rhythmic purr poured out of the speakers as the record needle began circling the vinyl and then "You Send Me" could be heard softly.

From the kitchen were double French doors that led out to a shaded crossbeam and wisteria-covered patio, a patio that showcased Kiki's green thumb and horticultural verve. Ceramic pots of all sizes, shapes and colors were overflowing with flowers and greenery. A low stone wall that outlined part of the patio had been constructed in such a way as to also function as a dramatic planter box; it too spilled over with flowers and small shrubs. A stone water fountain burbled, birds chirped, and an overhead circular fan slowly swirled jasmine and honeysuckle-scented air. The view beyond the patio was of the corner of her vegetable garden and then much further out was a breathtaking expanse of chaparral. Farthest out was the cliff side of a ridge; multicolored soil striations were in a diagonal upward thrust, delineating epochs in geological history.

We, Kiki and I, sat on the patio drinking her sweet lavender-infused limeade, quietly soaking up the serenity around us. The spot was so intoxicatingly beautiful that, to my surprise, I started crying. Without a word, Kiki got up and went inside the house. I could hear her talking and chortling with Mitchell, but I couldn't make out why.

When she returned, she was holding a box of tissues. She handed them to me with a knowing smile. "My husband died twenty-two years ago," she said. When I looked up at her in surprise, confused that she had perhaps read my mind, she added, "Regi told me over the phone."

"Your husband died twenty-two years ago?" I repeated, wanting her to tell me more.

A very subtle shift occurred in her face. Still, her cheeks remained high and full with a patient smile, but something in her eyes receded for a moment. She was thinking back. She became present again and smiled at me even more because she saw that I understood that quick mental visit to the past.

"Would you mind talking to me about what happened?" I asked her.

She pulled her chair closer to mine and took my hand in hers to get my full attention. "It doesn't hurt the same now as it did back then. You'll stop wishin' you were dead." She watched my eyes to see if what she had said registered with me. It had. I knew she was right, but it was precisely that fact, that the wound would heal, that was killing me. I didn't want to heal. I didn't want to go on. Life was too hard. In that moment, I forgot entirely why I was even there; my mother's pearls were the furthest thing from my mind. She put my hand down after giving it a rub. Her hands were firm and calloused.

After readjusting herself in her chair, she cocked her head to one side and she looked over to the slope in the hill Mitchell and I had driven in on. "It was a terrible accident," she continued. "Gerald was workin' the tractor over in the front field with Regina's husband, Carl. There had been heavy rains all week and it was the first dry day they could work. A corner of the tractor dug in and tipped it over. Both, both of them were crushed. Yes, that's the truth," she said when I clapped my hands to my mouth to contain an involuntary exclamation of horror. "Yes, that's what happened," she repeated, more to herself than to me.

I couldn't ask her to go on. The grizzly details of what happened next were none of my business. I was amazed that these two women I had just come into contact with had had such a devastating tragedy in their lives. Nothing of it showed on the surface.

"How awful," I eventually managed to say.

Kiki winked at me; it was an amended gesture to the wince I made inside when people had used that same phrase with me. Enough time had gone by for her that she didn't wince at sympathy from those who were not affected, as I did. She carried the moment with a perspective that I didn't yet have, with grace.

"How about helping me in the kitchen?" she said to steer us in another direction, to give my thoughts about her experience some time to steep. "We've got fresh eggs to make a big skillet omelet for dinner, add some chopped-up tomatoes and bell peppers, some potatoes and onions on the side, fresh from the yard, um, you never tasted something so good."

And she was right, the three of us ate together on the patio at twilight. I had helped chop vegetables, cracked the eggs, and set the table; she seasoned and stirred the meal to perfection. Mitchell hovered over his plate and wolfed down the food as if he had not eaten in a week. "This tastes great," was his contribution to the table talk. Much of the dinner hour was spent discussing my profession, which seemed odd and remote but strangely accessible. I could speak on the subject without effort. She wanted to know all about being a hairdresser, how long had I been doing it, did I like it, how much did I charge and what did I think about tips, did I ever have a difficult customer, and would I cut her hair?

I had never cut a black woman's hair, but I was sure I could do it. I told her that fact and she thought it was quite funny. "I'll cut your hair if you cut mine," I propositioned. It could be the evening's entertainment.

"Oh, Lordy, Lordy. I don't know how to cut hair. What if I make a mess?"

"You won't make a mess. I can teach you all you need to know. Besides, what if I make a mess of your hair?"

"I know you can't make it look any worse than it does right now," and she pulled her scarf wrap off. A chimney of hair sprang to life as she gave it a rough tousle, causing me to laugh. The sound of my own laughter sounded strange to me. It was the first time I had laughed since Grayson died.

"Can I be excused?" Mitchell interjected, feeling left out of the girls' beauty-parlor discussion. He wanted to return to her record-album and videotape collections.

I turned to him and lowered my voice, "Excused to wash the dishes, right? We cooked, you can clean."

After a slight, "Aw, man," protest, he picked up the plates and went to the sink.

I turned back to Kiki with a challenging grin on my face. "So what do you think? Do you have any haircutting scissors? I'll cut your hair if you cut mine?"

"I can't be held responsible for the results."

"Ditto."

Kiki went inside and gathered up a pair of scissors, comb, towel and a water bottle. In good humor we commenced to cut each other's hair outside. I went first, explaining some of the basic principles of haircutting as I went along. Reverting to a skill I had mastered early on in my career, I concealed the fact that I was afraid. I had never touched black hair before and I didn't know what it would feel like, if I would be able to get the comb through it, if my tugging would hurt her. I was expecting her hair to be coarse and wiry, but it wasn't; it was fine and soft, cashmere-soft and easy to cut.

When it came to her cutting my hair, I was glad we weren't in a well-lit room. I had absent-mindedly plucked at my hair to the point where there were some almost-bald spots behind my ears. I wanted it all cut off. To get her started, because she was intimidated by the length, I bent over and gathered it all into a ponytail that I then lopped off. With less to wrestle with, I guided her through the cut.

"Pull everything forward and rest your fingers on the bridge of my nose, that's where you cut. No, don't close your eyes."

When she had succeeded with that cut, she did a little dance; she was so proud of herself. Each time she cut a new section she whooped with delight. "You're a natural," I encouraged. At the end, I took the scissors, and by touch, did some finishing work. I sliced into the style to give it a textured, spiky effect. Afterwards, she was quick with a broom to sweep up the two contrasting textures of hair. She told me an old wives' tale that she had grown up with, that if a bird gets ahold of your hair to make a nest, you'll go crazy.

"That wouldn't take much," I told her. "We'd better get every piece." Then we went inside to look in the mirror. I had cut her hair into a wedge shape and it fell in finger waves around her face. She liked it. And I felt so liberated with my tomboy spiky do. I didn't want to look at myself in the mirror, but I wanted Kiki to know that I had seen and appreciated her work. We hugged at our success. "You're a regular Kiki Sassoon," I complimented.

"My sheep better look out. They got a new day comin', I'm tellin' you."

For dessert we brewed a pot of decaffeinated coffee and opened a bag of cookies from her pantry. Mitchell was watching a movie and falling asleep in the recliner. Kiki turned the patio light off and we sat under the stars, admiring the full moon. Uncountable numbers of crickets emitted their pulse-like beats. The sheep bayed occasionally from within their pen.

"Would you like to go for a short stroll?" Kiki asked.

"I'd love to."

The moon was so bright; we didn't need flashlights. She led the way along a path that took us behind the vegetable patch and barn, then along a dry creek and back up to the parking circle. We walked out the road for about ten minutes and came to the cattle grate and rock structure I had thought looked like an igloo or furnace.

"This is where Gerald and Carl are buried. This is where they died."

I then saw that what I was looking at was a monument to the two men. Driving in, I had only seen the back. At its front was an arched opening. Although it was not necessary at the center highpoint, I had the inclination to duck through the entry passage. Inside the dome were two cut crystal oil lamps flickering; they illuminated two ceramic tiles with photographic portraits of the men on them. Surrounding the tiles, embedded in the wall plaster was an elaborate mosaic made with colored glass, broken china, marbles, silver dollar coins, nuts and bolts, and various objects including a pocket knife, a watch face, a shoehorn, and a shot glass. A curved bench was inside the tiny alcove, and we sat down so I could study Gerald and Carl's faces.

Two handsome, clean-shaven, short-haired, men; one wore glasses.

"Let me guess," and I pointed to the man wearing glasses and said, "That's Gerald."

"Ha! You're right. How could you tell?"

I looked closer. His face was round and affable, in a way, similar to Kiki's. His smile was relaxed and genuine, as if it came easily. A good-humored man who enjoyed and told entertaining stories. Carefree? No. A muscle flexed across his forehead and lines radiated at his eyes; he was a thinker. The other man had a slightly intimidating face, lean; his aquiline nose suggested some Native American heritage. His complexion glowed like the polish on a fast sports car. His eyelashes were thick enough to make him look like he was wearing eyeliner, but not feminine, just fierce, catlike. He was lady-killer good looking, and I could imagine Regina, the Las Vegas sister, going toe-to-toe with such a fellow, and taming him.

"I don't know. Your husband looks like he was a nice man."

She looked from me over to the tile, and with admiration and pride she replied, "He was."

We sat in silence for several minutes. Kiki's eyes were closed, squinting in concentration. Her feet were planted apart on the floor. Her hands were on her knees, and her straight arms braced her upper body. After she inhaled deeply, she opened her eyes and turned to me with a questioning what-to-do-next expression.

"Kiki, how did you do it? How have you been able to go on? You seem so…at peace."

She looked back to the altar, bent forward, her elbows to her knees this time and she rubbed her palms together as she thought before saying anything.

"I forgave."

I wasn't sure I heard her right. "I don't understand. Forgave?"

"That's what I had to do. You see, I was thinkin' the accident was Carl's fault; Regina blamed Gerald. We couldn't speak to one another for the longest time. Our parents and grandparents, hard-working cattle folk who started ranching this land originally, had passed years before. We have another sister and two brothers; none of us were talking. Our aunties, uncles and cousins didn't know what to say. Nobody could talk about what happened. I hired a number of people to help me sell off the cattle and end the family business. It was a mess. And then I was here all by myself, just me and my misery. That was when I decided to build this temple. One evening I was in here on my knees, working on laying out some of the design, feeling especially lonely, angry, and sad when I just broke down. I cried out, 'God, please help me,' and instantly the word 'forgive' came into my head."

"What do you mean?" I wanted to hear more.

"God is the only place I could put my troubles. I gave it all to God."

"You forgave your husband for dying?" I asked timidly.

"That's not what I'm saying. What I'm trying to tell you is that I recognized that there is God in all things. God is the original source. I gave, forgave, it all to the grand source of all that is, was, and will be. That's what forgiveness is all about. Letting go... giving... to something bigger than all of the painful details."

When she said "original source" I flashed on the conversation I had with the pastor in that church, pastor James. To him, I had referred to God as the engine of evolution. It appeared as though Kiki and I had a similar sense of God, only she had put hers to use. I was attempting to assimilate her unique understanding of the word forgive but hadn't found the words to express my thoughts yet. Not wanting to seem impolite, I filled the swelling silence gap between us with, "Wow. You've really given me something to think about. Thank you." I thought I sounded rather feeble. I didn't want her to think she had wasted her time, or that I hadn't appreciated her effort to answer my question. She wasn't asking me to drop on my knees and pray to God the father. I had asked her how she coped, and she had told me. I needed to relax and let the meaning of what she was talking about sink in. I was free to take or leave what she had said as I saw fit.

Kiki got up and opened a small door in the altar's façade. In the tiny cabinet was a bottle of lamp oil, a funnel, a candle snuff, and box of matches. She adroitly topped off the two crystal lanterns with oil. "Shall we go back?" She offered me a hand to help me to my feet. We returned to the house in relative silence, the night sky pierced with thousands and millions of pinpricks of starlight. She could tell my head was swimming, and at one point took my hand in hers. It was a relief to know that I hadn't offended her with my silence.

Inside the house, Mitchell was sound asleep in the recliner. Kiki found a blanket to cover him with. He roused slightly, and she winked at him and gave his shoulder a tender squeeze. He pulled the blanket to his chin and rolled over to his side before sinking back into his deep sleep. Kiki showed me to a very comfortable room. French doors in the room promised a scenic awakening. We hugged goodnight. "Thank you Kiki. Today has been a day I will never forget."

"Me neither," she said, and my heart made a little spasm of joy. I believed her and found myself blinking back some more tears.

The next morning we were all awake at sunrise. As soon as the horizon lightened, I opened the French doors to let the smells and sounds of the garden in. An innocent jackrabbit entertained me until I heard movements from Kiki and Mitchell out in the living room. A peach-colored sky was quickly erasing the night chill. I got dressed and washed my face. My new haircut startled me in the mirror, but I liked it.

Kiki was in the kitchen. Coffee had been brewed, and a pot of oatmeal made with walnuts, raisins and cinnamon was simmering on the stove. Kiki was soliciting Mitchell to do a little automotive maintenance on her car before Aunt Essie arrived. She asked him if he could rotate the tires and change the oil on her Toyota Land Cruiser.

"It's possible," he said. "But it will cost you."

"Cost me! How much?"

"I don't know. I guess I could get it done for a bowl of cereal and a cup of coffee or two."

I scowled at his attempt at humor, but Kiki enjoyed it. How they had struck up such a casual rapport was somewhat baffling. I was jealous but didn't want to admit it. In between their good-natured banter, I asked, like a wet blanket, what time Aunt Essie would be arriving. Nine-thirty or ten was the short answer. When they went to the barn to get the car work started, I felt left out, like a third wheel. Full of self-pity, I busied myself with the righteous task of washing their dishes. Working the soap and warm water, I also began to ramp up what I expected from Aunt Essie. I expected her to be late. I expected her not to like me. I expected her to demand more than the three thousand dollars I had offered for the pearls.

I was alone with my misery when Kiki's words about forgiveness resurfaced to antagonize me. I didn't want to think about forgiveness when Mitchell had waltzed off with my new friend, when the lady who was scheduled to arrive in a few hours held all the cards, when my life had unraveled to a place I couldn't get my mind around. When Kiki returned to the house smiling, I practically pounced on her. I asked about Miss Essie. "Is your aunt coming by herself?" I launched into.

"Oh ya."

"How old is Aunt Essie? She can handle that road by herself?"

"Oh ya. Essie May Laws is a force of nature; no silly road could stop her. She grew up out here. She knows what she's doin."

"And you're sure she has my mother's jewelry?"

Kiki was doing her best to stay light, but a flash of annoyance crossed her face.

"I talked to her yesterday. She has your mamma's necklace and earrings, and she asked me to tell you not to worry. Now, I've got some weeds and vegetables to pick in the garden. Want to help?"

I was acting like an ass, and I knew it. Getting my hands in the dirt was just the antidote I needed. With the sun on my back, I told Kiki about resurrecting the yards around my own home, carefully sidestepping pieces of the story that involved Grayson because I knew it wouldn't take much to start me on a crying jag. Kiki handed me a large basket and asked if I could look around in the vegetables and pick whatever looked ripe, and I was happy to.

It was just after nine o'clock when I began to hear gears of a truck grinding and lurching off in the distance.

"Here she comes," Kiki said as she stood up and stretched and massaged her lower back.

Mitchell came out of the barn wiping his hands on an oil-stained red cotton cloth. We gathered and went to the parking circle to greet Aunt Essie. As she came around the bend in the road, an old-fashioned aa-oo-ga horn blasted incongruously from a relatively new-looking silver Mercedes G-500 SUV. She had her arm out the driver's side window and was waving joyously as she laid on the horn, then skidded sideways to a dusty stop.

"Hey Baby, what y'all think of my new horn. I had um put it in special just last week."

Before the dust settled Aunt Essie had jumped spryly from her silver steed and was giving her niece a robust hug. From within the squeeze Kiki looked at me as if to say, see what I mean, mouthing the words "force of nature." Once the older woman let go of Kiki, she shimmied her way between Mitchell and me and threaded her arms in ours and started us walking towards the house. "Here we go. My new friends from California. Girl, you is as tiny as a bug," she said to me, which I enjoyed. She then turned her attention to Mitchell. "Young man, you's skinny as a bean pole, tall as a pine tree. What's your name, son?"

"Mitchell, ma'am."

"Mitchell. That's one fine name. You look like a Mitchell. My grand baby's name is Mitchell. You two don't look anything alike, but he looks like a Mitchell, too. Go figure that. Mitchell, I like that name, strong, sensitive."

All of this was said with heightened congeniality. Once we ushered into the house, raisin toast and coffee was made for Aunt Essie and lots of catch-up ensued. She had come in without a purse or luggage and I secretly wondered when it would be appropriate to bring up my mother's jewelry. I was bursting with anticipation, and every new topic of conversation seemed to lead further from what was most pressing on my mind, holding my mother's pearls. I smiled and nodded through stories about her church, her neighbors, her family, but when she was beginning to discuss her travel plans, I had to interrupt.

"Excuse me. I can see you two have lots to share with each other. Maybe it would be best if we could take care of our little transaction, and then Mitchell and I will be on our way. I'd like to be back home before it gets dark, and that's a long drive still."

"Leaving! Stay over another day, stay a few days. Lord knows I can use the company."

The invitation caught me off guard, and was incredibly appealing. What flew through my mind was that if I stayed any longer, I would never want to leave.

"Oh thank you, but that would be impossible. I've already been gone longer than I thought I would be. I need to get back home; I really do."

"Then keep me in mind down the road, both of you will always be welcome," Kiki said with touching sincerity.

Then she asked Mitchell if he wouldn't mind bringing Aunt Essie's bags in. I gulped at the thought of him alone with the Mercedes, a purse and the luggage, and prayed he wouldn't do anything shameful. Kiki and Essie were going to trust him; I would have to follow suit. My stomach was cramping from tension, and I wiped at my upper lip where I could feel beads of sweat forming. I suddenly had the need for a bathroom and got up at the same time as my nephew. In the living room I said to him in a low voice, "Don't take too long," and I shot him a look that he understood. I didn't want him taking time to riffle through her belongings, and I wanted to get this over with as soon as possible. He got both points.

In the bathroom I tried to calm myself down. I washed my hands and splashed water on my face. I played with the new haircut and then splashed more water on my face. When I returned to the kitchen, Mitchell was back from the car. A large Louis Vuitton suitcase was inside the front door and Aunt Essie was pulling a luscious purple velvet sack from inside her Vuitton handbag.

"Here you go darlin'. I think this is what you're looking for." Essie's face had turned from good-time gal to warm compassion.

I took the sack and hugged Essie. Tears filled my eyes. I loosened the drawstring tie and shook the contents onto the kitchen table. Mitchell and I both gasped at the pearls before us; they were not my mother's. I tried to close my eyes and reopen them with the hopes that the whole thing would right itself, but the wrong pearl necklace and earring, lovely as they were, stayed motionless on the Formica tabletop. I stuttered in speechless confusion.

"A-Oh," Mitchell voiced, alerting Kiki and Essie that there was a problem.

"What's wrong?" Kiki asked.

I was still thunderstruck, so Mitchell told her they weren't the right pearls.

Kiki and Essie both exclaimed disbelief and showed instant concern for me by putting their arms around my waist and back. Kiki pulled a chair out for me to sit in before I fell.

Pearls my Mother Wore

I covered my face with my hands and sobbed. They were gone; the pearls my mother had worn were irretrievably gone. I had to face it. The two women rubbed my shoulders, arms and hair as I cried, hiccoughing spasms of grief. Even Mitchell did his best to try and bring me back, to try and soothe away my shock and disappointment. "Aunt Kelly," he repeated softly a couple of times, not knowing what else to say. He just tried to reach me by my name, "Aunt Kelly. Aunt Kelly, I'm sorry."

Essie spoke next. "Love, Sweetheart, listen to me. Child, don't let yourself hurt for something so alive and well in your heart. Just because you can't touch, don't ever mean it's gone. What you're lookin for is not lost, never will be."

It was all too big. I knew I was beat. I was fed-up with fighting Mitchell, and I was tired of fighting my memories. The why and how of it all was unbearable, and a way out included forgiveness. I needed the kind of forgiveness Kiki had been talking about the night before, spiritual forgiveness. I was ready to give-up. But instead of seeing this as an act of failure, I saw the possibility of it being an act of offering. I could offer my un-solvable problems to something bigger than myself, much bigger, the Driver Of All Creation bigger.

I had gone as far as I could, and I couldn't change what was. I was never going to see those pearls again. I couldn't bring them back any more than I could bring my husband and family back. Forgiving those facts meant I was to give them to a Greater Capacity.

What I got in exchange was a connection of sorts. Some might call this finding God. I don't know, the word God is so overburdened by interpretation. What I know is that I reached for something big, something big enough to handle the details of my life. The offering was not an instruction to fix, but to handle. I was ready to let the full arch of time work things out. In deference I took comfort. I gave to receive. I forgave.

The trip home was long and quiet. Mitchell never bothered with the radio. The whirring road noise hummed steadily through the car. Just before dusk, we rounded the corner into our neighborhood. There sat Mr. Finch and Mr. Ritell at their daily posts, two folding chairs in their opened garage. They waved to us as Mitchell parked in our driveway, and we both waved back.

Before Mitchell got out of the car I stopped him.

"Mitch, can I tell you something?"

He looked at me and tossed his head up in one assenting nod.

"When I was fifteen, my mother committed suicide. I've never told anybody that fact, not even Grayson. I want you to know that I now understand her suicide doesn't define her any more than those pearls did. I don't want you to feel bad about them. I don't."

About the Author

Terry Sue Harms has been a practicing hairdresser since 1977 and currently owns her salon. In 1992 she received a Bachelor of Arts degree in English from Mills College. In May of 2005, she was inspired, in response to the new reality TV craze, "to write a story where the losers were the winners." *Pearls My Mother Wore* was born of that inspiration. She lives in Northern California with her husband, Lutrell.

For much more about Terry Sue Harms and *Pearls My Mother Wore*, please visit: **www.pearlsmymotherwore.com**.